'*Private Rites* is lyrical, haunting, unsettling and J.G. Ballard-ian in apocalyptic scope. What makes the novel soar even as its world drowns are the sisters – Isla, Irene and Agnes – who are deeply, passionately, messily human'
PAUL TREMBLAY, author of
The Cabin at the End of the World

'*Private Rites* is committed to plumbing the depths of what might be unknowable: the monstrous, inexorable thrust of climate change and the delicate, dangerous tangle of family and sisterhood. Armfield writes the kind of books that stick with you for life' KRISTEN ARNETT, author of *With Teeth*

'Its end of the world weather seeped into my bones as I read – Armfield brilliantly creates an atmospheric state where comfort feels impossible'
AMY KEY, author of *Arrangements in Blue*

'The rainsoaked world of *Privates Rites* is one you'll want to linger in' SARVAT HASIN, author of *The Giant Dark*

'A beautifully crafted story of love and loss at the time of the apocalypse, Armfield's prose sparkles in the best novel of 2024' ELIZA CLARK, author of *Penance*

Private Rites

Julia Armfield

4th ESTATE • London

4th Estate
An imprint of HarperCollins*Publishers*
1 London Bridge Street
London SE1 9GF

www.4thestate.co.uk

HarperCollins*Publishers*
Macken House, 39/40 Mayor Street Upper,
Dublin 1, D01 C9W8, Ireland

First published in Great Britain in 2024 by 4th Estate

3

A catalogue record for this book is
available from the British Library

ISBN 978-0-00-860803-3 (Hardback)
ISBN 978-0-00-860804-0 (Trade paperback)

Set in Stempel Garamond
Printed and bound in the UK using 100%
renewable electricity at CPI Group (UK) Ltd

For Martha and Avery,
obviously and infinitely

we that are young
shall never see so much, nor live so long

King Lear

Softness, compliance, forgiveness, grace

Angels in America, Tony Kushner

Before

This will all be swiftly forgotten.

The sound of something opened up – a lock wrenched back, a transom rattled. A house, unlatched, is less a house and more a set of rooms through which one might be hunted.

To note: the wide dark room; the books shelved alphabetically; the photo of two children in a frame. The night is gentle, unremarkable. The house is glass and multiple with shadows, reflections rendered solid in the dark. Outside: the rain – the fifteenth day of it, and little sign of easing. The storm drains flooded out, the nearby green and football pitch and petrol station forecourt underwater. In the hallway, a barometer has been taken off the wall and leans, unmoored, against an incidental table, its former hanging spot a grey ghost-print, its value first contested, then dismissed.

What happens here? A silence, followed by the breaking of a silence. Intruders congregate, remove wet shoes, walk socked and single file from the entrance to the living room beyond. Someone is hearing this. Someone who ought to be in bed.

Soft voices – a woman, and another woman. Hard to tell, from upstairs, from another room, exactly who is speaking. Hard to tell what is happening or why. Dark corridors can seem longer than they should do, dark doorways too sinister to pass. A nightlight, greenish in an upstairs corridor. A doll divested of her skirt and left to contemplate existence halfway down the steps. Someone is sitting barefoot on the deep-pile carpet of the upstairs landing – someone small enough to miss. Downstairs: a voice, and then another voice, a hitching sound. The congregation gasps, breathes in and out, repeats the motion – rhythmic, heavy, measured – in and out.

What then? And who creeps downstairs to see it? In the central room, in the centre of the congregation, one woman grips the corners of another's mouth, claws inward, pulls as though to rip her face from side to side. She presses closer, dragging up and outward, grapples, muscles up, eyes smashed tight against the other's teeth. For a second they are connected at all points, inextricable, one figure emerging from the mouth of the other as if grown from the throat, from the gullet, pushing up and out. And then, a wrench of skin, bright rending give. *The gift*, someone says, *and the giving*, says another. What then? A grunt, a shudder. One woman pushing backwards, the other stumbling, choking, covering her bleeding mouth. The group exhales as a body. They raise their hands to cover their own mouths.

The house rattles, shifts, subsides.

If there is somebody watching, they will run back to bed and hide beneath the covers before the scene can resolve itself. The memory of what was seen, or heard, will fade the way memories do when they are only halfway certain. Hard enough, in time, to sort it from the drift of dreaming, from the sense of only being half-awake. Easier, instead, to remember only make-believe. After all, a blanket over the head can amplify a person's breathing, can make them think they hear things that aren't there. A mouth spilling blood can be unpleasant to wake up to, but the baffle of the darkness can be kind – can allow a person to imagine that they're still, in fact, asleep.

Part One

1.

Isla

On the afternoon of her father's death, Isla takes a session with a man who was exorcised of evil spirits at the age of seventeen. He is a new patient, referred from the counselling programme at the hospital – white teeth and a voice whittled down from a scream. When he clasps his hands around one knee, the veins bunch up between his knuckles, pale blue against the jut of the bone. Isla tries not to notice this, inspects her own hands instead and the bitten-off edge of a cuticle. Bad habits; both the tendency to chew the skin around her nails and to notice a tic or a physical trait of a patient and allow it to grow, blowing up until it becomes their entirety, the characteristic against which all else seems to pale. She lives in horror of slip-ups, practises saying their names aloud to counter her mental Rolodex: patients listed in order as *Bug Eyes*, as *Taps His Foot When He's Horny*, as *Big Hands*, as *Talks Like a Robot*, as *Tits*. She's good at her job, but the impulse to open her mouth and say something dreadful recurs and recurs. Not unlike the irrational desire to dash a contemplative silence to pieces or to climb to some high place and jump, so it seems a compulsion born less of intent than of the simple fact of its own possibility. The fact that she *could* do it is more than enough. She reels it in, always. Reels herself in tight. *Any minute now*, she thinks, *any second, I could crash this whole day into the wall.*

He tells her his parents were the ones who pushed for the ritual – the patient, hands unclasped, now sipping water. Isla pauses, looking up from her notepad, asks him to say that again. She's heard of this once or twice before, archaic practices resurfacing the way trends will, exorcisms like bootcut jeans, like mixing pattern with print. Two years ago: not her patient but a woman on television, face pixelated, discussing her experiences as a child of the Cult of Our Lady. And before that: a patient recalling how her parents would often wake her at odd hours and lead her out to their Japanese garden, let the blood from her arm and pray for deliverance. Not a rampant fad, but certainly a recurring one, things being as they are these days. A memory, briefly summoned and then swiftly, professionally set aside: Isla's own mother, white to the lips and muttering. Isla's own mother, her face very close: *this will only hurt for a second.*

Her sister Irene once said that, at pinch points, people always turn to the divine, or if not to the divine then at least to the well trodden. *It's a backup*, she said, *like a tested recipe. People love a ritual when things get hairy, to feel they're doing something that thousands of people have done before them.* And so, the patient, telling a story that Isla suspects he has told before: the blood on the bed linen, his mother inviting the priest, the sensation of something first beckoned, then wrenched from his guts. He believes both that the ritual worked and that it didn't, expresses appropriate levels of scepticism towards the concept of exorcism yet can't seem to set aside the idea that his parents did what they did for the best.

'I think they wanted to feel better,' he says. 'I think they got it into their heads that something was wrong that could only be solved this way. They wanted to feel like they were taking action, given how little they could do anywhere else. It's weird, because I don't remember them being that religious, at first.'

Towards the end of the session, Isla asks if he believes in the devil. 'I don't,' he replies – clasps his hands so the knuckles pulse as if filling and retracting – 'I don't, but I feel him anyway.'

'Thank you, Ted,' she says, thinks *Ugly Knuckles*, reels it in again, thinks that she ought to get someone in to look at the dark spot on the wall. The air conditioner purrs. Someone in a consulting room across the hall appears to be weeping. *D'you ever have the thought*, says a voice along the corridor, *that it might be getting worse every day but you're just so used to it that you aren't noticing? Like maybe it's really terrible and I'm just so cut off from it that I've lost all sense of size? Half the time I can't get back to mine because the transport's fucked or flooded or whatever. Last night I got home at ten to midnight and I'm just like … 'Well, that's not bad.' Fucking council.* Isla operates from a suite of offices shared with two other therapists, and the noises around her are never quite muffled enough. The building is crisp, masculine, yet somehow fleshly – its walls vibrating the way a creature might breathe in its sleep. On occasion, she will sit across from a patient and listen to the noise of other patients and other therapists in adjoining rooms, imagining them all held safe within the mouth of something vast and slumbering, unlikely to turn to one side, unlikely to swallow.

She sees the patient out, asks him to remember that their meeting will be half an hour later next week. *Did you know,* she hears a voice saying in reception, *that magnolia evolved before bees? They're one of the earliest flowering plants – as a species they're something like ninety-five million years old.* She heads back to her desk and removes her phone from the drawer, notes an unfamiliar number has called and left a message. She considers this for a moment, makes a mental list of probabilities: *Morven might have a new number (but I don't want to talk to Morven), Irene might have a new number (but why would Irene call), it might be the insurance company, it might be the bank.* She presses a button on her phone and waits, grinding one heel into the carpet. From her vantage point near the window, she can see down into the plaza below. The water is high today, lapping up against the edges of the elevated walkways, the sunken string of high-rise buildings sharp in unaccustomed light. It is mid-afternoon, threatening rain, agapanthus dying in a pot beneath the heating vent, and Isla hasn't eaten lunch. When the call connects, the voice on the line is kindly, professional. They would like to know her surname, her date of birth; they would like to tell her that her father is dead.

Irene

On the train, a girl at the other end of the carriage vomits into her handbag and passes it to her boyfriend. The boyfriend holds the bag away from himself, makes long and meaningful eye contact with the floor. *It's too early for this*, Irene thinks, then messages Jude about it. *Either it's too early or I'm getting old.* Jude responds that two things can be true and asks what Irene wants for dinner.

Three seats down across the aisle, a man is talking loudly into his phone while the woman beside him makes periodic tutting noises. Irene tips her head, tries to avoid the gaze of the woman sitting directly opposite. She hates making eye contact in public places, the idea of an inadvertent brush with someone best kept in peripheral blur. Some time ago, she accidentally winked at a woman while messing around with her contact lenses and the horror of that moment stayed with her well into the end of the day. Embarrassment, the potential for it, like something caught on the sole of the foot and hard to slough off again, a physical object she carries around at all times.

The light in the uppermost edges of the train windows is starting to turn, evening bleeding as if from a leak-sprung ceiling; incremental, then thickening, swelling as it falls. The afternoon is wide, peach-ripe – rain incoming as always and the windows greased with mist, the city grown porous and slack around itself. The gaps between rain are so few and far between that they barely count as gaps so much as temporary glitches. It will start again, she knows, before her journey is over, before she has the chance to disembark and enjoy the respite. The irritation of that, of having missed it, will simply be something to shoulder, like everything else. Irene often feels she can detect a certain amphibious quality in the people with whom she shares transportation, shares offices, shares the ingrown cramp of city space. Some days, she will squint her eyes and imagine a waterlogged sheen to the skin of the woman who hands over change at the newspaper kiosk, the man who touches her knee on the tram. People at work complain of bloated joints, persistent headaches, though only as one complains about anything that has always been the case. *I don't know*, Jude will say in the sanguine tone they tend to apply to things unrelated to the Now, *that I'd even know how to go back to things being drier. I don't know if it would suit me at all.*

But the whole point is that you were suited to it once, Irene replies on the days when she's feeling disagreeable. *When we were kids, when we were teenagers, even. The whole point is you were different once too.*

I know that, Jude says, *but what's the point in dwelling. Once you start, you'll never get to the end of it.*

Jude tends to operate like this, focusing solely on what's going on right in front of them, as if everything else is irrelevant and incapable of causing them harm. *That was Then, this is Now,* like a screen set up to block peripheral vision. Irene has tried it, has sat and reflected that the house was Then but this is Now. That her PhD and all she planned to do with it was Then but Jude is Now, that work is Now, that the sofa and carpet and special soft furnishings she's bought for the flat are all Now. The train is Now, she supposes, and the moment the girl at the end of the carriage recommences throwing up is Now, although then it is Now again and Now again and again until the girl is white and dry-heaving and the boyfriend sets down the still-reeking handbag, gets up and moves towards the door. They are two stops away from the end of the line. This train route used to be longer, but old ends to old lines have long since been abandoned, stations drowned and duly cut off, trains diverted, raised above the water where possible or else supplanted by boats and water taxis, journeys thrown off course. Irene thinks about calling her sister and then dismisses it, thinks less seriously about calling her other sister but then leans her head back against the window and sighs.

She was trying to get to the end of a thought about souls, about the strange internal silence of something one might assume to be essential and yet which serves no tangible purpose. This happens fairly often. Thoughts crop up, unwanted, despite the fact that her PhD is a relic, discarded long ago in a panic that feels foreign to her now. She works, these days, for an office which administrates payroll for remote staff and agile workspaces, and the memory of her studies operates rather like an atrophying muscle, unconditioned but still prone to spasm when pressed a certain way. She'll think that if one assumes that the soul is distinct from the physical form, then the soul cannot communicate, for it has no recourse to speech or any other form of expression with which to sign out its meaning. She will think that if this is the case then one might extrapolate that the soul has no *need* of language, which poses questions about how it enacts control or influence over the human body and what the divide between silence and language means in terms of spirituality. She will think *I should write this down*, but then find that the notion recedes the more closely she looks at it, until it reveals itself as little more than a muddy act of pointillism. It's depressing, all this thought that has nowhere to put itself, all this context and research with no place left to go. *Give it a rest*, she will think to herself. *You have a job and it isn't actually this.*

The train rattles over a series of point blades. The sky is closing in. Later on, the summer constellations will sharpen into being, though too far back behind cloud to be seen.

Her phone vibrates in her pocket. She slides it out and checks the number, feels surprise quickly curdling into annoyance as she realises her older sister Isla is calling. *What*, she thinks, irritably, *do you want. Whatever it is, can't it wait.*

Agnes

She's in charge of the music on Wednesdays, which is what makes the Wednesday late shift bearable. She picks music to smooth the afternoon along: inoffensive country or pop songs that obsess over long drives, over loving, over women who move a certain way. Jason describes the work as *senseless killing labour*, which is overdramatic and typical of the way he refers to almost everything. In Jason's parlance, Mondays are *a fascist rite of passage*, commuting *a soulless death parade*. Possessed of a sort of beady-eyed anticharisma and no sense of volume control, he makes an art of rendering every interaction nine times as difficult as it needs to be. Not to say that Agnes doesn't also find the work tedious, but it hardly helps to go on about it.

The way it works, most days, is that he takes the orders and she makes the coffee. On Tuesdays and Thursday mornings, they have Svetlana, who fills in for Agnes and siphons sugar off into a takeaway container, an ongoing act of blatant theft that Jason is always just about to deal with. On Fridays and alternate Saturdays, they have Liam, who fulfils his duties immaculately and with a rather bone-chilling intensity, walking the cafe at closing time with a broom that he often appears on the precipice of turning on the customers. Agnes doesn't mind the job, works her shifts and goes to the swimming pool, eats her lunches in the back room sitting on an upturned crate. It's work, in that it requires just enough concentration to keep her mind from wandering without demanding very much. She has perfected the art of pouring shapes into the top of a latte but doesn't often bother to do this. She enjoys writing the wrong names on the sides of people's takeaway cups.

The tips of her fingers still smell like chlorine from the pool, a smell that never seems to leach away in its entirety. She likes to swim before the late shift, though the pastime has turned out to be an expensive one. There used to be places to swim that didn't cost eight pounds fifty, but the municipal pool closed years ago and the swimming club never reopened after a billboard came down in an electrical storm and took out most of its cafe. The leisure centre situated on the thirteenth floor of the apartment block near work costs too much for what it is, but Agnes pays the entrance fee three times a week in order to swim in comparative silence and not have to think, for an hour, about dinner or her taxes or the number of times she's rescheduled her cervical smear. She is not always lucky enough to be the only person at the pool, although the nature of her work allows her to pick odd times. There are any number of ways to be annoying in a public pool, even during designated lane swim, and Agnes is fairly sure that the list she's compiled is more or less exhaustive. Men who join the medium lane, swim two incredibly dramatic lengths and then stop at the shallow end to breathe loudly for twenty minutes. Women in swimming caps who spend what seems like hours adjusting their goggles poolside only to overtake you with a school-teamy front crawl the second they start. People who swim too slowly. People who swim the wrong way. Anyone who chooses to do the butterfly, which is a stroke for cunts. Agnes can never tell which of them she hates the most and tries to avoid them all indiscriminately.

Swimming can be exceptionally calming, but only if conditions are right. Agnes swims only breaststroke, the way the majority of women without swimming caps tend to, and when she swims she thinks about things too insubstantial to stand to attention on dry land. Her mind moves with the pointless rolling momentum of B-roll, flicking blandly from songs she used to listen to, to actors who died, to dinner, to the fact that Dylan Thomas, when young, looked like literally every ugly boyfriend of every straight friend she's ever had. Thinking when swimming is not thinking, but something more like elevator music. It comes as secondary to the fact of her body, to the bald imperative of motion, and it makes her feel easier, more physical, and less liable to come upon a thought that will cause her to scream and to never stop screaming. It is in this frame of mind that she has occasionally fucked someone in the swimming pool changing room – her brain, still buoyed along on this trivial pathway, allowing her to catch the eye of a woman in a tan-coloured bathing suit, a woman with a nose ring, a woman with a buzz cut and legs of no appreciable shape. Earlier this afternoon, she pushed two fingers up inside a stranger, discovering in that moment an ugly tattoo just south of her pelvic bone, and moved her hand in a rough, hectic rhythm until the moment of release. It is very easy, she has found, to present herself as simply a body, to take her towel off in a changing stall and think of nothing and to feel much better for the break.

'Do you think,' Jason is saying now, 'that it's maybe a cultural thing? Like, Svetlana steals the sugar because she somehow *values* sugar? *Cappuccino to take away for Stephanie.* You know what I mean? Like maybe it's something her *family* do.'

Agnes sets about pulling a shot of espresso, rolls her eyes as Jason leans back against the counter to look at her. Her fingers, she has realised, smell both of chlorine and a little like the woman she fingered at the swimming pool, which is likely some kind of health and safety violation, though she isn't particularly minded to do anything about this.

'I don't know what you mean by *cultural*,' she says, tamping down the coffee and locking the filter into the machine. 'Svetlana grew up in basically the same place I did – she's always going on about how we would have competed at county indoor athletics if she hadn't broken her leg in Year 10 and I'd ever done any athletics.'

Agnes pulls the shot, sets it aside and starts steaming milk.

'Well, I don't know,' Jason says. 'Maybe it's a learned behaviour. Whatever the case, it's got to stop.' He holds up a hand to a new customer, who is now leaning across the counter trying to get at the biscotti jar. 'Sir, if you could just stick to your side of the counter, I'll deal with that for you.'

Agnes pours the milk over the espresso in the takeaway cup and scribbles *Jeremy* on the side, slides it down to the pick-up window where the customer is waiting. 'Takeaway cappuccino.'

The girl is tallish – dark hair – and Agnes immediately wants to fuck her. It happens like this sometimes; impulse driven sharply upwards and into her gut. She looks at the stranger now inspecting the name *Jeremy* on the side of her coffee cup and thinks *yes, that* and then can't remember the name she was supposed to have written.

'Sorry,' Agnes says, 'I have this thing where I just – I don't write names correctly.'

The stranger looks at her, white collar point sticking up on one side. She has a backpack, foldaway umbrella, good tits from the little her outfit chooses to advertise. *I'd like,* Agnes thinks to herself, *to do all of that. I'd start at the collar and figure it out.*

'Oh right,' the girl says.

Agnes nods, shrugs one shoulder. 'Always been a problem.'

'So you just' – the girl raises her eyebrows and Agnes notes the new way her face arranges itself, the gentle upward kink to one side of her mouth, preparatory to a smile – 'you just pick any name?'

'Usually, yeah.'

'Is it sort of a spite thing or a dyslexia thing?'

'Depends on the day,' Agnes says, and the girl snorts.

'*Cortado to have in, for Lionel.*' Agnes looks at Jason, who is now handing three bagged biscotti to the man at the other end of the counter.

'I'd better get on with that.'

'And what are you going to write on his cup?'

The girl is grinning at her now and Agnes aims for nonchalance.

'See where the spirit takes me, I guess.'

'Well, if you need a name,' the girl says, reaching for a napkin from the box beside the stirrers, 'mine's Stephanie.'

The day has been a throwaway thing – hot too late into the afternoon, tables sticky with spilled coffee, with packet sugar opened and emptied and mashed with the back of a spoon. Agnes mops while Jason deals with the shutters. She is tired in a way that seldom leaves her; a tight, acidic exhaustion. She can catch her reflection in the polished chrome of the Gaggia and find herself surprised to recall the arrangement of her face, that her eyes and mouth and all her features come together quite in the way they appear. It is raining again, of course; downpour after a very brief respite. The front window is opaque with water and the certainty of that feels deadening – the wet walk and the inner-city ferry, the trudge up nineteen flights of stairs. She takes out her phone and holds down the button to wake it up, pulls from her pocket the napkin with the number scribbled sideways up one corner: *Stephanie, call me (by my name)*. Agnes doesn't like to have her phone on, treats it with the general apprehension due to anything prone to bite. Phones are how people reach you, and nothing very good can come from that. She plugs in Stephanie's number to save it, ignoring as she does so the rush of messages and missed calls that burst across the screen: landlord, bad date, *FREE delivery on six-pack of our award-winning doughnuts, use code FREE003*. She is about to turn it off again when a series of more recent messages flash up, each attributed to the number saved as *I (1)*. She schools her face, holds her hands very still – though this is pointless as no one is looking at her – thinks *be quiet* nonsensically to herself.

Hello Agnes, I have tried to call a number of times now, I need to talk to you.

Agnes, please can you turn your phone on.

Agnes, I'm not sure if the grey tick means you're not reading this or you simply haven't seen it but either way, please can you give me a call.

Another message follows, this one sent from a different number, labelled *I (2)*.

Agnes you stupid bitch answer the phone.

She looks at this for a second, swipes a tea towel across the surface of the serving counter, and wonders which of her older sisters she ought to call back. Soon enough, she will leave work and make her way across the elevated walkway to the point where the stairs lead down towards the jetty, and pause for a moment at the highest point of the slope. You can see a long way from here – rainclouds interspersed at irregular points by narrow bursts of early-evening sun in far-away parts of the city. *People getting raptured*, she thinks whenever she sees this, *always somewhere other than here.*

City

Remember this: the world as it once was. The way things appear in the instant before they go under: first assured, then shipwrecked. The ease with which facts presumed permanent can change. There was dry land, once, and also the concept of drowning as emergency, a thing to be thrashed against. Now, there is simply inevitability, the narrowing gaps between floodplains, islands of viable space on which people build doggedly, insistently, upwards, away from the mess of below. There is a horror movie adage that people are always running up stairs when they should be jumping out of windows, but what is a person supposed to do when all obvious exits are underwater? Places stack up, clench inward, people forced into ever closer proximity, one on top of the other on top of the other on top of the other. People can afford real security or else they simply cannot. Those who can't live wherever and however they can, bunched together in tower blocks ill-equipped for modern circumstances, renting well over the odds, losing power, existing.

It has been so many years – a decade of this, another decade before that of almost this. People take supplements, for vitamin D, for energy, complain the damp has reached their bones. It rains constantly and the fact of the rain, of the rain's whole great impending *somethingness*, runs parallel to the day-to-day of work and sleep and lottery tickets, of yoga challenges, of buying fruit and paying taxes, of mopping floors and taking drugs on weekends and reading books and wondering what to do on dates. It's exhausting, as it always was, to live with such a breadth of things to take up one's attention – exhausting, the way there can be too much world, even in its final stages. Exhausting, to be so busy and so bored with no time left for either.

Isla

Their father built houses, which is to say he designed them and let someone else construct them. He was responsible for great portions of the city as it stands today, the upward heave of a population trying to scramble out of water. Stephen Carmichael: the man, the myth. He believed in building up, in building away – his structures allowed their inhabitants to ignore their surroundings, turn inward and forget, though for a price very few could afford. He was difficult – increasingly so at the height of his renown and then equally, if differently, after. He listened only ever with the affect of one attempting to maintain his train of thought over unpleasantly loud music, repeated the ends of people's sentences with an irritable upward inflection when asked if he'd been paying attention – *you said that you're unsure if that's the direction you want your career to go, I heard you.*

When Isla first told him she was going to marry Morven, he looked at her with the considering expression he employed before being flatly dismissive. It was an attitude that came across as both intentional and thoughtless – the squint, as though he couldn't understand what it was you were doing in front of him, much less what you were trying to say. The tilt of the head. *Well, I can't see why you'd want to go about doing that, but I suppose it's your life and we all have to bow to it.* This *we* was not uncommon, an assumption of plurality, as though he spoke not just for himself but for others, though everyone he might have spoken for had been jettisoned long ago. That Isla got married despite this was an act that she held, at the time, as proof of having moved past him and claimed ground for herself. That she is now in the process of getting divorced from Morven is something she never communicated to him, but that's a separate issue.

She thinks about this, thinks and then sharply stops thinking. Rolls her ankles, tries to focus on a single point on the wall. Her mind feels scattered and sorely needs to be less so. *I'm not sure—* she wants to say, but can't think of an end to that sentence. Her breathing might be a little off, or potentially her vision. Her phone sits blank in her hand. *We've been trying to get in touch with you for hours*, the voice on the line had said, *but we've been having issues with the hospital switchboard – lines down due to flooding, poor reception on several floors. I'm so sorry for the delay, and for your loss, of course.* She had snagged on this phrase – *your loss*. She had pictured holding her loss in one hand and then the other, pictured opening up a window and lobbing out her loss to see how quickly it fell. *You're dissociating*, she had thought to herself, *don't do that. Don't panic, for God's sake.* She had shaken her head, picked up her phone again and called one sister, then the other. That was a while ago.

She is still in her office, though the day should have ended, though the downpour has long since settled in for the night. She had been meaning to set the afternoon aside for paperwork, glances sideways at her in-tray and its jumbled stack of notes. *Exceptional circumstances*, she thinks, trying to imagine explaining to Jenny from reception. *I meant to file my paperwork but then my father died, which threw me off my schedule.* The sentence sounds wrong, oddly comic. *My father died*, like the tag to a joke. Her breathing feels funny, or maybe it's her heart rate. *Don't panic.* On the phone to Irene, she had tried to come straight to the point but found herself prevaricating. Asked Irene how she was, what she thought of the weather. *D'you remember*, she said, *Dad's high-rise project – the one with all those glazed walkways and glass dividers? This was early, I think, when he was still with Williams Hardy. It was a mirror house. I mean, the façade was mirrored so it sort of melted into the sky around it, like if you looked too quickly it almost seemed to not be there – what was that project called?* Irene said nothing, static rustle on the line. *I don't remember*, Isla continued, *it was something like* Invisible House. Invisible Space. Invisible *something. I should just look it up but that feels ridiculous.*

Irene cleared her throat. *It was called* Unseen. *Why are you calling me?*

The project in question had been a series of high-rise apartments huddled tight within a building whose bright glazed exterior reflected back an often louring sky. The contractors eventually had to smoke the glass to prevent unwitting birds from flying smack into the panelling and killing themselves, though this design flaw had gone unnoted in the architectural press.

I remember it being a sort of failure, Isla went on to say, ignoring her sister's question. *I remember we weren't allowed to bring it up, though I don't know if I've made that up. I need to call Agnes. I'm sorry. I'm not getting to the point.*

In her office, now, Isla leans back in her chair and tries to breathe normally. She rotates an image in her mind: a bird, a smooth trajectory, then the crack, the broken neck. *Your loss.* She tries to breathe, to breathe to breathe. It would, she thinks, be useful if she could plan. Make a list of things to be done, actions to be taken. *I'm not sure—* she tries to say again, then lifts herself from her office chair and hurries to the bin to be sick.

Irene

There's a protest going on along the upper bank of what used to be a public thoroughfare and is now a poorly demarcated stretch of open water. Irene can see the majority of this from her bathroom window, although the point of the protest is unclear to her, the placards indistinct from this distance.

She has been drinking a beer in the bath and periodically standing up to peer out of the window. She has been doing this for upwards of an hour – since she returned, in fact –

topping up the hot water, standing up and sitting down again. Her phone lies on the lid of the toilet and she is, for the moment, happier to ignore it. *We should go to the hospital tonight*, Isla had said when she called, *shouldn't we? Maybe we shouldn't. Would tomorrow be better? I'm not sure. I should get hold of Agnes first. That's going to be a nightmare.* Irene had listened and nodded and tried to imagine saying something useful. *I'm already on my way home*, she had said instead, and then felt weird about it. Dull shock followed up by nothing, by a sense that there should be more to the news than was coming across. *I mean, it's going to be hard to get anywhere tonight, isn't it? I don't even know how we'd get there.* She hadn't said *he won't be any less dead by tomorrow*, though the thought had occurred to her.

She stands up again, peers out at the protesters. One of the figures on the upper bank has set fire to what looks like an effigy and is holding it over the water, suspended from a longish pole. Protests are not unusual – there was one on the viaduct only yesterday about border control and another last weekend about spiralling energy prices. Twenty or thirty people zip-tied themselves to lamp posts and railings and were eventually taken away by law enforcement. Irene tries to keep up with politics wherever possible, attends talks on police intervention, participates in mutual aid, though increasingly she can't help but feel that her will to be seen taking part is not matched by her actual desire to do so. She used to rage, to get involved with direct action and instigate chaos, but her anger has waned over time, the way laughter eventually becomes forced, and what is left feels unpleasant but nonetheless easier. Isla used to say that Irene's anger felt relentless, a term she employed in a voice that seemed to avoid saying something ruder: *you never come to the end of it*, she would say, *it just goes on and on, like a valve you're choosing not to close*. Irene had never known what to say to this, not only because it seemed so obviously an insult but because, with the passing of each year, it became less and less true. *I **am** angry*, she has thought before, *I just don't know that I'm angry twenty-four hours a day*. Isla once told her, conversationally, that she often saw people in her practice who felt that if they stopped looking out into the world, stopped responding with what they perceived to be the proper degree of outrage, they'd die. Irene replied that she was most likely thinking of sharks.

There are, Irene has always felt, few frustrations to match that of being read a certain way by family members. To be misunderstood is one thing, but the curious hostility of a sibling's approach lies less in what they miss than in the strange backdated nature of the things they choose to know. A person can be thirty, thirty-five, and yet still largely described by her sisters in terms of things which happened to be true at the age of seventeen. Irene, then, at the age of seventeen: first blonde then a crispier, bleach-fried blonde, self-consciously furious in every direction and seldom polite enough to let anyone reach the end of a sentence before starting one herself. An Irene who, to this day, lingers like a supplementary presence, superimposed over the top of the current version, making her harder to see. *Well*, Isla will say, affecting the older-sister voice that implies an age gap of decades rather than barely a year, *you've always been political, you get upset, you never let anyone speak.* Will turn to her wife, Morven, and say *Irene's spiky, she's always been spiky. You have to watch what you say*, as though Irene is not in fact in the room. (Morven, an anthropologist turned office worker, will nod along as though this makes perfect sense, as though it's not a ridiculous thing to do to someone, nailing them down forever to one particular scrap of floor.) The sensation, then, not so much of being misunderstood as of being understood too well at one time and then never again. Too hard to explain to her sister that she *does* know how to listen, that she's too old or too spent to be angry all the time.

There is a nastiness to you, Jude has said – not unkindly, holding Irene's cheek in one hand – *you're not always very nice, but I don't think you do it on purpose. And I don't think that makes you* angry, *per se.* Irene's turn-ons include being bitten until her neck bleeds, being told her flaws by someone who understands them, and being fucked hard and brutal until she's able to go to sleep. Jude has often asked her why she cares so much what her sisters think of her, or why she hates them thinking things that only used to be true. She doesn't say, though she thinks it, that it's because too much of her is already confined to a state of past tense – to the PhD and her plans for it and the many small things that only used to be – though she imagines Jude may know this already.

Irene drains her beer and thinks about ordering pizza. Jude is making dinner in the kitchen and the impulse to undercut this feels rooted in the teenage spite that Jude calls her *goblin side*, miming Irene stomping a foot through the floor. *Good thing I love you.* Jude is too good for Irene (this is not subjective), too patient with the pettiness, the little obsessions, the things she can't let go. On coming home this evening, Irene had explained the news and the phone call with Isla as lightly as possible. *We're trying to get hold of Agnes now, or I mean, mainly Isla is. But I sent a text message. It's the usual Agnes thing – she'd drop off the face of the earth and you'd never know about it.* She didn't add that, until this point, it had barely occurred to her to think about Agnes in six months. Agnes is only their half-sister and the distance between them is keenly apparent even outside crises. Jude, who had sat down on the arm of the sofa to listen to all of this, pulled a neutral face that appeared only a fraction constructed. *I know you'll feel weird about all this*, they said, *but don't get pissed at me if I tell you I'm sorry.* Irene shook her head, felt confused and then vaguely irritated. *I won't get pissed*, she said. *It is what it is, isn't it? It's a weird feeling, I don't know. I can't tell if I'm waiting for it to hit me or whether this is just it. It's not like when Mum died.* Jude nodded, squeezed her hand, and Irene wished they wouldn't. *I think that makes*

31

sense, given the way you left things with your dad. Jude, too tall and too attractive, with their easy manner and unfailing ability to produce a spare pen or chewing gum. Jude has always made Irene want to be better, or at least to appear to be so, to be calmer and more generous, easier and less enraged. Not the furious Irene that Isla clings to or the weary Irene that is but another version, a third version: best-case-scenario Irene.

'D'you think you'll be wanting a salad dressing?' Jude in the bathroom doorway, wiping their hands on a tea towel. Irene blinks, tips her head back against the lip of the bath.

'What's that?'

'A dressing,' Jude repeats, 'for the salad. I could throw some oil and balsamic at it, I'm not feeling fancy.'

'Whatever you like,' Irene says, scrubs a hand over her face and then shakes herself. 'No, sorry, I'm paying attention. Dressing would be nice – I can do something with a lemon when I'm out of the bath.'

Jude nods, cocks their head to the side. 'How are you doing in there? Want me to come and install a coffee bar? Couple of pillows? Really make that place a home?'

Irene snorts, registers a moment of desperate relief at being treated as she would on any normal night. A small, sickish feeling persists at the pit of her stomach, though she is finding that, if she ignores it, it seems happy enough to stay put. *I called the hospital back*, Isla had said on the phone. *They said the housekeeper found him and brought him in.* Irene has been playing a constructed version of this image in the back of her mind since hanging up. Subsequent to a stroke and cardiac arrest four years ago, their father had quickly deteriorated, had come to favour a wheelchair for getting around and become semi-dependant on bottled oxygen. Housebound, he had maintained a level of frigid hauteur which would have made it difficult to assess how he was really doing, if any of them had particularly tried. As it was, the housekeeper had become their proxy and their father had receded from them. The thought, then, of their father, collapsed, frozen and unfindable, somewhere in the depths of the house. A picture jutting sharply up against the more overbearing blankness, the certainty that she feels nothing, and the splinter at its core. She prefers to ignore this – the pain and the blankness and the sickish feeling in her gut – and the permission to do so feels like a small sort of grace.

'I'll be out in a minute,' she says. 'It hasn't been *that* long.'

Jude waves a hand – *yeah yeah* – already half-turned out of the room again.

'Ok, well, dinner in fifteen.'

'No, wait—' Irene beckons with the tipped neck of her beer bottle, leaning up as Jude leans down. 'I missed you today.' She kisses them quickly, before hoisting herself up out of the bath with a sudden movement that displaces more water than she was expecting; tidal spill over the edge of the tub.

Agnes

Agnes is not a sleeper. This is something she likes to say, mostly to women she's trying to have sex with: *I don't sleep very much. In general, I find it's much easier to just go on being awake.*

She has fucked women who envy her this – not her type, desperation fucks – women who like to watch videos which tell them to get up earlier, to do Pilates at 5 a.m., to hustle. *I know what you mean*, a girl once said in response, *it's something I'm trying to be better at – using my time more effectively. We all have the same twenty-four hours, you know?* Agnes had nodded and pulled on her t-shirt and not bothered to say that this wasn't what she'd meant at all.

Sleep has never been easy because sleeping brings with it the possibility of dreaming, of faces that turn queasily towards her in almost-familiar settings, of eyes leering down upon her, a sense of being watched. In dreams, she packs herself tight into a box and hopes this will be enough to evade some questing creature, holds the lid shut with two fingers and tries to ignore the sound of something breathing nearby. In dreams, fabric grows across her mouth to prevent her from screaming, and when she tries to do so she wakes and wishes she had never slept and turns the lights on to obliterate the memory.

These are the strangest times, the times between waking and sunrise. Her flat is too high up to see much from the window – damp city sprawl, low cloud obscuring tower blocks. Now, jolted from sleep, she leans her head against the windowsill and allows the sweat to cool, noting as she does the pieces of recollected nothingness that often surge the moment after waking, like dust thrown up and dancing as it dissipates. Disconnected memories: dim sheen of hospital lighting; her sister handing her a lemon and claiming she could eat its skin; her father's hands; her sister lowering her voice to say *it's only a pot plant, move it closer, move it into the sun*; the smell of Brasso metal polish; fingernails clipped short; the sense of something hidden in a closet, thrust beneath a bed, too swiftly dealt with not to re-emerge. A sense of her mother, too, hidden somewhere amongst all of that; a woman she never knew and who does not now reveal herself, except as an absent spot on the floor. *She was nothing*, she once heard her father saying, *a miscalculation. No need to waste another thought.*

Agnes rubs her temple with one finger and replays Isla's message, voice distorted by weak phone signal: *We're going to go to the hospital to see him first thing tomorrow. I thought you'd want to know.* The day dawns thin, sky like the skin of a drum, and her father has now been dead since yesterday.

2.

Isla

She is sitting in the booth of a place that sells doughnuts, trying to drink a cup of tea. Atmosphere redolent of hot oil and sugar, wet windows, ageing Formica. She has recently stopped drinking coffee, which unfortunately feels more unchic in practice than she had imagined it would. There is something, she can't help but feel, deeply juvenile about walking up to a counter and ordering tea, not unlike getting to the end of a meal at a restaurant and asking for a glass of milk. She hasn't felt particularly tired since giving up coffee, but nor has she felt particularly anything. Another therapist on her floor promised lessened anxiety, better sleep, improved digestion, all of which is hard to assess when the baseline was already so abysmal. It is perfectly possible that she feels less anxious, perfectly possible that she sleeps better now, but this doesn't mean that she isn't still anxious when judged by any relevant metric, or that she doesn't still wake nine times in the night with the sheets tangled round her knees. It would be nice, she can't help but think, to order a coffee. It would be far nicer to order a beer.

The door swings and it isn't anyone – a man hustling in with a swiftly sheathed umbrella, lick of sweat up the back of his shirt. Makes for the counter, orders coffee and a doughnut, exclaims loudly over the price. Isla watches him, pleased to keep her eyes off the door. It's too early to eat, she thinks, but she's ordered doughnuts anyway; damp trio of fried sugar rings in a plastic basket, one cinnamon, one vanilla, one coconut. Extortionate, of course, but then what isn't these days. Someone towards the back of the shop is smoking a cigarette, which is something she still can't get used to. It's been legal since last October, or possibly November, although whether the reversal of the ban came before or after everyone started ignoring it is a question few seem quite prepared to answer. Events are tricky to remember in constituent pieces, a symptom of submerged chronology, of a timeline moving fast and incoherently, too much unpleasant daily news. The facts, as far as Isla can recall them, are that no one wanted to smoke in the rain, so either they didn't or were told they didn't have to, and in either case, that seemed to be that.

Isla is still watching the man at the counter, now wrestling with the lid of his coffee cup, which is how she misses Agnes at the window, Agnes at the door, Agnes now beside her table, wet from the rain and looking down at her.

'Well, hi.'

Isla blinks, half-stands and catches her elbow on the table, sits down again and rubs her arm. 'Ow, shit.'

Agnes with different hair, hacked back to her chin and currently plastered to her forehead. Agnes who never seems to remember her umbrella. She offers the corner of a smile and slides down into the opposite seat, nods her head towards the doughnuts.

'Big morning?'

'They're for all of us.'

'Irene's going to be a dick about you ordering for her.'

'Well I'm sure she'll be grateful for something to moan about.'

Agnes rests her head against the vinyl back of the booth. 'Shit I'm tired.'

'Have you been staying out late? Your lips look awfully dry.'

'Gee, thanks.'

Agnes reaches for the cinnamon doughnut. Isla watches, tries to remember how old she is. A rogue image swimming through her: their father eating dinner, imitating Irene to make Isla and Agnes laugh, his elbows on the table, imagined snap of teenage gum – *you see the thing is,* **Dad,** *the work you do is actually so* **elitist.** A tiny Agnes, pressing both hands to her mouth as if to stop the sound of laughter, though as Isla looked at her she became less certain that any sound was trying to get out. Agnes is twenty-three now, she's pretty sure, or possibly older. It's hard to tell and nor does she have any means of calculating, since she can't for the life of her recall her birthday, only other incidental moments: Agnes, collecting ladybirds in aluminium tins which always killed them, the piss smell they secreted when she tried to pick them up; Agnes, with her baby voice and poor sense of direction; Agnes, oyster-solitary and never in need of orthodontics.

'So,' Agnes says, wriggling her hand through her hair in a gesture Isla recognises, 'you said you hadn't actually seen him yet.'

Isla wishes they could wait until Irene arrives. *Nothing like 'How are you, Isla?' Nothing like 'Long time no see.'*

'No, the housekeeper called the hospital when she found him and they took him down – I wanted us all to go together, if you're ok with that.'

Agnes nods, shrugs, finishes her doughnut. Isla waits for some show of emotion, watches as Agnes wipes sugar from her chin.

'I don't mind if you don't.'

'Why would I *mind*?'

Agnes looks at her for a second, bright knife briefly flashed then stowed beneath a flat expression. Isla tries to find a voice for what she's thinking. *Why does it always need to be so oppositional? Why do you enjoy it being so fucking hard?* She wonders, for a moment, whether this isn't something she more typically thinks about Irene, whether she's simply covering for having almost no clear idea about Agnes at all, most of the time. With Irene, only one year her junior, she knows where she is. With Irene, it is easy enough to be pissed off and leave it at that. A thought she once had: if she sent the same message to both Irene and Agnes, Agnes would ignore it, whereas Irene would send her thirty messages about a word that she'd misspelled. *Why can't you both just be nice to me*, she thinks, and then feels pathetic. She remembers, all at once, that Agnes is eleven years younger than she is, recalls the gape of time between them like something taken from her body, the ache like stolen flesh.

Agnes is her sister – is their sister – in the sense that all three of them share a father, but the concept of *sisterhood* is not one that Isla has felt able to extend to Agnes. The problem, perhaps, is the distance – the years and the fact of their separate mothers, the blank space where there should be shared history. Their mother was named Allegra, Agnes's mother was named Marie. They came first and she came second, and the weirdness of that has never gone away. She has often thought of Agnes as something that *happened* to her and Irene: a small and squalling baby, abandoned within a year of her birth by her mother and left to be managed by everyone else. The house disarranged and inhospitable, their father telling Isla daily to clean up the mess, as though she had created any of it.

At the table, Agnes pulls on the sleeve of her jacket and Isla thinks about when she contracted chickenpox at age two or three and Isla spent several long afternoons cooling her down with sponges squeezed into iced water because she didn't know what else to do. Such early closeness coupled with deep resentment, with panic that no one else was going to help. Perhaps natural, then, for their adult relationship to have struggled, for the distance to have grown insurmountable the second that Isla escaped that house. On the rare occasion they meet now, she will look at Agnes and feel surprised to discover that she looks like that or sounds like that; every feature and mannerism one that Isla is somehow always just discovering again. *I don't think*, as she once said to Morven, *that Agnes likes me very much*, to which Morven responded that she doubted Agnes thought about her sufficiently to form any so strident an opinion. *And anyway*, she added, *you never think that anybody likes you.*

'Ok, well' – Agnes shrugs again – 'I'd like to come then, since he was my dad and all.'

Isla opens her mouth to reply but then the door swings back again and Irene comes bowling in, wearing glasses and a worsted coat that seems all but calculated to absorb any moisture in the atmosphere and end up five times heavier. Isla blinks over the top of Agnes's head and Agnes turns, rolls her eyes when she spots their sister.

'It's like she works to be as pissed off as humanly possible. She treats it like a fucking job.'

This last: delivered in the offhand fashion of her more astute remarks. Agnes, opaque to a point and then suddenly offering an opinion so in tune with Isla's own that Isla struggles with attribution later. The two of them briefly united, each taken up with the absurdity of Irene's coat.

The pleasant sting of this, but then Irene spots them and the moment is over and the three of them are what they are again.

'I don't know why you had to pick somewhere so out of the way.'

Irene, throwing herself down next to Agnes. Irene, yanking her coat off, holding herself like a fist. Isla sighs. *Long time no see.*

'It was equidistant.'

'As the crow flies, maybe. But you can take the train in. It's all ferry from where I'm based.'

'Right, well.' *The next time our father dies I'll pick somewhere more convenient.*

'Do you have coffee? Are these yours?' Irene gestures to the doughnuts, scrubs a hand across her face. Pale collarbones, the star-white hair, the impeccable jawline. It has always seemed unfair that Irene gets to be the pretty one, somehow against the natural rules: it should be first sister – pretty one; last sister – special one; second sister – miscellaneous. As it is, Irene has always been the one who's seen to best advantage in the harshest lights, whose hair takes in the rain without issue. It's a fact that Isla should be too old and too well trained to resent, and yet which slides beneath her surface like a splinter nonetheless.

Irene flags down a waitress to order coffee, gestures round the table to confirm three cups. Isla bites her tongue, pushes her tea aside and leans forward as the waitress departs.

'Well, I'm sorry about the place but I'm really grateful to you both for coming.' Irene looks about to interrupt so Isla presses on, in the way she long ago learned to be wisest. 'I don't know about you both but I'm feeling pretty … confused about things, so I thought it might be better if we met before—'

'Confused how?'

Isla closes her eyes, considers counting to ten, but Irene just carries on talking.

'I'm not being a dick, I just mean – well, confused how? You know how it's been. You know the relationship. I've barely spoken to him in four years, you got him that house-keeper so we wouldn't have to see him or look after him. I don't mean it isn't sad, I just mean … well … it doesn't feel like much to me. You know? I just don't think there's any point sitting here trying to get it up for each other when it's just … it is what it is.'

Isla remembers Irene, aged thirteen – a brief period of replying *but is it though?* when anything was described to her as complicated.

'Alright, fine, I'm sorry I spoke. I just thought it would be good to see each other—'

'There's absolutely no need to take it personally.'

'—somewhere neutral—'

'I'm just saying what I think.'

'—where we could just talk like adults.'

Isla spreads her hands. Agnes picks at a fingernail. Irene reaches for a doughnut. A brief silence. *But we've done all*

this before, Isla thinks. *I swear to God we only just did this.*
Four years ago, the first time their father died. The stroke,
which led to several days in hospital. The ICU smelling of
Dettol and eucalyptus chewing gum, the vending machine in
the corridor stuck on some malign kind of random mode,
dispensing only Scotch broth and peanut brittle. The scene
as follows: Isla by the bed; Irene in a chair; Agnes standing
by the door with her backpack on. *Take it off. Are you not
sticking around?* Irene said to Agnes in the exasperatingly
reasonable tone she sometimes employed with her sisters,
like she was speaking to someone partly unsocialised or
unusually dense. *Why*, Agnes replied, and Isla looked
between them both, thinking as she did so of the year that
Irene developed pica and made herself sick eating blackboard
chalk every morning before school. *I know all about you*,
she wanted to say – wanted to tell Irene to keep her reasonable tone in its holster, stick to eating chalk and being quiet.

I know it's not an ideal situation, she said instead, *but it's
so nice that we can all be here together.*

In the chair, Irene looked up. *What's that supposed to
mean?*

*I just mean it's nice that you've both been able to get
here, even if the circumstances aren't that great.*

*What exactly do you mean by 'get here' though – I've
been here literally the entire time you have.*

Yes, almost – I know, and I'm saying that's great.

Yes – Irene narrowed her eyes, chewed her cheek before
speaking – *but I'm not particularly clear on what direction*

this praise is coming from. I'm not sure who made you the arbiter of who's doing a good job 'getting here' – it's not like you've been here every day with a pocket watch waiting for us to arrive.

No and I'm not saying that, am I? I'm saying it's nice you've managed to be here.

Why are you saying 'managed' like I'm somehow just now learning to walk?

Isla looked around, bewildered. By the door, Agnes shifted from one foot to the other but otherwise refused to come to her aid.

I don't understand what it is you're so offended by, Isla said. *I'm saying you're here now, and that's really nice to see. I'm saying it's a good thing.*

You're saying it's a miracle, is what you're saying.

Irene, I have honestly no idea what you're talking about – if you're feeling guilty I suggest you work on that yourself.

I don't need to work on anything.

Well, then don't take your anger out on me.

And don't take your therapy out on me.

Isla opened her mouth to reply, but at this point their father – unheeded until now in his hospital bed – chose to go into cardiac arrest. A cardiac arrest functions much the same as any series of mechanical actions – the obstruction of blood flow to the heart, the heart ceasing to pump effectively, the circulatory failure leading to oxygen starvation of the brain – but death itself, as a fixed point in space, happens not as a result of this process but just as the process begins. In a purely clinical sense, death occurs not in the five minutes it takes the brain to starve but in the second that circulation stops and, along with it, breathing. Death, then, as an immediacy, as something pulled out of air. Of course, he did not truly die that day. Or rather, he did, but only for a grand total of three minutes and thirty-five seconds, before the crash team managed to revive him. *Long enough though*, Isla thinks now, looking across the table at her sisters, *long enough for all of this to feel familiar.*

'D'you remember' – and this is Agnes, out of nowhere – 'D'you remember what he'd say when you talked back to him? *Don't get twitchy. Don't get twitchy with me, young lady.* And you could never tell what he meant by that, whether it was just a cover for calling you *bitchy* or whether he really did think you were … giving off a twitchy vibe. You'd be like *Dad, I don't want to do the washing-up* and he'd be like *don't you get twitchy with me.*'

She pulls her neck to one side and pauses that way for a second, apparently waiting for a click that doesn't come.

'Yeah. Yeah, I do remember that,' Isla says.

Agnes goes on. 'He'd say *don't get twitchy* over and over and then when you got annoyed, he'd change it to *don't get glitchy*, which was even more irritating because it didn't make sense. Just over and over – *think you're being a bit glitchy, darling*, and you'd want to put your fist through a wall.'

'Only sometimes it wouldn't be that,' Isla says. 'It would just be *ooh, is somebody sulking?*'

Agnes grins – that half-suggestion of a grin, like a trick she's been working on. '*Ooh, is somebody **sulking** back there?*'

'*I think someone's **sulking**.*'

'*Quick, everyone put your forks down and appreciate the terrible sight of Miss Irene Amelia Carmichael **sulking** across the majestic plains of the dinner table.*'

This last delivered with no particular sense of malice by Agnes, who sits back in her seat and looks down at the table. Irene wrinkles her nose, finishes her doughnut. She has left the coconut one for Isla. It sits in the plastic basket, sweating its sugar.

＊　＊　＊

Outside, then. Brief beneath the awning – Irene taller than Isla, who is taller than Agnes. The rain and the thick city smell that is reminiscent both of rot and of metal. Isla looks at her phone, tries to decide the best route to the hospital. Her map presents a number of options, at least three of which take them past buildings designed by their father: *The Seeley-Lessner Building. Blue Glass. The Undertow.* She zooms in on her map, scrutinises the coloured lines indicating ferry routes.

'I think,' Irene says, pushes her hair from her face with one hand, 'that it's best if we walk to the jetty. We can try to catch a ferry from there.'

'I know that,' Isla says, still squinting at her phone. 'I'm just trying to figure out which one.'

Irene sighs loudly. 'Well, if we just head there it'll be easier to tell what's running.'

'Not necessarily.'

'Yes necessarily.'

'Irene, for God's sake can you just let me look?'

'There's no point,' Irene persists, 'going by the times you see on your phone. It's all so unreliable, so why don't we just walk to the jetty?'

See this building here? And this one? And this one? Isla wants to say, pictures herself turning her phone to Irene. *I don't want to go by them, I just want to find a safe way through.*

The promenade is busy despite the rain, the usual shrouded crush of people rendered headless by umbrellas. Isla gazes out beyond the awning for a moment, tries to focus her mind on the task at hand. *I think all of this is my fault*, she thinks to herself, looks down at her phone again and finds it has locked. *I think I was supposed to sort this out.* Doesn't know what she means by this. Pulls her map up again and squints at the route.

Irene

You learn to roll with it – this is something Jude is always saying. *Sure it's shitty, but you learn. It simply doesn't help to be overwhelmed all the time. Does that make sense?*

I guess it's all about perspective. Irene will narrow her eyes and quote a movie they both like – *yes, too much fucking perspective.*

Irene tries to focus on this – tries to focus on the image of Jude, pinching salt over watery GM tomatoes, fixing her a cup of tea, *ok but what are you really angry about?* It helps when she can feel herself working up to exasperation – helps now, in the lobby of the hospital, with one sister demanding to see someone in a position of authority and the other sister chewing her nails. It took them so long to get here that it's barely even morning any more – first the ferry then a series of clippers, Isla drumming her fingers incessantly on her knees.

Isla once told Irene that she had absolutely no idea what someone as nice as Jude was doing with someone like her. Isla pretends not to remember this: the two of them drinking together four years ago, the first time their father died (and then didn't). Isla leaning on the bar, ordering a fifth martini. *This needs **lemon!*** Spill of hot sauce down her shirt. They had set up camp in a by-the-hour hotel near the hospital: white lights, the bar upholstered an indifferent aubergine. Agnes, pleading work, had left them some hours earlier. *We're all busy*, Isla said, not to Agnes but later, to no one in particular; *how **busy** can she really be.* The rain-washed window showing slivers of the evening, spring-dark, infrequent passers-by, not late enough for streetlight. Isla drank too quickly, ordered food only as an afterthought. Leaning forward, an interrupting gesture despite the fact that no one was speaking: *I've never understood what you're doing together.*

Jude tends to talk about family the way one might refer to the temporary closure of a favoured restaurant: a shame, but hardly something to get worked up about. This isn't to say that Jude isn't sympathetic, but all the same there always comes a point at which they will nod and smile sadly, say *I know, babe,* and then, *but fuck 'em, right?* Irene has often felt that Jude has tranquillity hardwired the way others have tastes and obsessions, sensitivities to certain kinds of light. This is tranquillity as distinct from apathy, as distinct from not giving a shit. Seen from the outside, it can feel easy to read their almost preternatural ease as something approaching lassitude, if not to say idiocy. *They're maybe a bit woo-woo, I'm not sure,* Irene texted a friend after their first encounter. She has paid for it ever since. *How's the yogi,* the friend continues to ask even now, even after everything, and Irene is running out of ways to tell her to give it a rest. The truth is not that Jude is calm to the exclusion of all problems but rather calm in the face of them, calm as a method of attack. It helps, Irene supposes, to have a job which actually means something, a job in which Jude spends each day dealing with people whose homes have been flooded out, who have nowhere to put themselves, whose foundations are coming apart. It doesn't do, in that context, to always be getting so angry. *Does that make sense?* Jude will ask after explaining this again, explaining the day they've had, with the family of five who've been moved to a bedsit just above the waterline, with the woman trying to access adequate end-of-life care for her grandmother after her previous assisted-living arrangements were declared unsafe. *You just have to be getting on with it.*

The rain today has a temporary quality, as though it might quite easily evaporate on point of impact and rise again; moisture moving in the wrong direction. The journey to the hospital was uncomfortable and beset by delays, waterways blocked by downed pylons and other, larger things. They strung cable cars along broad sections of the city once, years ago, and then abandoned them. The pylons still rise out of the water at intervals, half-drowned, the cables hanging slack. It was a solution applied thoughtlessly, no one stopping to realise that the mechanism wouldn't be able to withstand rising water levels, that the pylons couldn't be appropriately secured. They passed one of these on the ride over, collapsed and impassable halfway across a thoroughfare. The city is littered with follies of this nature, relics of a very recent history; a place first throwing itself into resistance, then management, then damage control.

The hospital smells of disinfectant and cheese sandwich. Irene considers the hospital lobbies of her teenhood: track lighting, swing doors and the knowledge that a body can be tricked into eating itself, that a piece of chalk held under the tongue can last you eighteen hours or more. Her father in his leather gloves, coming to pick her up: *imagine, a daughter of mine.*

Isla marches back from reception, arms folded. 'They're sending someone up to check.'

No one seems to know what's happening. The housekeeper who phoned emergency services is nowhere to be found.

Isla has spoken to three receptionists, a nurse and a doctor, all of whom have given her contradictory information: their father is still on the ward; he's been taken down to the mortuary; they never admitted anyone under that name at all. Isla throws herself down in a plastic chair and recommences tapping her fingers on her knees. *Can you fucking stop it?* Irene wants to say. Wants to say, *do you remember when they took me to hospital because I ate all those cherry stones and couldn't stop throwing up?*

Standing beside the plastic chairs, refusing to sit, Agnes finishes work on one hand and starts to chew the nails on the other. The air vibrates with activity, doctors moving back and forth. *Maybe they'll just leave us here*, Irene thinks – a dirty thought, pulled up by the root – *maybe we don't have to do the next bit.* She is worried, extremely worried, that no matter how flat her reaction has been, no matter what she said in the doughnut shop – *it doesn't feel like much to me* – what comes next will reveal her as a liar. The image, again, of her father as he must have been, frozen somewhere in the house and waiting to be found. She thinks about saying a prayer and dismisses it, wonders why the thought occurred to her.

'Ms Carmichael?'

The doctor could be referring to any one of them, though Irene and Agnes both look to Isla, who stands. The doctor is youngish, grey about the eyes. He has come to explain that their father was brought in yesterday afternoon after a suspected stroke, that the team worked hard but were unable to revive him. *Was it far to travel?* he wants to know, an apparently genuine question that feels to her like it comes with its own footnotes: *was it too much to ask that you turn up last night, do you not care, what kind of night's sleep have you had?* She imagines raising her hand, sitting up straight as if in a seminar. *We didn't come last night,* she wants to say, *because it didn't feel like an emergency. We didn't come because we've done this bit before.*

Isla asks when they can see him, and Irene remembers the prayer for the dead; the brief patter she learned at the age of thirteen when googling *catholic stuff* on her father's computer and clearing the search history afterwards – *in company with Christ, who died and now lives, may they rejoice in Your kingdom, et cetera, et cetera.*

'If you'd like to come with me, I'd be more than happy to take you to him,' the doctor says. His skin is like news-print, untold hours into a weekday shift, and Irene realises he wasn't wondering why they didn't come last night, that it probably never even crossed his mind.

'I think that's fine,' Isla says – a strange thing to say – looking to Irene and Agnes. 'Is that fine with you?'

Irene nods, doesn't look to see if Agnes is also nodding. Thinks *Daddy* – the line from the old movie – thinks

Daddy, my Daddy. Thinks *every minute, every second, our bodies are eating themselves.*

Agnes

Don't look at it.

She holds one thumb between the fingers of her other hand, squeezes tight and tries to focus her attention. If she had a hair tie, or a piece of elastic, she could string that round her thumb and pull taut, stop the circulation and watch the skin grow white towards the knuckle. Just to hold her concentration. She wishes she'd thought of that.

The room is cold, which makes sense. Patients, the doctor had explained, are taken to the viewing suites to allow relatives a more comfortable experience, an opportunity to sit with the loved one in peace. *Patients* is an odd word to use in this context, implying as it does that the situation may still be developing. *So what's the prognosis*, Agnes had thought of saying, and bitten the tip of her tongue.

Irene and Isla had bickered dully all the way up to the room but now appear to have run dry. The clock on the wall is fast, though perhaps it doesn't matter. Agnes holds on tight to her thumb and tries to plan what she'll say to Jason. *My father died*, she imagines, and then, *I mean, my father is dead now.* She remembers her father's face, impassive in the hall light, in the mirrored glass of his house, the unrelenting tic of the vein in his forehead. She remembers him looking at her – opaque expression of one thinking of something else – imagines she is eight again, thirteen again, and the nothing she always was in his company. She glances to the right and imagines she sees him standing where Isla is, at her elbow, the dark hair and uncomfortable posture of a man grown too important for the people who surround him day to day. Agnes draws in a breath, squeezes her eyes shut and opens them again. Isla shifts and there is nothing beside her at all.

'It's freezing in here.' Irene is still wearing her stupid coat, yet now scuffs her hands up and down her arms.

Isla looks at her sharply.

'Can't you think of something *nice* to say? Right now, of all times?'

'I didn't—' Irene starts, and then stops herself, looks around, looks forward. 'It doesn't matter.'

Her voice sounds funny and Agnes wishes her sisters weren't both so incapable of keeping their mouths shut. She watches as Irene continues to slough her hands along her arms in the corner, watches as Isla takes an uncertain step towards the gurney, reaches up to touch her own hair. Agnes lets her gaze drop to the left and then shakes herself.

Don't look at it.

She doesn't want to, absolutely doesn't want to. She looks at her thumb instead, the place where the skin has reddened, the flesh beginning to blanch. She presses down harder with two fingers and ignores the noise coming from nearby, a noise like someone sniffing, another noise like someone fumbling in their pocket, pulling out a tissue, blowing their nose.

'Fucking hell' – and this is Isla's voice now, and she is the one holding the tissue – 'fucking hell.'

Agnes wonders whether Isla really said the same thing twice or whether Agnes heard it once and then replayed it. She thinks about the time Isla tried to cut her own wrist with a Venus razor – her sister aged eighteen, wandering out of the bathroom with a horizontal cut already clotting at the corners, asking someone to come and see what she'd done. Her gaze is drifting again – towards the gurney, towards the shape beneath the sheets – and it's imperative, absolutely imperative, that she doesn't allow this. *Don't look at it.* She releases the hold on her thumb. *I told you not to look.*

It takes a second or two to realise that she is moving towards the door, that Irene is asking where she's going. She moves without full control, steps out of the room and walks calmly down the corridor towards the nurses' station. Here, she stops, raising one heel and then the other, clicking them together and then setting them back on the floor. It is warmer in the corridor than in the room and easy in the brief collapse of time between one place and another to think of nothing, to recognise the taste of the chewing gum she swallowed earlier and the acid of her breath behind that taste and to wait for something new to happen. Bolted to the wall above the nurses' station, a television plays the news on mute: a group of protesters collected outside a half-drowned municipal building, then cut to a piece on a pair of missing siblings, then cut to the ads.

'Are you cold?' A man's voice, directly behind her. She turns and finds him standing there – perhaps a nurse, wearing scrubs and identifiably weary, strong smell of canteen coffee on his breath and a polystyrene cup in his hand. She looks at him and feels nauseated in a way she can't fully place. He has the look, she thinks, of someone pulled from water; a certain sallowness around the edges of the face, a sense of something tending towards salt and bloat. She rocks back to put an inch of distance between them and gather up the scatter of her thoughts. He is looking at her benignly enough – with the red-rimmed eyes of someone either recently out of bed or many hours away from it – and she registers an unwonted impulse to turn on her heel and run.

'What did you say?' she asks, as he takes a casual sip of coffee.

'You look chilly,' he says, nodding his head towards her. 'I'm always saying we keep the rooms too cold.'

'Oh, yeah,' she says, her voice weak for no justifiable reason.

He nods again, continues to look at her. She tries to remember how many times a minute a person is supposed to blink.

'Bad form, that,' he says, smiling at her, and as he does so she becomes unusually certain that the smile is wrong. That this man, in fact, is wrong and the corridor is wrong and everything about this moment is fundamentally wrong. On the television above the nurses' station an advert beams the praises of a Teflon pan that's actually seven pans in one. The man holds her gaze, the smile like something plastered over an absence, a hole in a wall.

'I was sorry to hear about your father,' he says, and she wants to ask how he could possibly know who she is, or who her father is, or anything about them.

'Oh, well,' she says instead, stepping back another couple of inches and trying to remember why it was she came out into the corridor. 'I should probably be getting back.'

'Everything will work out for the better, you know,' he says as she turns to move off down the corridor and back towards the viewing suite. 'It all comes good, in time. We'll be thinking of you.'

Later on, Agnes will feel sick with herself for reacting so strongly to someone who, in however strange a manner, was only trying to help. As it is, her response to this last exchange is to turn and take in the man's smile once again, before crossing back and knocking the coffee out of his hand.

She is back in the viewing suite some thirty seconds later and her sisters do not ask where she went. The air is cool again, the walls clean and featureless. She squares her shoulders, pictures the splash of coffee down a shirt.

Don't look at it.

She keeps her hands loose, her expression neutral.

Don't look.
She looks at her father.
There you are.

City

Unpleasant to say, but there's no way to bury a body in earth which is flooded out. Customs change, of course; it has long since been held quite unfashionable to plant a body that could instead be burned. Less cost-efficient, less space-efficient; far better to collect the remains of a loved one to scatter or keep them close in some cool and private place. Even before the previously buried bodies started floating up, unearthed and mutely hostile, most people were already choosing to burn their dead, a choice that was first recommended and latterly enshrined in law. Morbid, but still a subject requiring attention, the administration of death as due an update as anything else in unprecedented times.

It is easy to forget matters like this; easy, amidst the monotony of supermarket sandwiches and damp subsistence, to forget the chippings and scrapings that come attendant on a world fundamentally narrowed in scope. One *could* bury one's dead, once upon a time, and now it is impossible. Hardly something to be grieved in itself but still a lessening, a fact consigned to history along with almost everything else.

3.

Agnes

Someone is yelling *fucking amateur hour* over by the bar and Agnes holds onto the neck of her beer and tries to remember how long it's been since she did a line. Too many bodies in one place, dark heave of bass. The pipes behind the bar, painted orange and peeling. She tips her head, lets her hair fall forward and notes that she's sweating. Takes inventory: feet – sore; tongue – swollen; teeth – filmed over with something slick. Dyke Night at the Compendium is usually easy enough to navigate, easy to move through the crowd with the slippery purpose of something jettisoned or otherwise thrown with no thought as to where it will land. She picks up scraps of conversation as she moves, grinds her teeth, passes women with geometric haircuts; rakish butches, femmes playing it low-key in denim shorts and bustiers.

People can turn any old shit into an omen

All I want is to sit in a room with someone and let the world end

I'm obsessed with Beckett right now

Did you hear about Jennifer

So I said we should start our own splinter group

All I want is an Aviation and a fuck

All I want is some decent storage space

All I want is for it to be ok

Agnes shakes her head, rocks her foot where her heel is coming out of her shoe, tries to wriggle it back and misses. Her bare heel brief against the floor – tacky nightmare, too disgusting to contemplate. She hops up on one foot, grabs her shoe and jams it back on, feels briefly dizzy. A butch in a harness palms her back to move past her and she considers catching hold and asking to be rescued. *Someone help me, for fuck's sake.* It passes, the way it always passes, and the music is loud enough to let her forget.

Club nights haven't survived in any meaningful sense, though those that have can be found hunkered down in abandoned places, forced into strange dimensions, the better to cling on tight. They grow the way wasps fashion nests beneath eaves, in the slips of wall cavities: puckered makeshift shapes, built to fill the spots they inhabit. Easy enough to locate, once you know what you're looking for. The Compendium, for instance, is a warren of rooms on the second level of a former office block now partially underwater, the companies it once housed long since resigned to inflated rents in more hospitable areas, further out and higher up. Whoever first took over reinforced the windows against the water, then blocked them off with plywood and black tape. You can worm your fingers into gaps between panels and look out: queasy aquarium light offset by the disco balls. Someone installed a bar, then a stage, then a generator and ventilation system, in that order. No one is entirely clear as to who pays the rent and to exactly what entity. They run queer nights four times a week and dyke nights every Thursday. You have to take a water taxi to get here, stagger up across the rudimentary jetty built to wrap around the outer structure of the block. This is a washed-out area, a dip in the city. No one realised that cities are as variable as any other landscape, as made up of peaks and valleys, until the rain arrived to fill them in.

Agnes wipes her mouth, tries to collect herself. There is someone in the crowd to her left looking directly at her – blue eyes, unfamiliar, older – and she feels simultaneously too exhausted and too wired to follow the gesture through to its obvious conclusion: the eye caught, the change in music lending itself to dancing, pressing her mouth up against the neck of someone solid and anonymous and shivered over with salt. She wants more coke, wants to drink exactly two more drinks and stop replaying pointless scenes from earlier: *it's freezing in here – can't you think of something nice to say?*

It's too hot, her skin too loose or tight or too ill-suited, and she knocks against someone, staggers sideways and comes up short against another girl.

'Hey, there you are.'

Agnes blinks and Stephanie grins at her, lurching forward with the movement of the crowd and grabbing on to Agnes's shoulder for balance. She is dressed differently from yesterday, her hair scraped back, fine clamber of gold along her upper ear cartilage. Agnes's confusion is rendered quickly moot by a drunker recollection: her phone, switched on outside the hospital and almost immediately off again, enough time to send a message and then forget about it.

'Ooh, yeah,' she says, stumbles back and then rights herself, wonders how long is too long *not* to look at someone's tits when you know they know you're thinking about it. Too long seems studied, like you want to look more than you do and are just trying to stop yourself. She looks quickly, looks back up. Stephanie still grinning at her. Hard to tell how drunk she might be.

'You texted that you'd be here and I thought, well, *serendipity*. I'm here with friends,' she adds, 'in case you're thinking I made the trip for you.'

Agnes tries to focus. Distracted by the thought of one sister, sometime between arriving at the hospital and being shown to the viewing suite, chewing her hair and snapping at the other sister. The two of them going at it in a play of hostility that is still a greater intimacy than either has ever shown to her. Agnes shakes her head again, tries to force down the feeling that occasionally arises, of wanting to be wanted more than she pretends. *I've been trying to call, I can't believe you'd have your phone off at a time like this*, Isla had said when Agnes first rang to ask what was going on, ignoring the fact that Agnes did not yet know it was a time like that, but also failing to acknowledge that neither she nor Irene ever usually tried to call Agnes anyway.

'Hey' – and this is Stephanie again, leaning forward and miming a knock, definitely a little drunk and giggling. 'Where'd you go – I think you wandered off.'

Agnes leans back, tries to take her in despite the bleary club light, despite the fact that they are packed in by bodies on all sides. Stephanie is taller than her, a fraction heavier, good hips, great tits in a tank top, and Agnes thinks to herself *I'd sleep better on top of that*, thinks *I'd sleep better with that on top of me*, and she puts a hand out to catch at the hem of Stephanie's top and isn't refused.

Later on, after dancing and drinking and kissing the way people do when they know each other's names and nothing more – after that, Agnes will drag Stephanie out to the entrance where the music is quieter and tell her to come home with her. *I don't think*, Stephanie will say, *that I need to worry about you being a psycho.* Testing look, her mascara sweating sideways off her face. *I mean, I've seen your place of employment.* She will smile – her mouth, kissed thing, attempting to recall its secondary purposes – and Agnes will want to tell her where she spent today, that her father died and she saw him and then left without speaking to her sisters. That she had been so afraid to look at him but that, when she did, the sight made her feel such a heap of nothingness – not a nothingness brought on by grief but by an absence of grief, an absence of anything at all – that she had to leave or risk opening her mouth and speaking the void aloud. She won't say this, will only bring Stephanie's hand to her mouth and bite it, just gently, just in the place where the thumb meets the pad of the palm. *Not a psycho*, Agnes will say, and Stephanie will grin at her. *Well, you would say that, but sure, I believe you. Although who knows what it is you've got planned.* Agnes will say something she remembers from early childhood, something once said by Isla or Irene or her father or the television, something she was never actually planning to say: *Well, people won't often kill you.* She will say this and watch Stephanie play it back, tilt her head and decide to find it funny. She will say this and not, for whatever reason, say the next part, though the sentence is meant to come in two pieces: *all it takes is for someone to decide to kill you, of course, but usually you'll find that they won't.*

Isla

The house is both transparent and impenetrable – a hard balance to strike, but then on a purely technical level their father was always passed master at the art of building a home. The coffee table book published some seven years prior to his death bore rapturous witness to this particular Midas touch. *Stephen Carmichael: A Retrospective* – a glossy collection of prints and elevations, photos of their father with his back to the camera, surveying the mess of a site. *The true genius of Carmichael's design has always seen its best expression in the domestic; he is the hero of the domestic space, its veritable caped crusader, snatching homes from sites grown uninhabitable and lifting them up out of harm's way.*

Isla still has the book in her possession, batch-signed by her father at point of printing with the anonymous greeting that feels somehow more appropriate than if he had signed it to her directly: *Best wishes, SC.* She used to flip it to the page bearing a photo of her father poring over a blueprint with two tiny girls, the caption running rather to sentiment: *Carmichael and his daughters Isla and Irene discussing their Substratum project.* A peculiar act of fan fiction on the part of the book's editor, this. Isla and Irene were of course far too young to have had anything to do with the Substratum project and their father too deeply protective of his work besides. This is not to say he was private, exactly, for he frequently held court on his ideas and the thinking behind certain projects, but never with the sense that what he wanted was anyone's input. His work was something he appeared to discuss simply in order to have discussed it, his tone always that of a man who expected to have his words reflected back at him more than he actually longed to be understood.

As a child, Isla always called it *the floating house*, though its title is *White Horse* and their father liked to refer to it as *the stable*. It was built to rise above water, a high-functioning pastiche of Le Corbusier and the mid-century stilted houses which hung in the air for no other reason than that their design permitted it. Larch-clad, steel-framed and slender, strung with ribbon windows that run to fifty feet on either side, it streams from north to south as a single linear form, a straight line intended to play-act the flow of a river. Its legs are mechanical, extending as necessary to match the rising water levels. Unseen when submerged, these legs support a concrete base and surrounding platform that sit swanlike and unconcerned upon the surface; an affect of something about to drift away. Easy to watch the water lap against the bottom of the windows and miss the fact that the house is rising higher to account for this encroachment. Once, sifting through papers in her father's study in search of a magazine, she came across a sheet of trial marketing copy for a series of commercially produced buildings intended to be modelled on this one: *the design allows for a sizeable margin of error, raising the structure as necessary to contend with potential flood depths of well over 10.9 feet. This is above the 1:50-year-plus predicted change in water levels, protecting your investment even in a worst-case scenario.* She isn't sure whether the replicas were ever actually realised, though the thought is a peculiar one – this house, but not itself, elsewhere.

She hadn't intended to come to the house without the others, had turned to Irene at the hospital and promised to meet her here the next day. She had said this to herself several times even as she planned the route, booked the water taxi which took her from the hospital and out beyond the limits of the city as evening fell. Open space, still flooded out but cleaner, wider, better sanitised, a place that might once have been referred to as suburbia but which now more typically falls under a newer umbrella term: *the millponds.* The trains still run here – slow local lines elegantly raised above the water – and the houses are expensive, low-lying structures, built to float or rise as necessary. This, of course, is only one of several ways the wealthy choose to live, to raise their families. Those who prefer to avoid the floodplains entirely build their houses in the hillside enclaves: gated, high places where it is still possible to stroll or drive a car. Others remain in the centres of cities, spread across the highest levels; storeyed penthouses built like self-sustaining life rafts able to generate their own power, some connected by private walkways along the roped-off corners of the sky. Their father was responsible for a number of these places, celebrated for the knack he had with buildings which wore their emergency functions lightly. Life-preserving structures, built for people who could afford them.

Irene always said it was showy that their father chose to live out in the millponds, where the water had already taken hold. *Very 'Look at me, look how well my house works, look how easy it can be to live.' He could just as easily have built himself a high-rise and ignored the problem, but he loved the illusion of harm's way.* This was not strictly fair. Isla's memories do, after all, account for times before submersion, early times in the house's history where rain was frequent but not a constant, where the lawn was often visible beyond the exposed metal struts built to hold them above it. Exactly when the tipping point came is tricky to pin down. It was always a Bad Year, always a bad situation, but the point at which it became notably worse was probably fairly late on, in the scheme of things. Perhaps around the time she was eighteen, perhaps sooner. There were certainly times in her childhood, twenty years ago or more, when Isla remembers clambering down from the house onto marshy grass, remembers standing palms-up in the rain and feeling grateful for what could still be relied upon to grow in wet weather. She remembers the Lebanon cedar on the far edge of the property before it succumbed to rot and Sirococcus, before it dropped its needles and bled translucent gum. She remembers this, but even so Irene's accusation does hold. Perhaps building a house like *White Horse* anticipated what was to follow, perhaps the point in settling where they did was always the long game.

Now, Isla stands in the wide rectangle of the living room and tries to decide what to do. The overhead light is dim and the evidence of her father's taste is everywhere, muscled oddly up against the wheelchair and oxygen canisters, a final meal left out to go bad. *Why has the housekeeper not dealt with this*, she thinks, and then remembers that she still doesn't know where the housekeeper is. She has called and left a message, called again. *I should get on top of that.* She is not, it occurs to her, here for any concrete reason. Morven might lump it in with what she refers to as Isla's *first-man-on-the-moon* habit – her need, in Morven's words, to always be somewhere first and then look around for messes made by subsequent arrivals. It might be this instinct. Or it might be an urge to ensure a place is safe before her sisters can come striding in to see for themselves.

She sits down on one end of the sculptural velvet sofa and jangles the keys in her hand. Briefly considers crying. But what, after all, would she really be crying about? This impulse had also hit her at the hospital, hard enough for her to take out a tissue only to find no tears to mop up. She had blown her nose to cover the moment, stowed the tissue away again. In the viewing suite, her father's body had appeared to her like a strange anomaly, an ugly chair or table in an otherwise well-presented room. She had looked as long as she felt able, then glanced away to see Irene scratching the back of one of her legs, to see Agnes staring stupidly at the wheels of the gurney on which their father lay. *What are we doing here*, she had thought, and then looked back at the body – understood *the body* as somehow distinct from her father, yet felt little about her father's technical absence from the room. This lack was not a new sensation. How, she wondered, is one supposed to grieve an absence when that absence is familiar? What, she wondered, was grief without a clear departure to regret?

Dark windows, eerily reflective where the blinds stop halfway, mirror her back to herself in a murky black and white. The house is cool, evidence of the swishly unobtrusive air conditioning, and she thinks about all the tricky little operations necessary to hold the house in stasis: the legs calibrated to extend just above the waterline, the air conditioning and dehumidifying systems, the microturbine that nixes the need for mains electricity. It's no wonder, she thinks, that her mother came to feel that something terrible was coming down upon her, in a house which seemed always to anticipate disaster. This is a bad thought, unanticipated, like something against which she has barked her shin: her mother, standing by the window in her dressing gown, her hair caught up in one hand and pulled taut as if preparatory to lifting her scalp away. Isla gets up and crosses to the fireplace, puts her hand around the side of the chimney breast and encounters the panic button intended to trigger an alarm that connects directly to the police, a button their father had warned them never to play with and which Irene had frequently feinted towards but never actually touched. She turns around, leans back against the mantelpiece and surveys the room from this vantage, chases a memory through the upper storey of her mind and abandons it.

A patient she has taken to seeing on alternate Wednesdays talks not infrequently about the fact that his father set himself on fire on the balcony of their apartment complex one night and that shortly afterwards the remainder of the family moved some hundred miles south, presumably to outrun the smell of burning flesh. She isn't sure why she thinks of this now, or why she then moves through the house as though propelled, turning on lights in every room and checking them as if for ghosts, as if for interlopers, even going so far as to look under beds and behind curtains, keeping one hand always clasped around her phone, held before her as a torch. She makes a loop around the central corridor, going briefly up the stairs and swiftly down again. By the time she's finished, all the lights in the house are on and she feels better, sits down at the circular table in the main room, which used to function as both their breakfast and homework table.

A new message pings and she finds it is Morven asking for her to reply to her lawyer's last email. She drops the phone into her bag and sits back, tries to recollect telling her father about her first girlfriend and then stops and thinks instead about her recycling and why it is you have to separate the recyclables from the non-recyclables and why can you not just throw them all away together, because surely there's technology to pick out the unsuitable bits and send them to landfill, and surely that's easier than throwing the cardboard exterior of a sandwich box into the ordinary bin because the cellophane window won't recycle and you're not sure if you can throw the whole thing in the recycling with the plastic still attached. But then again, maybe the things that get thrown away wrong don't only go to landfill but somehow end up somewhere worse because you didn't put them where they were supposed to go, and even overlooking all of that who even really *bothers* recycling any more anyway when the whole projected point appears to have been to avoid a situation which is long since past? It's the kind of thought that comes to her with a whirring regularity, the fact of how little she knows about the needful things in life.

She closes her eyes and smooths her hands across the surface of the table, finds the little sigils she and Irene must once have scratched into the wood with drawing pins and protractors, despite repeated exhortations to leave the good furniture alone. She finds the little *IC* and another, bigger *IC*, finds the crown and the tiny set of teeth and a mark she doesn't recognise: little holes for eyes and something like a face scratched around it, slash of mouth like someone has taken the metal corner of a ruler to the table and dragged it across. She moves her thumb over this image, tries to recall Irene carving it into the wood and can't, then leans closer, picks out what appear to be words scratched in the tiniest text to ring the face in several widening circles: *in time in time in time in time in time in time in time in time*. Jagged

73

shape of each *t*, scored sharply. What a strange game one of them must have been playing, though exactly what it was escapes her memory. It occurs to her that Agnes was alone in the house a lot longer than she and Irene were. A small child might do all sorts to keep herself occupied.

She shifts back in her chair, takes in the expensive lamps, the side tables, a large Persian rug she doesn't recognise softening the cold poured-concrete floor.

The rain appears to have picked up since she first arrived and is now hammering hard against the side of the house. Spit of something like hail, like heavy weather. *That's a bad sign*, she thinks, and wonders whether she should have asked the taxi to wait.

※　※　※

Once, Irene crept into Isla's bed and asked her to tell a story about their mother. It was late, heavy rain behind curtained windows, and Isla's room was warmer than the hallway. The house was always cold along its central corridors, a chill like something passing through the veins. Sometimes, in summer, Isla and Irene would press their cheeks into the hallway floor to absorb some fraction of this coolness, lying flat as overheated animals might when they tumbled down to pant and twitch their legs.

Beneath the covers, Irene slithered an arm around Isla, who kicked out but didn't shrug her away.

'I've been counting backwards, and counting sheep,' Irene said. 'I still can't sleep. The baby keeps crying and crying and I can hear it all the way from my room. It'll work better if you tell me a story.'

Isla sighed. 'Yes and then I'll be stuck with you here all night.'

It was a week after Isla's twelfth birthday, an event rendered awkward by Irene, not quite eleven, declaring that she didn't see why it couldn't in fact be *her* birthday and then sulking the day away. Their father had presented Isla with a water balloon of exotic fish and she had asked him several questions about their provenance, which appeared to irritate him, for he plugged the bathroom sink and poured them out to thrash about in shallow water, telling her that all that mattered was where they found themselves right now. Later on, he gave her a tank to move them into, though by this point she had been crouching by the sink for several hours with her hands in the water, trying to ascertain which of the fish was still alive. The tank now sat in the corner of her bedroom, casting a dim nightlight glow over a narrow strip of carpet, a single fish moving idly about the gravel at the base.

'I'll tell you a story,' Isla said, 'but I want you to get out when I'm done.'

Stories were easy enough, if you started with details. *Mum was so beautiful*, Isla always said, though she hadn't been in her last few months. Narrow face like something pared unkindly back, the eyes and mouth revealed almost indecently. *That dressing gown she had*, Isla would say, *her hands. The notes she left us around the house. Her way of talking like she only meant for you to hear.* Stories were fine if you knew how to edit. Isla could talk at length about the day their mother brought boxes of ribbons up from the spare room and twisted their hair into braids, without mentioning the way she'd also looped a ribbon round her own neck and held it there too long. She could tell the story about the time their mother read aloud from an article about worsening weather patterns in the Global South and omit that, late that night, she'd heard her sobbing in the bathroom, then retching, then washing her hands.

She was well practised at leaving things out: the parts where their mother and father fought, the shouting that Irene never heard because Isla had put her in her room with a record playing and shut the door. She never said that their mother had been increasingly subject to night sweats and frenetic impulses, long periods of agitation that found her outside at odd times and in uncertain weather; that she had paid people to rake their hands across her skull, to realign her aura, to hold her down and slap her back and forth across the face. She had spent hours on the phone to women who charged by the minute to hint at what her astrological chart meant for her future prospects, had filled one room with candles that melted when she lit them and stuck to the floor. *I don't know,* Isla had once overheard her saying to their father, in answer to some question offered in too low a voice to catch, *but I think the next thing will really be what sorts it. I feel I'm very close to cracking this, I'm really on the edge of something good.* That this was seven months before her death was frankly not a point on which it did much good to dwell.

Isla also never said that, one morning when playing alone in the living room, she had seen a woman coming around the side of the house and making for the back entrance. She never said that she had heard the back door opening and wondered what to do because her mother had said she was going out and wouldn't be back until later and her father was never much good at receiving unexpected guests. She never told – never related the footsteps she heard, another door opening, closing, the movement deep within the house. Later on, when introduced to the woman who was to be her stepmother, she would look at her and put some things together, though by that point there was little use in saying anything at all.

'I'll tell you a story,' she said to Irene now, and Irene settled down on her side, counted back from one hundred and fell asleep.

City

It's hard to tell if it's worse or just business as usual. Unseasonable heat followed by days of roiling weather, rain that barely ever stops, that curves hard into hail and then loosens again like a fist clenched tight and released. People go out on the roofs of their buildings only to hurry back in at the threat of thunder. Ball lightning bouncing down fire escapes, heavy rushes of wind, pushing the weather sideways. People pile sandbags against the leaking windows of apartments rented out too low and too close to the waterline.

It is difficult, these days, to know how to be. Not a new phenomenon, of course, but one lent a certain urgency by the situation. People protest, or forget to protest. People hoard food, hoard medical supplies, use them up and hoard them again. People get on, shop, work, attend lectures, complain that there is never anything good on TV. They suspect that there is less time than predicted, throw parties to celebrate the endless ending, pretend the coming on of something new. It's always been this way, always worsening. A contradiction: the fact of something always being the case and yet that case being flux, deterioration. Best not to recollect that once there were any number of options and now there are fewer. That once it might have been possible to drive a car in a city, take a plane to a foreign destination, that once there were green spaces, cinemas, coastal towns, Tube lines, Tube posters for *The Phantom of the Opera*, cheap rents, cheap fruit, skylights, free healthcare, beaches, public art, bumblebees and all the rest of it. The world has a way of erasing its own history. It can be easier to participate in this – to forget that one could once quite easily buy red meat, take the bus, visit certain countries – easier than it is to resist.

* * *

Of note: A group of women are briefly featured on the lunchtime news for orchestrating a boat race in a flooded-out neighbourhood which is subsequently broken up by police. A man sleeps overnight in his office only to find on waking that water is spilling through the heating vents and service elevator. Another man drowns, quite by accident. A whole series of people quit their jobs on the same day and take to the internet to decry the need to work in a designated end time. A woman films several videos in which she etches sigils into her skin with the tip of a cheese knife, claiming that doing so in a certain sequence will work as a guard against harm. These videos are taken down some thirty minutes after posting, though in the window before this happens they are shared upwards of a hundred thousand times. *Thing is*, someone comments in response to the final video, *she's clearly a fucking fruit loop but I get it.*

A news reporter conducts interviews with a group of people clustered around the foyer of an apartment building – the stairwell is roped off with police tape, officers shuffling back and forth in the periphery. *You don't like to think of these people being where you can see them*, a woman in a dressing gown nods into the camera, *right under our noses, you know.* There has been what the reporter keeps referring to, perhaps overzealously, as a *Jonestown-style occurrence* in one of the flats in the building, and the neighbouring residents have been penned downstairs in the lobby at the mercy of police and reporters until further notice. *I don't think*, one man says, *that it can possibly be that unsafe for us to go back to our beds if all they did was poison them-selves. It's not like there was a gas leak – why did they even get us down here at all.* A girl in a long sleep t-shirt bearing the legend *women want me, fish fear me* elbows her way into the frame. *They want to check we're not all going to off ourselves too, that's my theory. Want to make sure it's not a building-wide pact, like you read about sometimes.* The man snorts. *Where are you reading that? What are you talking about? They were a bunch of silly kids subletting a too-small flat and they killed themselves for attention – stop being so dramatic.* The girl rolls her eyes towards the camera. *What do you mean, 'for attention'? Pretty hard to enjoy the attention if you're dead.* The man shrugs. *Weirdos all over the place these days.* The girls nods her head. *But that's exactly what I'm just saying. There's a lot of it about.*

Agnes

Waking suddenly – the jack-knife all-at-once motion of a woman in a novel, thrown out of a dream that was perti-nent to the plot. Sitting up in bed, she looks sideways at the figure beside her and passes a hand across her face. Shot of memory: kissing in the foyer of her building, outside the broken elevator, the way the inside of another person's mouth can feel at once unseemly and correct. Stephanie had asked her which floor they were heading for and Agnes had forgotten, said seventeen and then twenty, started laughing when Stephanie pulled a pained expression – *you're saying you want me to walk all that way*. Fingering her in the stairwell between seventh and eighth to stay her impatience; Stephanie curling forward, curling inward, Agnes sharing second-hand the liquid pleasure of something like a gutting, like the pulling out of lungs and stomach, shriek cut short by a hand across a mouth. Afterwards: the flat, and Stephanie asking questions about the flat, about the room and its self-contained kitchen, the bathroom that she shares with her neighbour along the hall. *You don't need to tell me it's disgusting*, Agnes had wanted to say, *I already know that it is*. She hadn't said this, only managed *I didn't want to be beholden* before stopping herself, turning instead to the cupboard where she keeps the tequila, to get the evening back on track. *I love kissing*, Stephanie had said, at some later point, *I could kiss all day and not mind what comes later*, and Agnes had told her that was no way to live.

Now, she rolls out of bed and crosses to the window, looks out at heavy rain and something like a fog beneath it. Dirty city morning; miasma, sticky in the throat. In bed, Stephanie turns towards the wall and goes on sleeping. Agnes glances at her, registers the horror movie beat of someone trying to evade the killer and thinking they've been caught. It's not a nice quality (and, more to the point, it is not an interesting quality), this tendency to react to the prospect of intimacy with immediate panic. She is aware, painfully aware, that there is nothing more tedious than a person who turns to another and says *I don't know, I just find it hard to stay interested in someone who actually likes me.* Nothing more tedious than a person who wears their aversion to commitment as a blazon of their own originality. *I don't know what it is, why I find things harder than other people. I guess love is just different for me.* She knows all this, and still finds the impulse to run from the room as fresh as she always finds it. The need to be free from what she did and afterwards to change the sheets and forget about it, to go for a swim and eat a bagel and read the Wikipedia plots of violent movies on her laptop until she feels more or less alright again. She considers her options, tries to decide whether it would be better to wake Stephanie up on purpose or simply to cause such a commotion in the kitchen area that she can't stay asleep, but then of course Stephanie blinks awake before she can make a decision and, what's worse, looks over at her.

'Oh, hey,' Stephanie says, and then wriggles her shoulders into a yawn. 'I'm sorry, I didn't mean to sleep over.'

'Oh, yeah,' Agnes nods, realising she's naked about the same time Stephanie seems to and reaching for a shirt.

'Don't change on my account,' Stephanie grins, and Agnes makes an indistinct noise, pulls the t-shirt over her head. 'I had fun,' Stephanie adds.

'I don't have any coffee,' Agnes replies, and immediately feels embarrassed, though Stephanie only smiles at her.

'That's fine,' she says, 'I wasn't going to stay.'

Agnes turns away to fish a pair of jeans out from under her desk. She considers the flat as it must appear to a newcomer: the plywood wardrobe and the dying spider plant, the black mould clambering down the stucco to the corner of the windowsill. *This is a choice*, she wants to say, and doesn't, directing her attention instead to dragging on her jeans and ignoring the sounds of Stephanie pulling on her clothes behind her. *I'd like to see **you** try it*, she thinks, and doesn't know what she means by this, and then Stephanie clears her throat, which means she has to turn around.

'Sooo …' Stephanie fixes Agnes with a testing expression which dissolves into something easier as she meets her eye. 'I'm just going to say the thing I might as well say, which is that I find you very hot and I'd happily take you to breakfast.'

Agnes blinks, steps unconsciously backwards and bangs her ankle on one of the desk chair castors.

'Um.'

'Yes, I know,' Stephanie says, as if naked alarm was exactly the reaction she was after, 'but I made this little pact to at least *ask*, you know. Just feels so fucking stupid not to, given' – and here she waves a generalising hand. 'Anyway.' She pushes herself up off the bed and claps her hands together, looks around for her jacket and locates it, turning to punch a gentle fist against one of Agnes's shoulders in a gesture that is entirely too sexy for its intention. 'You're pretty weird.'

'I am—' Agnes sputters to a halt in advance of saying *not*, puts her hands on her hips and then drops them after thinking for a sudden and horrified moment that it might make her look like Irene. Stephanie laughs, tips a hand to her forehead in mock-salute.

After she's gone, Agnes isn't entirely sure what to do with herself, settling at first for pulling off her jeans and t-shirt and walking the flat in a wide circle, stopping in the centre to tilt back on her heels and then resettle before putting the t-shirt back on again. She feels odd, prickled over, the comedown combined with a feeling like skin being removed from hot water; shrink and tingle, the sweat through the lines of her palms. She surveys the deflated form of the spider plant in a pot beside her bed, impulsively crosses to the kitchen and fills a glass at the tap to water it, watches in some dismay as the water simply runs off the impacted surface and onto the table beneath. She sets down the glass and crosses to the window, looks out and then down the long drop towards the entrance of her building, the elevated walkway and the long jetty that allows easy access to the front of the block. There is, it appears, some-one down there – possibly a man, though it's hard to tell at this distance and through the haze and the rain – someone standing a little way from the entrance and with their neck angled back as though trying to get a good look at one of the higher windows. Without quite knowing why, she steps back, glances over her shoulder into the flat before peering out again, though by the time she does this there is no one there at all.

* * *

At the age of eight, unencumbered as she was by mother or sisters or very much in the way of distraction, Agnes stole a scale model that belonged to her father and used it to stage suicide attempts for stuffed animals in her bedroom at the top of the house. The model was that of a tower her father had proposed for a grant early on in his career – proposed unsuccessfully, though he kept it the way he kept all his creations, consigned to a toytown of models laid out across the long baize table in the hall. At the time, Agnes had only the sketchiest idea of what a suicide attempt actually entailed. Late one night and unattended, she had watched a programme in which a woman talked a man off the ledge of a building and had enjoyed the theatre of the interaction so much that she had started trying to parrot it, staring into the mirror while she brushed her hair and intoning *don't do it, imagine how your children will feel.* The live-action replay had been the obvious next step; a line of rabbits and bears stacked up along the side of the miniature tower, queuing up for a chance to fling themselves into the void. It was Agnes who took on the role of mediator, demanding that one animal after another think of their wife and all they had to live for. Sometimes her tactics would work, and sometimes they wouldn't. When an animal chose to throw itself into the sky, she would set it aside with a pat on the head and move briskly on to the next one.

I just think she's weird, Irene once observed. Isla glancing up from a magazine, pushing her hair back from her temples. *Irene, you just get angry when anyone acts contrary to how you personally would act.* A reaction which Agnes, at the age of six, still recognised as being less rooted in a desire to defend her than in a desire to antagonise Irene.

Ten years, eleven years: too great a gap to be properly bridged between sisters. Isla and Irene already a mystery to her in the brief period they spent in the house together and receding further the older they got. *Look after Dad,* Isla had said the night before she left for university, hugging Agnes in an odd, one-armed way which Agnes would repeat, as if experimenting, on the same toys she would latterly fling to their deaths. The concept of looking after her father was never something with which she managed to reckon – her father a figure she saw predominantly as impervious, a structure much like those on which he spent the majority of his time, unaffected by weather or external stressors. As a very young child she had often imagined her father to be in some sense carved or otherwise artificially constructed, while the rest of the people she knew she assumed to be hatched from eggs. After Isla had moved out, she had sometimes tried to imagine bringing her father a blanket or putting together a sandwich to take to his study when he was deep in his work. She had never done either of these things, of course, had instead only chosen to follow Irene's lead and ignore him, until Irene had in turn moved out and left her to fend for herself.

Sitting back on her heels in her bedroom that afternoon, she found that she had run out of soft toys to talk off the ledge. Those that had taken her advice sat huddled together in a makeshift support group around the foot of her bed. Those that had not been so circumspect lay elsewhere, to be ferried some short while later to the graves which Agnes would parcel out beneath her duvet covers and the rug beside her desk. Before that, however, she wanted a drink.

She made her way down to the kitchen, the stillness unconcerning to her, the chill only proof that the house was working as it should. Her father, she knew, was most likely in his study. She preferred this – to be elsewhere, even if elsewhere meant being by herself. The two of them existed in this house very much as roommates might, meeting for dinner and the occasional evening film which they would watch together, Agnes on the rug and her father on the low-backed velvet sofa, neither commenting much on proceedings unless it happened that Agnes had a question to ask. *It's nice that he does that*, Isla had said, when Agnes recounted a film she had seen with their father. Her sister's voice had strained towards casual and Agnes had known without quite understanding that Isla considered these movie nights to be some point of contention, of competition or jealousy. She had not known how to say that the ritual meant nothing to her, that she would have been happy to watch the movies alone, willing to trade the time with her father if Isla had something she wanted to swap. Hard enough, at the age of eight, to speak aloud what she knew of their father: that he accepted her presence only because she was already there.

He's different to how he used to be, Isla had gone on, and Agnes had taken a moment to consider what it was this could actually mean. Her father as she knew her sisters saw him: the ego and the temper that disguised itself as something glacial, swift rages caught in ice and thawing only slowly, anger running down like meltwater, first a little then a sudden chilly surge. Her father, younger, involved in his career. Her father, famous, and spiteful in a way that journalists excused as caustic wit. *So am I supposed to call you Doctor?* he had said when Isla chose to study psychology, and she had looked at him, bewildered. *Of course not.* It was a version of her father that had faded, though flashes remained. He liked, Agnes knew, to push you to excel and then to cut you down when you did so. *Well done*, he would say when she used a word he had taught her, *now let's find you one that's actually difficult.*

He's calmer now, Irene had said in response to Isla's assertion that he was different, and Agnes had wanted to shake her head, to explain that this wasn't calm but something else, something to do with his older daughters leaving, with Agnes's mother disappearing, with having taken too much, having too little left to take. And something else besides – a change only Agnes was aware of. Agnes knew, these days, not to scream or cry, not to react in any way, whenever possible. She had learned by trial and error – responded to her father's irritation, to being hefted from a room with a hand around her wrist, to being slapped without knowing the reason. She had wept, once – in the way a little kid will weep, operatically and without cause – and her father had put his face very close to hers and told her, if she continued all that noise, someone would come along in the night to take her away. She knew, now, how to hold herself, how to keep herself very quiet. Her father was calmer now, for that reason and for many others.

In the kitchen, she fetched a glass of orange juice and then wandered into the central room and thought about switching on the television. It was raining again, a hard persistent rain that followed three weeks of something similar. The garden beyond the deck was flooded, originally marshy and now simply overrun, the water rising, the big tree at the edge of the property bending inward, turning black along its trunk. She sat down on the sofa, fiddled with the remote, and it was at this point that she realised there was a woman outside, a woman who might have been there for some time, looking in through the long ribbon window that wrapped around two sides of the wall. A woman looking in at her.

Difficult to know what to do, in this situation. At the age of eight, and with no experience of anything similar. Difficult to know whether to call for a father who would most likely be annoyed at being interrupted, to go to the window and look out at the stranger, or simply to turn and run upstairs. Agnes stood for several moments, frozen between the television and sofa, staring out towards the window where the woman stood, her hair matted with the rain, her face difficult to make out through glass which ran with water. Agnes stood where she was, felt her hand tense around her glass of juice, release and then tense again before she could drop it. She did all this – little as all this was – and then she turned around and ran upstairs to her room and locked herself in until dinner.

Isla

She is awake and Irene is flicking water at her, standing by the sofa in her ridiculous woollen coat.

'Looks like you slept over,' Irene says, setting down the glass she has apparently carried over from the kitchen for this express purpose. Isla sits up, wiping her face with the flat of her hand, bleary with the realisation that she has, apparently, fallen asleep and woken again to a grey, inclement morning.

'It just ended up being easier to come here last night.'

Irene raises an eyebrow. 'Were you afraid I was going to take something?'

'Oh, please stop it—'

'No I really want to know,' Irene carries on. 'I mean, it was apparently of paramount importance that you got here before I did, despite the fact that we *agreed* at the hospital yesterday that we'd meet here this morning.'

Isla leans forward over her knees, noting as she does the awkward fact of having slept somewhere unfamiliar and woken disarranged and all at once.

'Well, there wasn't,' she says, but Irene is already talking again and it feels easier just to let her get on with it, to tense her shoulders and feel them both pop into place. *Your sister*, her father once said, *is the kind of person I always imagine hanging around in corridors trying to catch people talking about her.* As an observation it had been accurate enough, if the very kind of talk it accused Irene of being paranoid about. Isla had been fifteen, possibly fourteen, and had laughed in the way this kind of confidence always invites, then gone away afterwards and worried about it.

'If it makes you feel any better' – she tunes back in on Irene, who is still talking, just as Irene can always be relied upon to still be talking – 'you can follow me round the house and film me, for your records? You can go through my bag before I leave, to make sure I haven't taken anything?'

'Oh, for God's sake—' Isla drops her head into her hands for an instant but reels back to look at her sister, who has now paused and is staring at her as though surprised to find her still there. 'For once in your life, can you just let it go?'

Irene opens her mouth, seems about to react in typical Irene fashion, then deflates, sinking down onto the sofa beside her. 'Yeah, ok,' she says, and shrugs off her coat.

Isla listens for the reassuring whir of the house around her; discreet burble of fridge and generator and air conditioner to signal they're still alive.

'I don't know why I came last night,' she says, without meaning to say it, looking directly in front of her at the circular table with its messy scored marks. 'I mean, I guess if I were groping for an answer I'd say part of me felt like I needed to check that he was dead and another part of me felt like if I came by myself I'd find him, and he'd still be alive. But I don't know.'

'Thought you were supposed to be a therapist.'

'I am, that's why I'm trying to parse my own motivations.'

Irene nods and leans briefly sideways, knocking a shoulder against Isla's. 'So did you find anything?' she asks, and Isla shakes her head.

'He's definitely dead, if that's what you mean.'

It feels true, too, in a way she had failed to fully grasp last night. The house that is in one sense so automated, so crisp and contained as to seem incapable of possessing a character, nonetheless feels newly devoid, newly stripped of its personhood. Without the animating element of her father, it amounts only to a sequence of rooms, a construction of walls and windows, like something staged for a game. It has been almost four years since she was last here, settling her father in with the new housekeeper after his heart attack, noting the way the woman looked around the house with professional curiosity – *we might need to set up a bed for him on the ground floor.* Isla had nodded and smiled and not looked at her father, had left and not come back again, though she often glanced at her calendar with the intention of blocking out a visit, just as soon as she had time. She straightens her spine and tries to imagine the house struggling to life. Tries to imagine – as she did when she was very young – the house straightening its own spine in imitation, declaring an effortful *I, I, I*. She tries this and hears only the air conditioner, looks at her sister instead. 'How did you sleep?'

'Not very well.' Irene is staring across at the wall of windows, picking idly at a spot of something crusted on the knee of her jeans. 'Jude says I'm sleep-talking again, which is sort of annoying.'

'You've been doing that since we were kids,' Isla says, and Irene flicks at a speck of something on the sofa.

'Yes, well, I'm sorry to bore you with old information.'

'I didn't mean that as a dig—' Isla says and then stops, sighs. *Just let her have it*, Morven said once, back when Morven was still liable to take her side. *What's the point in trying to win all the time?* 'D'you think we should have asked Agnes to come with us?'

'How could we?' Irene snorts. 'She took off before we could organise anything.'

'I know, but still ...'

'She's an adult, Isla. We don't always have to be carting her around after us if she doesn't want to come.'

Isla looks at her sister and registers a certain splitting, a tear between the way she knows she ought to be and the place her impulse more naturally leads her. It is, after all, just so *easy* to allow herself the fun of resenting Agnes, as easy as it was when they were kids and she was first thrust upon them: small and unacceptably their sister, the sudden end-stop to a former life. The first time you lose a parent, a part of you gets trapped there; trapped less in the moment of grief than in the knowledge of the end of childhood, the inevitable dwindling of the days. It is a concept that Isla often explains to her patients, leaning forward to describe the various forms of stasis. *One can start to more fully understand oneself as finite, as coming from a person who was finite and having to inherit that trait*, she has said on more than one occasion. *When my mother died*, she is more careful not to say, *I became aware of the limits of things, of the fact of my own ending*. It is a feeling she associates, somehow, with the nagging suspicion that Christmas is not what it used to be, with the knowledge of the end of promise, the lessening of real surprise. She pictures herself and Irene as fixed there forever, aged eleven and ten and with no mother and newly awake to the way of things. It is a feeling that unfortunately extends to the way they both relate to Agnes; Agnes, who came so hard on the heels of this death, this sudden stasis, that it is almost impossible to extricate one from the other. Agnes exists – everything dies. Unfair, but then having a child with one's second wife not ten months after divorcing the first was never going to work for everyone.

'I thought she looked skinny,' Isla says now, offered as conciliation to the conversation Irene actually wants to have. 'I wonder if she's doing ok. It's hard to tell, I feel like she gives away so little.'

'She's always looked like that,' Irene says. 'She's just taller. Hair's gone very *dykes to watch out for*, though.'

'Yours was like that at her age, to be fair.'

'It wasn't at all like that,' Irene sniffs. 'My hair was Debbie Harry.'

'Your hair was radioactive.'

'Well, that was the point.' Irene cocks her a look and Isla finds herself startled into a smile. 'I'm sure she's fine,' Irene continues. 'She's twenty-two, being twenty-two is nothing.'

'I think she's twenty-four.'

'Is she?'

'I think so. I mean, I'm thirty-five, so I think she must be.'

'I never remember.'

Isla stretches her arms over her head, then looks at her watch. 'I don't know if this is in bad taste but do you think there's anything in the fridge? I didn't check last night but I really need to eat something.'

She finds the wilted remains of a salad in a Pyrex mixing bowl, two chicken legs, the skin shrinking back from the flesh from too long spent refrigerated, several blocks of expensive unopened cheese. Hardly breakfast food, but she feels off-kilter from last night and willing to eat anything that might wake her up. Leaning into the fridge, it occurs to her that there is nothing to eat at her own house, that she has forgotten to buy anything in, or for that matter to pay the bills she promised herself she'd pay before getting the call about her father.

'I'm getting divorced,' she says to the inside of the fridge, although the next second she wishes she hadn't because Irene is standing behind her, holding out a hand to take the Pyrex bowl.

'I did wonder,' Irene says, and Isla grabs for one of the blocks of cheese and hands off the salad without looking at her. 'I'm sorry, that's shitty.'

Isla rolls her eyes then feels bad, laying out a couple more things on the counter and closing the fridge.

'Yes, well.' She wants to say something more, wonders whether it would be in some way insensitive to break into a salt-cured ricotta her father will never have the opportunity to try.

'I mean,' Irene continues, and her voice has that awkward conciliatory tone it sometimes takes on when she's worried someone might be about to cry in front of her, 'I know Morven could be a bit tricky —'

'I was thinking we need to speak to his lawyer,' Isla interrupts. 'Dad's – about the will, and about funeral arrangements. And we also need to think about whether anyone's going to want to write about him. An obituary or something. I feel like the guy who wrote the retrospective on his work would probably want to know.'

She looks at Irene, who nods and then looks away.

'Yeah, I suppose so.'

Isla watches her for a second, resists the urge to drum her fingers on the counter. *Come on, be helpful, please.* To distract herself, she pulls a knife from the tastefully hidden cutlery drawer and stabs it into the corner of the cheese packet to help peel the plastic away.

'Do you remember,' Irene says, 'Dad's thing about noise? When we were kids running around the house and we'd always have to play with our socks on because he said the sound of bare feet was worse than being murdered?'

'*Sticky feet on perfect floors,*' Isla replies. 'And the way he'd go around pointing out marks you'd made on the concrete.'

'Weird thing to be so obsessed with' – Irene looks down at her feet – 'and yet look at me still wearing socks.'

Isla glances down at her own feet, nods, tries to picture Irene at seven, racing around the upstairs corridor in socks too soft to prevent her from skidding, crashing into the banister and weeping piteously over a knocked-out tooth. She looks at her sister now – her sister who only yesterday had sat across from her at the doughnut shop and snapped that *it doesn't feel like much to me*, her sister now standing in their father's house, contemplating her own socks with a face expressive at least of ambivalence. She looks and imagines she sees right through her to some pulpy inner place. When Irene lost the tooth, Isla had gone digging around at the bottom of the stairwell and found it for her, carried it back and presented it, though when she did so Irene declared that that was a disgusting thing for her to have done and she didn't want it now anyway. Isla had persisted, nevertheless, in placing the tooth under Irene's pillow, although since she forgot to inform either her mother or her father about this, the tooth remained where it was for several days and was never exchanged for money.

She takes a slice of the cheese and assesses it, finds herself with less of an appetite than she previously assumed. The sorry state of these abandoned provisions – the deeply ordinary salad, the ridiculous luxury of the cheese – hits her briefly, squarely, and then fades again. Her father is dead, she thinks, and no one has bothered to clean up after him.

Irene

Their dad liked to talk about Venice. Long gone, of course, even before things really started to slip. They never saw it, only knew it from their father's descriptions. He often found it necessary to rhapsodise about places his daughters would never get to see.

Sitting in the kitchen, picking at cheese and crackers, Irene looks at a photograph on the counter of a Gothic lancet window half-hidden by water which rises up to cover the bottom of the glass. Their father visited Venice in its last twenty years, took a boat around its swiftly flooding corridors, witnessed San Marco overflowing. He took pictures, framed and arranged them later as a kind of monument to failure. *See here*, he would say, gesturing to a palazzo tottering sideways, a bridge dipping down. *Shoddy work.*

Across the table, Isla is making a list. She has written *funeral, caterer, lawyer, cremation* and is now chewing reflexively on her pen.

'You know, what we really need to do is get hold of the housekeeper,' Irene says. 'It's pretty weird to bring him in and then just take off like that. Weird just to call and then drop off the face of the earth.'

'I've tried to get hold of her,' Isla says, not taking her eyes off the paper. 'She's busy – she had other jobs besides this one, we don't know her schedule. It must also have been difficult, finding him like that. She might need some time to decompress.'

'Well, you hired her,' Irene says, feeling irritable – the image, once again, of her father dead in the house and no one coming quick enough. 'It can't be *that* hard to get through.'

'We'll get hold of her,' Isla says, waving a hand. 'She'll want to come to the funeral anyway.'

'If there was an inquest she'd need to come to that.'

'Why would there be an inquest? He had a stroke, he was unwell before, it seems pretty cut and dry.'

'Yes, *I* know, I'm just saying, *she* doesn't know that – it's unhelpful to just drop off the face of the earth.'

'She hasn't dropped off the face of the earth.'

'Well, you can't find her.'

'Oh, Jesus *Christ*,' Isla hisses, slapping a palm down on the table in annoyance, 'don't you ever get tired of going on like this?'

Irene sits back in her chair. *Only you make me like this,* she wants to say. *You think I'm like this and that makes me worse.* She looks at her sister, the square chin and long green eyes, the way she holds her head like something heavy she is trying to carry back from the supermarket with both hands already full. She has always felt Isla might quite easily turn out to be keeping a hunchback in a bell tower, or a wife in an attic, or whatever else it is extremely upright people often turn out to have been doing in private. Nettled, she pushes her chair back from the table, crosses to the fridge and pulls a bottle of vodka from the long chest freezer. An instinct, something she expected to be there; heavy bottle, over halfway full. She doesn't look at Isla as she tumbles a glass from a shelf and pours a splash of imported Beluga, turns to fix Isla with what she hopes is a candid look. Isla looks back impassively, one corner of her mouth twitching, then reverts her attention to her list and to chewing her pen.

Irene pictures Isla at sixteen, swinging around the living room after getting into their father's vodka to celebrate the end of exams. *He says I'm **not allowed**, well here I am **doing it**.* Their father had found the bottle in her bedroom the next day and made her stand on the landing and count while he administered a smart set of cracks to the backs of her knees with a ruler.

Irene imagines offering Isla a glass, pouring one out and presenting it to her. She watches as her sister draws a tick box against each point on her list. *Your sister takes after your dad a little*, their mother had once said. *She's so purposeful, sometimes I worry about what would happen if she ever stopped.* Irene had felt, at the time, oddly torn at the thought of this distinction – Isla taking after their father being, of course, tacit confirmation that she, Irene, did not. Difficult, on the one hand, to regret her lack of similarity to a man so prone to unkindness, but, on the other hand, who was she supposed to resemble? *You're so interesting*, their mother would say to her, *your mind moves in all these different directions*, and Irene would want to tell her that actually she could be capable, that she could do what Isla did and move in one direction at once. *I don't know*, she would think and not say to her mother, *that I really want to be like you.*

She feels abruptly deflated, unsure what it is she's trying to prove. She necks her drink and grimaces – *bad idea* – refills her glass with water and pours one for Isla as well. Whether this is intended as an apology or something else feels unclear, but she nudges the glass across the table anyhow. Isla thanks her and sets her list to one side, tells her that they both really ought to eat something.

'I think,' Isla says a little while later, 'that the problem is going to be the house.'

Irene tries to ignore a brief blurring around her peripheral vision and wonders whether she ought to eat more cheese.

'You mean in the will?'

'I mean in the will.'

Irene watches as Isla taps her pen against her teeth, scratches a number onto her paper and then scribbles it out.

'Maybe he left it to the housekeeper the way old men do in magazines,' Irene jokes, and Isla snorts.

'I'm sure he could have.'

Irene looks around as though becoming freshly aware of her surroundings. 'Do you ever think about Mum here?'

Isla looks at her; an expression like something wiped abruptly clean, whatever was written across it too swift for Irene to catch.

'What d'you mean?'

'I mean' – Irene shrugs, looks around again – 'I mean do you ever think about her – living here? Do you remember what that was like?'

'Well, of course I do,' Isla replies evenly. 'She lived here until I was nearly eleven years old. It's normal to remember a lot from that age.'

'No, I know that,' Irene says. 'I just mean ... what do you remember?'

Isla says nothing for a moment, looks down at her empty glass and then refills it.

'I remember her trying,' she says, 'I remember her trying to make it work.'

I remember that too, Irene wants to say. Wants to say *I remember her moods and the way they fought and the things you tried to keep from me. I remember when she got really into crystals and the time she said she thought she saw a dangerous aura floating around the top of my head and how much that freaked me out until she said she'd exorcise it for me. I remember the way she'd touch her cheek to mine and then withdraw it. I remember the morning you found her outside in the rain in her nightdress and took her back to her bed without saying anything.*

'I don't want it,' she says instead. 'I don't want the house.'

Isla takes a sip of water. 'I don't either, but I'm worried about conditions in the will, anything that wouldn't let us sell it. I don't think he'd be happy with just anyone living here. I'm not sure what he's set up.'

Irene shakes her head. 'I think you're being paranoid.'

'Maybe I am,' Isla sighs, and rests her head on her hand. 'I don't know why I keep expecting something to jump out of a corner and give me a nasty surprise.'

Irene thinks about four years ago. About the money her father insisted on splitting between them just after his heart attack, the way he had contacted each of them separately as if hoping they wouldn't confer. It had been huge money, money enough to carry with it the possibility of ease, of improvement, and it had been almost impossible to know what to do. The problem, of course, has always been her father, the sense of him shattered across her – first broken and then embedded. *You act like this*, as Jude once said, *because you were raised by a psychopath who made you believe that everyone was somehow in opposition to you or out to con you or waiting to abandon you.* Irene had told them this was pop psychology and then gone away and brooded on it. The problem has always been the way that her father treated her mother, that he loved her and then ceased to love her, the way this withdrawal caused her first to unravel and finally to die. The problem has always been the way he left them alone in the house for long periods, the way he spoke to his daughters, the way he pitted one against the other – left each to struggle for a love they should have known they couldn't earn. The problem has always been squaring one fact with another, her father's great ease and easy cruelty. *That's good*, he would say, in response to something Irene would tell him about her work, and the sun would shine.

She thinks about this now and then stops abruptly, finds herself wanting to smear her hands across the floor, to renounce all claim to it, to push the glasses from their careful recessed cupboards and make a chaos of the place she used to live. (She wants this and yet, at the same time, she very powerfully wants to cry. The image of her father's body – wide dark void of a shape half-obscured beneath sheets as if, for whatever reason, someone had felt the need to tuck him in – has played in her head uninterrupted since yesterday. *Can we touch him?* she had wanted to say in the viewing suite, and found herself unequal to asking in a normal voice. *In company with Christ, who died and now lives, oh God oh God oh God.*)

She has a headache. Only a dribble of vodka, but still a stupid idea this early in the morning. She stands up, ignoring Isla and staggering slightly, moves quickly down the corridor towards the bathroom, where she slides the door shut and splashes water on her face. Her reflection is discoloured, her eyes unpleasantly red around the rims. She wipes her face with her shirt cuff and tries to remember the last time she got a decent night's sleep. *You were talking,* Jude said this morning, passing a hand over her head, tilting her up to meet their eyes. *You kept going on about noises, you said there were noises downstairs.*

She reaches up for the light switch above the sink in a vain bid to improve her reflection and knocks the mirror as she does so. It is screwed to the wall from the top and shifts only slightly, swinging sideways so that a sliver of wall is uncovered, a little darker and bearing a series of scratches, as though someone tried to score into the concrete with a sharp object. Irene squints at it, still moving her cuff over one half of her face. The shapes are odd, inconsistent and tightly packed, not the marks made by a drill when hanging the mirror but smaller, stranger. She looks closer, makes out a face, or something resembling a face, wonders how long this could possibly have been here and, more to the point, who put it here. The first and best bet seems to be her mother, though the more she thinks about it the surer she feels that this mirror wasn't hung until long after her mother died, that there didn't use to be anything on this wall. So not her mother then, but someone else, someone armed with a tool sharp enough to score into concrete. She reaches out a finger to trace across the largest of the scratches, but then the mirror slips back as the house emits a sudden rumble, the floor beneath her trembling in the manner of something gliding backwards on wheels. Irene blinks, stumbles and reaches for the door handle, moves out into the corridor to find the pendant lamps swinging – an odd, narcotic motion, gold glass casting queasy shadows on the floor. The house shivers again, tics like a cramping muscle and then subsides. It would barely be discernible to the untrained eye but the house, she knows, has risen a little, just as it is calibrated to do.

4.

Agnes

The Monday shift is hectic, people placing complicated orders and then changing their minds and needing to be rung up again. Agnes holds her weight in the balls of her feet, scrapes her hair off her forehead and thinks about nothing. Jason rambles on about Monday commuters, refers to them as *the wall-eyed death parade* and appears to enjoy this so much that he repeats it twice more. Mondays are his day to pick the music, which means the ambience is awful and the customers on edge, skittish as barn animals and prone to cutting in line. *You know it's too early for this*, Agnes has said more than once and Jason has looked at her seriously. *Never too early to feel.* At one point a little while before noon, a woman outside the cafe slams herself up against the window, splays her hands and stares in at Agnes, pushing her forehead hard onto the glass. A customer at the till takes a step back, clutching at his collar and staring out at her, though Jason only shakes his head.

'Fucking weirdos,' he says, and tips the customer's change out over the counter.

The woman moves off shortly after, though the streak from the drag of her forehead remains on the steamed-up glass.

Agnes's father's obituary ran in the paper this morning but Jason thankfully seems unaware that anything out of the ordinary has happened. He asked her to bring a fresh sack of chicory blend in from the storage room first thing and she shouldered it easily, letting the weight press down like a dead thing. She isn't sure how obituaries work exactly, whether one of her sisters dictated it or whether someone was simply waiting around with an essay ready to go. She remembers a girl she once fucked talking at length about how Liz Taylor's obituary was written twelve years prior to her death and updated at regular intervals. *Kind of ghoulish when you think about it*, the girl had said (red hair, talked about her ex too much), *the idea that someone's out there just waiting on your death to get themselves another writing credit.* Agnes had looked at her, tried to remember where it was she had picked her up and why exactly she had bothered. *I mean, sure*, she had said, *or maybe it just shows that someone was thinking about you.*

Her father's obituary ran to almost half a page, hagiography needled through with a glimmer of truth: *Pre-eminent architect whose devotion to the home preceded his complicated domestic life.* She read it on a stranger's phone, peering over their shoulder on the morning ferry, glanced over phrases like *simplicity of form* and *unrivalled precision* in search of something else. *In respect of their gentle austerity, it may be said that the buildings reflected the man, for Carmichael was severe in his manner, if not quite the type to earn the familiar epithet of one who 'did not suffer fools'. A tall, strident man, he combined the intense modernity of his design vision with a marked conservatism of dress and, some would argue, ideas. He was renowned for touring building sites in full three-piece suit and fob watch and known for commencing all correspondence with a scholarly, if not to say belligerent, 'Sirs.'* Coming down to the end of the piece, the person whose shoulder she was reading over paused upon the following line: *Carmichael was married twice. He was predeceased by his first wife, Allegra. He is survived by three daughters, Isla, Irene and Agnes, and his second wife, Marie.* Agnes read this segment over slowly, wondered whether it was worth informing the person whose phone she was sharing that things were more complicated than that. *No one knows where Marie is,* she imagined the article ending. *Read more on this exclusive story on page 6.* The photograph below the byline: her father at thirty-five, too young to seem anything but a fiction of a person. The dark hair so like hers, the set mouth, and broad features, like Captain von Trapp without the residual warmth. She looked at the photo for several long seconds before the person in front of her pulled up their messages and started to text someone logged in their phone as *Chloe DO NOT TEXT*.

Agnes hasn't turned on her phone since Saturday evening, when Stephanie texted to apologise for asking to take her for breakfast. *Obviously I meant it*, she had said, *but there was no need to give you a heart attack*. Agnes had considered responding that it was fine, that her father had died and she wasn't in a wonderful place emotionally, but then clicked out of her messages and chucked her phone under her bed.

She makes a chai latte, a cappuccino, serves a man who asks for a teabag dipped twice in hot water and then thrown away. The last of the morning drags and people complain about prices in the usual futile manner, mishandle lids and spill across the counter. At twelve thirty the rain stops – out of nowhere, simply ceases the way it sometimes does, switch flicked and the day unrecognisable.

'Flip the sign,' Jason says, and Agnes moves to the door, spins the sign from *Open* to *Closed* and steps out, leaving Jason to ring up a last customer. The sky is a polluted pink, the sun like an eye half-stuck with sleep. All around her the day has ground to a halt, retail workers and cafe workers and office staff pouring out of their respective buildings to take in the pause. People stand with their faces upturned and Agnes thinks of photographs from the 1950s: men and women in goggles watching nuclear tests from Adirondack chairs. She shields her eyes, turns towards the sun and finds she cannot tell if it was always this colour. She tries to remember how it feels to be warmed by something other than the wet-flannel press of humidity. She looks around. Two men have brought sandwiches out from the shoe shop across the way and are sitting on the pavement to eat them. The pavement is wet and Agnes wonders whether they will regret this later, walks a little way, sees a woman across the concrete who seems to be looking at her. She looks away, looks back and finds the woman still looking, finds that she may have changed course as if to approach her. Agnes turns around, unnerved, and finds another woman coming from the opposite direction, younger, eyes locked on her. She realises it's Stephanie before she has a chance to course-correct, tries to decide whether to turn again, but by this time Stephanie is all the way up to her and the moment is already happening.

'Of all the gin joints …' Stephanie says, and then pulls a face. 'Sorry, that was weird.'

She is taller than Agnes remembers, perhaps because she mainly remembers her lying down. She is dressed in office clothes, dark hair pulled back, and Agnes thinks about her hips and about going down on her and then stops herself, shakes her head and glances to her left. The other woman, the one who had also seemed to be moving towards her, is nowhere to be seen. She turns back to Stephanie.

'Do you, er – are you here because you work around here?' she asks, and immediately feels embarrassed.

Stephanie frowns. 'Yes, not too far. I came out because' – and here she gestures around her in a manner Agnes recognises from the morning after; Stephanie waving her hand about, saying *I made this little pact to at least **ask***. She feels affectionate, the way familiarity can feel like complicity. A gesture shared in private, now out here for anyone to see.

'My boss lets us bunk off whenever it's like this,' Agnes says, 'which I guess doesn't mean much these days, but you know. I think his theory is no one's going to want to skip dry weather for coffee, so why bother.'

'The pragmatic approach.'

'What do you do, if you work around here?'

'This and that,' Stephanie says, and Agnes raises an eyebrow.

'And you just – happened to come by the shop?'

Stephanie hesitates for a second, then starts to laugh.

'Ok, first of all, I happened to be at the Compendium last Thursday with friends but also *you* invited *me*, if you recall – and secondly, I'm temping around here. I'm a temp. I do admin work for law firms and I work the phones for insurance companies and I do whatever, in whatever location. So *that's* why I came in for coffee the other day and *that's* why I'm here right now. Nothing more sinister than that, I promise. Not a psycho,' she adds, and it takes Agnes a couple of seconds to recognise this as another echo – Stephanie's hands on her shoulders, tilting back when Agnes asked her to come home with her.

Agnes tips up her chin. 'Well, you would say that, but sure, I believe you.'

They end up walking the length of the overpass and it feels strange; strange in the wrongness of the weather, in the abnormality of sunshine. Without the unifying feature of the rain, their conversation is rendered somehow incorrect, ahistorical. Things feel unmoored and it is perhaps for this reason that Agnes finds herself more able to simply accept the walk, the conversation.

'My dad died,' she says into this space. 'I mean, like, recently, which I could argue is why I've been acting so weird except it isn't, really.' Stephanie is looking at her now, has stopped in the middle of the pavement, which means that Agnes has to stop too, leaning awkwardly over to one side and holding her left wrist in her right hand as though feeling for a pulse. She looks over Stephanie's shoulder, thinks of a bedroom the colour of egg yolk, about her sisters and the distance between them and the fact that, at one point in her life, she was unable to tell whether Isla or Irene was actually the older one.

'I'm really sorry,' Stephanie is saying, and Agnes nods, tries to remember how much coffee she's had today. Her father, once: *Agnes isn't very bright, she gets that from her mother.* Her father, once: *You must protect yourself, my love, because trouble tends to find you if you don't.*

'It feels silly, doesn't it,' she says now, 'the idea of being sad about one person, given' – and here she waves a hand around; a borrowed gesture that makes Stephanie smile.

'I don't think so,' Stephanie says, and seems sincere as she says it. 'I think we all have to live our own lives. We can't constantly be comparing things that happen to us to worse things happening all over the place.'

'It would be a good excuse though, wouldn't it,' Agnes says, 'to say that I don't feel sad about him dying because everything's gone to shit.'

The rain is coming. Agnes can see it already: pink sky bleeding down into darker colours over some far-flung part of the city, blur of buildings plunging back into cloud.

'Maybe we should go inside,' she says now, and looks at Stephanie like it's simple. 'I can make you a coffee or something. For free, I mean, not to pay for. If you don't need to rush back.'

Stephanie nods, shields her eyes and looks directly into the sun in a way that Agnes knows, from YouTube videos of old children's television, one is not supposed to. Footage from a programme preparing children to view a solar eclipse, hosts explaining how to make a viewfinder out of a box, a flat mirror, a white envelope: *Now remember, ultraviolet light floods your retina, burning the exposed tissue, even if you only look at the sun for a short time.* Agnes looks at Stephanie instead, which seems safer.

'I could do a coffee,' Stephanie says, and lets her hand fall from her eyes.

Isla

The patient is in her early thirties and talking about how her housemate will only eat certain kinds of food at certain prearranged times of day and night.

'I guess it's what you'd call clean eating,' she says, 'only it's, like, *pristine* eating, eating as devotion, like it's going to save her. I don't know her very well – she moved in when my cousin moved out and I didn't have much of a say – but, like, I once found her drinking chicken stock from a juice glass in the kitchen at one in the morning. It's weird. She has this thing about how we're all out of whack, somehow, that people didn't use to eat the way they do now and that's why everything's so fucked up. I don't know what any of it's about, but it's pissing me off to have to live with it.'

Isla tries to work out a kink in her neck discreetly and asks the woman why she thinks another person's eating habits appear to be bothering her so much. The afternoon is grey and warmer than she likes it – unkempt about the edges and shifting underfoot. She feels tired, stupid, uncomfortably stuck on the idea of softening the day, of having a drink. A man she saw earlier talked about a recurring dream in which his windows burst inward from the pressure of water, and the flood, when it came, was all miniature pieces of glass.

'People can find ritual comforting,' Isla says now, adjusting the notepad she keeps on her lap during sessions. 'Acts to organise their days around, acts to cling to. Don't you ever find yourself doing that?'

'Not drinking stock in the kitchen at midnight, no,' the woman says, and Isla starts to bite the skin around her fingernails, notices what she is doing and sets her hand back down.

People allow therapy to work when they want it to, but the point of the process is seldom the end result. She has patients who come to her twice a week only to repeat themselves, to detail the same obsessions, same behaviours, same indifferent little squalors and embarrassments. People like to feel that they're working on something, to feel exonerated by the simple fact of self-reflection. *I know I can do better*, one woman has been known to say to her on average seven times per session. *No one ever gives me credit for the fact that I'm **aware**.* Isla likes the practice, in the main. She likes to work with people, to trace her finger down between two points of connection. Only sometimes does she find it hard to muster up the patience needed for mistakes repeated to the point of imbecility, the afflicted sighing of *I know I need to change.* Morven once said she was too wedded to this repetition, that her job was becoming a waste of her, a slow sinking in the mud. Morven, who had studied anthropology for years only to end up in whatever job would pay her, who had seemed to awaken to this squandering all at once, not only as it applied to her but as it applied to everyone. *You're going to spend your whole life with these people who never seem to get a lick better. Your whole life on their* *problems and then it's going to be over and you're never going to have breathed real air.*

Morven, who left five months ago because she wanted, in her words, to live while the world was still liveable. Morven, who had never spoken like that before, who made fun of the people who did. *I'm really scared of wasting it*, she said one morning over toast and imitation eggs, as if she'd been repeating herself for weeks without being listened to. *I'm really scared and I don't think you are, like maybe this is enough for you. Or like it's all you're capable of wanting. And I don't know what to do with that.*

Isla had messaged Morven from the hospital – Irene in the corridor, talking to Jude on the phone and making her feel in some way deficient. *Dad died*, she texted, and then, *Hope you're well x.* Morven responded several hours later. *I'm so sorry, love*, she said, and that was all. Morven, who had said she wanted to travel, to see how other people were living, who is somewhere north, where it isn't supposed to be quite as bad, who is doing what she feels is necessary. Not uncommon, in its way. Isla sees enough from the news and from her patients – a current of rising impermanence, into which people now routinely disappear. Families vanishing wholesale, trailing unpaid debts and hints about better lives in better places. A patient Isla sees more occasionally recently lost touch with a sister who's joined a quasi-religious enclave established in the hills outside a midlands city. *I don't know what the deal is exactly*, he said when trying to explain it, knitting his fingers together and then unknitting them. *From what I gather it sounds a bit like homesteading – they all dress like the nineteen-fifties, she does her hair a weird new way. They took her phone away last week.*

Things progress unevenly, at the so-called end of things. Patients quit their jobs and tell Isla they did it to rest or to travel, then find they don't have the money to do either. Patients tell stories about friends swallowed up by bad crowds, by panic and self-delusion, by the sense that things cannot be quite as bad as they are. Even Isla herself wakes up in the dead of night, on occasion, confronted by blackness, by thoughts that refuse to arrange themselves into legible shapes. A recollection of herself, aged five, watching the rain and listening to a man on the radio saying it was good for the garden. Attempting to recall when it was that people realised the emergency was already upon them, the warning signs noted then duly forgotten in favour of squabbling about small things, about taxes and football championships and protests that caused offence or caused traffic, of doggedly ploughing a course.

After her last patient departs, she checks her phone, throws her notebook onto the Barcelona chair she bought for her office last December. A text from Irene, outlining the times she's happy to come with her to see the lawyer, another message from Morven, which she looks at but doesn't open, choosing instead to check her calendar, to adjust the papers on her desk. At their wedding, Morven said that she felt relieved to love her, that loving made everything easier. *Enough to just be us,* she said, *despite everything,* though this of course turned out to be untrue.

It takes longer than it used to do to get home from the office – Jenny waving her out at reception, warning her the train line's down near the bridge and she might want to think about walking to the jetty. Isla lives in a relatively sheltered part of the city; a neighbourhood perched high and above the water, houses built in step formation up the hill towards the west. Seven thirty – sticky evening heat, a smell like something dredged from water, minnow-stink, a dank unwelcome breeze. She lets herself in, steels herself as she always does for the silence, the heavy quality of air that has gone undisturbed since she left. She slips out of her shoes and walks in her socks to the living room, where she sits down on the sofa and allows herself a moment to do nothing but press her palms against her eyes. She does this for eight seconds, nine, then pulls her phone out of her pocket and thumbs through the contacts to her father's housekeeper, presses the call button and holds the phone to her ear. The call rings out, as it has done every time she has phoned since her father died, and she leaves a message as usual, asking the housekeeper to please get back in touch. This is becoming a sore spot, not to mention one of some concern. Isla has only ever met the woman once, the first time she showed her around her father's house – a smallish woman, she thinks now, good posture, can't remember anything more. It had been directly after their father's heart attack and Isla had thrown herself into the task of acquiring

119

home help to detract from the guilt of not being around to take care of him. *Now that Agnes isn't at home any more*, as she had put it, *now that things might be trickier to manage*. Irene had rolled her eyes at her, asked how much help she really imagined Agnes would be even if she were still at home. Isla had ignored her. She had thought, at one point, about querying the continued suitability of her father's house and then dismissed it, recognising a losing battle when she saw one. The housekeeper had been selected for her by an agency that matched domestic help to specialist situations. They had sent across a CV, citing useful sidelines in first aid and CPR and attaching a supporting statement in which the candidate detailed an interest in forming connection, in classic cinema, in modernist architecture. Isla had spoken to her twice on the phone – warm voice, long story about a former client who had tried to gift her a full and very ugly dinner service – and had hired her on the basis of this and a set of excellent references. They met to settle her in with her father and Isla watched the house-keeper introduce herself – businesslike, professional: *my name is Caroline, Mr Carmichael, I'm a great admirer of your work*. It felt like a transfer, of sorts. *Every day for a few hours*, Isla said to her father, *just to pick up around the house, to see to your food and medicine, just to make sure you're ok*. Her father, unfamiliar in recovery, lessened in a way she found uncomfortable to look at; a shape in a chair. *It'll be better*, she said, *just to have someone around*. An unkind flash: her father, younger and listening to her tell him about herself, about a girl she'd met at school and how she felt about her and what she thought that meant. Her father, waiting a long moment after she'd finished, then saying he really wasn't sure why she'd felt the need to tell him a thing like that. She felt cruel, entitled to be cruel.

You'll be fine with Caroline, she said, *you won't need us.*

At first, she received periodic updates – *good day, good appetite* – but after a while these petered and Isla didn't chase them. It felt good to know she had sorted a situation that didn't need constant checking, though now she feels like perhaps she should have kept a closer eye.

She sets her phone down on the table, eyeballs the unopened message from Morven again and then gets up, crosses to the sideboard and opens a bottle of wine. She had sneaked it from the house without telling Irene, which accounts for its label, its provenance. She pours a glass, then opens a drawer on the sideboard and pulls out a stack of photographs. She had taken them out of a box in her spare room the previous night and stored them here for a more leisurely assessment when she had five minutes. Some kind of content, she thinks, for the funeral, for people to look at, so they don't just have to look at her. *I'll need to find something to say*, she thinks, and feels sick at the thought, imagines reading the back cover of her father's biography or taking along a copy of his obituary, eulogising him with words written solely by somebody else. She finds herself back on the phrase *your loss*. Her father once said that a funeral was no place for children, though in a voice that less implied it might upset them as that they might make noise. *Your mother did something very selfish, Isla* – she remembers this statement without warning, without any sense of how or why – *it's worth your knowing how selfish she's been.* They weren't allowed to attend their mother's funeral, though she doesn't recall what they did that day or whether anybody stayed with them. Isla looks down at the box in her hand, at the wine glass, tries to gauge the mess she would make if she dropped them. She starts to cry just like that, with her hands full and unable to wipe her face, cries about her father, or about her mother, or about herself in a pointless, waning present. She cries – perhaps – because her father once told her she was spiteful and parents, she has always felt, should have to like their children more than that.

Once this is over, she feels better. She leaves the wine in its glass, doesn't touch it, spreads the photographs out on the coffee table and hopes for some kind of inspiration. Flicks through one and then another: Irene aged five and leaning precariously out of a window, Isla next to her, aged six and up on tiptoes, craning back to be caught by the lens; their father, looking up from his desk and apparently unhappy to be interrupted; her mother, hands on her hips in the kitchen, the light from the ribbon windows white-gold and refracting in amber across the crown of her head as though she is on fire.

Agnes

They are halfway to fucking in the lift of Stephanie's building, which feels like a weird choice, but then it has been a weird week. Blank yellow light from the overheads, mirrored wall scribbled over with sticky green pen: *flat 3 shut yr dog up or ill come up there and give it something to howl abt*. She tips her head back, lets Stephanie kiss her at the pulse, at the secret place where her jaw meets her collar. Jeans unbuttoned, shirt untucked. Easy enough, with three fingers inside her, to forget the sunshine that had arrived and departed, to forget the day and simply be as she is, driven back against the wall and with four floors still to go.

She hadn't meant to come here. At the cafe, this afternoon, she had made Stephanie coffee and ignored the woman who came in behind her – long hair and a difficult demeanour, asking Jason about their chicory blends. *This is good*, Stephanie said when Agnes slid her mug over, and Agnes rolled her eyes. *It's crappy*, she said, *but I threw in some chocolate*. Stephanie looked at her. *You're a little ray of sunshine, aren't you*. She hadn't meant to come back with her, hadn't meant to let Stephanie wait for her after closing time, loitering on the rainy overpass with her backpack and umbrella, an even look on her face. *I thought we should celebrate the weather*, she said, *I mean the weather from before*.

Sixth floor. Stephanie removes her fingers, licks them quickly and then hoists up her backpack. In the long second between the lift coming to a halt and the doors opening, Agnes looks at her and finds that she wants to tell her something. Wants to hold on to her arms and tell her that sometimes she worries she's never felt anything but a blanketing sense of dread.

'Come on,' Stephanie says, takes her hand like it's nothing. Her flat is tiny and bears the hallmarks of absent roommates: a chore wheel on the fridge, mismatched crockery, a comfortable sense of disorder just barely under control. Stephanie leads her to a bedroom towards the back, kicks the door shut and pulls her down onto the bed. A brief impression: mildewed wall and windowsill covered over by strings of golden lights, a thick rug, a poster of Whistler's *Nocturne: Blue and Gold*. She closes her eyes, lets Stephanie pull her trousers and underwear down around her thighs, lets her use her mouth and then her fingers, tight acid pull of too much, just for a second, the strange little bundle of nerves in her stomach that seize and complain until Stephanie shifts her fingers around. She opens her eyes, finds Stephanie leaning over her, long sweep of her hair and her mouth like something freshly inked on paper; wet and clean and somehow mutable, as though kissing it too quickly might cause it to lose its shape. Agnes registers the fingers paused inside her, the frankness of Stephanie's gaze. *I read somewhere*, she wants to say, *that humans used to be telepathic but then we lost it.*

'Is this ok?' Stephanie asks her, and she nods, tips her hips up a little.

'If you can move your fingers around about forty-five degrees, it usually works better.'

Stephanie grins at her – roger that – and moves her hand obligingly. Sweet spot, a prising sensation, like something inside her giving an inch. Agnes settles herself a little, tilts her hips. Thinks *the world is fucking ending*, swiftly followed by *God, stop being a twat*. Holding herself tight for another second and then relaxing, the evening suddenly all uncurled: chaotic, tender, quiet.

* * *

Later on, they share a cigarette and address the subject of Stephanie's hipbones; Agnes with her head resting idle on her stomach, tracing her finger back and forth. The little scar to the left of the navel and just below, slightly darker than the skin all around it. Stephanie explains that they took out her appendix when she was eleven years old.

'My mum didn't believe me,' she says, 'for two days. She was like *it'll be your period finally* – I didn't get my period till I was fourteen – *you're just having your first taste of cramps*. On and on about how I was becoming a woman, about how it was all the first step in the beautiful journey of being in pain and complaining about it for the rest of my life. Then on the second day my appendix burst and I started throwing up all over and they had to drain an abscess under general and I was on antibiotics for weeks.

All of that and Mum was just like *well, you should have been more specific when you said that it hurt.* Sorry, I'm sure this is extremely sexy,' she adds, passing the cigarette down to Agnes, who leans up on one elbow.

Stephanie in the half-light: loose black hair and the gentle curve of her hips, easy in a way Agnes finds unnerving, like she has nowhere to be, nothing more unpleasant to be thinking about. During sex, she had said *Agnes, Agnes, Agnes* and Agnes had thought about the way some people know how to say your name better than others, say it like a fist rapped smart against a door. She had come and then had looked at Agnes dizzily afterwards. *You're fucking great at that*, she had said, and asked her to fetch her cigarettes.

'Are your roommates around?' Agnes asks now, tilting her head as though listening for evidence of life. Stephanie shrugs, takes back the cigarette and leans over to mash it out in a mug sitting on the bedside table.

'I don't think so. Everyone'll be out leading their squalid little lives. Beck does shift work, Casper's got a cleaning gig, I can't remember the new person's name yet. Ships in the night, et cetera. I guess at least what I'm doing at the moment keeps me to fairly social hours.'

'Do you like temping?' Agnes asks, resettling herself slightly so she is lying with her head on Stephanie's stomach, looking up at her.

'I mean, *no*, obviously. It's terrible and when it's not terrible it's boring, but I have to pay for shit, so this is what I'm doing.'

Agnes nods.

Stephanie looks at her. 'What's that face?' she says.

Agnes shakes her head. 'Nothing, honestly – it's just a bit weird.'

'Weird how?'

'I don't mean – I mean I get it, obviously. It's just you said you made this pact with yourself to go after the things you wanted – to at least *ask*, you said – but you're doing a job you don't like.'

'Well, sure,' Stephanie says, equably enough, 'but there's things you want and things you want, aren't there? I mean, there's things you have to do to stay alive and then any space you have left over to make staying alive feel bearable, you know?'

'No, I get that,' Agnes says, embarrassed for bringing it up. 'I mean – I know people have to *work*, I just … I figured if you were thinking in those terms, about wanting to do things *now* because of everything, then maybe it would make working a job you hate harder.'

'Do you feel like your job's a waste?' Stephanie says, not in any particular tone but looking at her with interest. 'Do you feel like you should be doing something bigger?'

'*I* don't,' Agnes says, and then tries to form the second part of that sentence. *But I don't think I'm as hopeful as you are. I don't think I'm so set on making the most of things.*

'Way I feel,' Stephanie says after a not uncomfortable pause, 'is that there was never going to be a situation where I wasn't going to have to work, so the least I can do is have a job that invades on the actual substance of my life as little as possible. In some ways I think it would be worse if I had a job that was more interesting but that encroached on my downtime more. At least this way I can have as much of my life as possible to hang out, to go dancing, to do this, whatever.'

'As much of your life as you're allowed,' Agnes says without really meaning to, although Stephanie only shrugs again.

'If you like.'

Agnes pushes herself up and crosses to the window – high up, the rain coming down, blue-grey swim of early evening. She acknowledges the tangle of a number of things she might say and doesn't want to: the fact that she could have taken her father's money and didn't, the fact that she had a mother who left before she could commit her face to memory.

'You know when I said my father died recently,' she says instead, picking a flaking piece of paint from the windowsill and then realising she shouldn't be doing that in someone else's home. 'I meant he died last week. Is it weird I didn't say that?'

'Well' – the sound of Stephanie shifting in the bed behind her, the sound of another cigarette being lit – 'only weird if it feels weird to you.'

'I don't know,' Agnes says. 'It's maybe weird to me.'

'My mum's still alive,' Stephanie says, 'but the way she goes on you'd think I personally killed her several years ago and have yet to be tried for my crimes.'

Agnes laughs in surprise at this, and in approximately the same moment the lights in the room flicker and go out. Sudden clasp of darkness, close as muslin held across the face. Stephanie curses.

'Fucking third time this week.'

She clambers out of bed, hands her cigarette off to Agnes and pulls on a dressing gown before leaving the room, coming back a minute later with a handful of tealights which she arranges not at all artfully around the room.

'Grid keeps going down,' she explains. 'This building and then like twenty or thirty more in that direction.' She gestures vaguely towards the window. 'Just one of the many daily joys of living in exciting times. I don't know about you, but it feels to me like it's sort of worse at the moment, or getting worse, or something. But then I also don't really know what we're supposed to judge that against, or do about it, so I guess what's the point in worrying?'

Agnes watches her light the candles, feels a passing self-consciousness about still being naked and then dismisses it. She glances out of the window again and is taken aback by the absence of light; the rain and the dark and nothing in between to interrupt it. The evening washed clean, uninhabited, the colour of outer space.

City

Dark nights are more common these days. The power is unreliable and spotty, blackouts not infrequent, occasionally scheduled, other times brought about by the weather or by bad luck. Power is expensive, light parcelled out at a premium and frequently easier to go without.

A group of teenage boys sit together in a darkened bedroom, recounting the plot of a movie they are now unable to watch: *so this guy finds an eye in the ground – just the eye and part of a skull – and I forget how the rest goes but point is, it turns out it's Satan's face.*

A man rolls over in bed, still groggy from shift work, unable to tell whether the darkness is a power cut or simply due to the time of night.

Somewhere in a built-up part of town, a straggle of protesters bed down in an office foyer for a twenty-four-hour sit-in, holding torches to their faces to exaggerate the point.

The long blue of a hospital corridor, backup generators whirring to life.

You haven't asked – one woman to another – *how my day went.* Her companion looks at her – *I imagined just the same as always, to be frank.*

A stretch of unilluminated water, gentle break and drop of something like a body slipping down – a midnight swimmer, or the sound of something else.

Two girls run around their dark apartment burning sage together and singing a song they heard on the radio.

A woman forks tuna from a can, asks her boyfriend where the hurricane lamps have got to. *You always ask this,* he replies, *and I always tell you the same exact thing.*

A group of people contemplate a photograph – dark-haired girl half-turned towards the lens.

The evening struggles, darkness borne down heavy and replete. The rain falls, the night continues – black horizon and the pull of what's beneath.

5.

Irene

Early Tuesday morning, shifting onto her side and already awake, quick cluster of thoughts: *call Isla, speak to lawyer, speak to work about my hours, improve attitude, clean out airing cupboard, commit to the concept of being a sane and productive member of society.* Jude's face in the back of her neck, the narcotic sensation of a sleepy kiss briefly distracting her. She lies where she is for several seconds, counts *one, two,* waits for another kiss not forthcoming. A line from one of her father's obituaries occurs to her: *Mies van der Rohe said architecture was the will of an epoch translated into space, whereas Carmichael appeared to believe that architecture was the panic of a slightly different epoch translated into a different sort of space.* She shifts a little, pressing back against Jude, who hums into her hair. Awful, she reflects, whenever Jude goes off to sleep and leaves her alone.

When she was young, Irene had been a failure at sleeping, had grown into it only via an aggressive self-determination. Lying in bed aged seven or eight, she would count belligerently down from one hundred and, on finding herself still awake at zero, simply proceed to count back up again, only in more disappointed tones. The ultimate result was that, by the age of eleven, she was more or less able to put herself to sleep in a matter of seconds. Sleep, to teenage Irene, was like New Year's Eve or something launched into space: pointless at its heart but still significant enough in its build-up. She was seldom refreshed in the morning, dreamed oddly and often woke overheated and stuck through with worries, like someone who had rolled over on pins. The issue, of course, is that going to sleep is one thing but staying asleep another. Even so, the control she exerts over the beginning of sleep has always cheered her. *I'm going to sleep now*, she said to Jude the first time she stayed over, and then proceeded to do just that. *I always thought that was weirdly sexy*, Jude said to her later. *It made me feel like you had your shit together, which obviously wasn't the case, but you had me going for a while.*

She sighs, sticks one finger into the corner of her eye to extract a sliver of last night's make-up, then struggles out from under Jude's arm and pushes herself up off the bed. She is working from home today, finishing up payroll templates for a new client, but she doesn't need to be online for hours yet. The morning has a frazzled quality, rain like something sifted, turned halfway towards mist. She wonders what to do, whether she should read or watch television. Television these days confines itself largely to constructed reality, to game shows where people compete to pay a month's worth of bills or audition potential room-mates. On a show Irene has found herself watching from time to time, the host conducts a series of contestants round a flat, then asks what they'd be willing to pay in rental fees. After all the contestants have entered sealed ballots, the host takes the top two bidders into a head-to-head. Irene can't remember the last time she watched something interesting. She can't remember the last time a new film came out. She has a friend who, at an early stage in her life, wanted to be an actress but was informed around age eighteen that there wasn't a lot of call for that these days.

She puts on her dressing gown and wanders into the study – *study* in itself a generous term, since what they have is more akin to a box room filled with junk and papers. The agent who showed them the flat said he wasn't legally allowed to list the room as a bedroom, since it couldn't fit any furniture conventionally resembling a bed. Instead, he simply noted it on the floor plan as a 'bonus room' and expounded on its myriad possibilities until Jude asked him to stop. They use it for storage, although Irene has recently taken to going in there when she can't find anything to settle to, sitting down in the single armchair which they have managed to wedge into one corner and spending a little while doing nothing. She does this now, curling up in the chair and looking around her aimlessly – narrow window grimed with something resembling verdigris, warm-toned tan of the carpet and stuccoed white walls. The room is haphazardly stacked with folders and boxes of mostly useless papers and she nudges the closest box with her foot, leans down to lift the lid and peer inside. Jude, typically an orderly person, regularly notes that they need to invest in a filing cabinet, or at the very least start throwing things out, but Irene has always registered a low note of panic at the thought of getting rid of any possessions. She is prone to treasuring her most trivial items, ticket stubs from the ferry, old water bills, books she didn't really like. This is never so much in the belief that they'll one day come in handy as that the act of throwing them out will somehow trigger their long-withheld purpose, a sudden and obvious use revealing itself only as she watches the item fall from her hands.

The box she has picked is almost overflowing, mostly with ancient bills. She sifts through it, still half-curled in her chair. She pulls up several old receipts and discards them, the rental agreement on a flat they no longer live in, flicks past the manual for the vacuum and then pauses, pulls out a plastic wallet ringed around with rubber bands. She looks at this for a second, turns it over in her hands and tries to recall where it came from. Her father's house, maybe, throwing things in at random before she left for university; the sort of relic that follows you around through much of your adult life. She flips the rubber bands off the corners, undoes the clasp and slides out a handful of papers, pages through them one by one. A copy of her birth certificate, clearly filched from her father's study under the misapprehension that it might come in useful, a sheaf of drawings from a brief period when she thought drawing could be her thing. Notes, too, for an essay she no longer remembers writing: *the First Great Christian Disappointment might be categorised as the sixty or so years directly following Jesus's Crucifixion and Resurrection when it became increasingly obvious that he wasn't about to return imminently after all.* She looks over each item without much interest, dropping one after another into the box at her feet.

The last handful of papers are initially unfamiliar too, scribbled on sheets of A4 that she squints at for several seconds before the handwriting clarifies. Holds them a little away from herself, sets them down in her lap. *Sweet girls,* reads the first, *I'd tell you not to misbehave while I'm away but you'd only ignore me. In place of behaviour, then, please at least pretend to be the kind girls I know you to be.* A kiss at the end of this note, single *x* sketched in with green pen. *To Isla and Irene,* runs another, *since you asked so nicely, here is what I remember from the article about White Horse that I said I enjoyed reading so much: 'a fumed oak front door marks the entrance to a home that doubles as refuge, the sheltered point of arrival preceding a generous inner sanctum whose windows reach back and up towards the sky'. Isn't that wonderful? Now if only I could remember which magazine I found it in.* Irene sits still for a moment, looks down at these little notes that their mother used to leave around the house for them to find and fight over, each addressed to the pair of them, never left for one and not the other. *Dearest girls,* reads one folded down towards the bottom of the pile, *I know it won't seem like it now, or even later, but things will begin to make sense in good time.* She looks at this last, turns it over as if expecting more. No idea of the context that would have explained this, her mother's writing listing sideways as if keen to be up and gone. She shrugs, stacks the notes and drops them into the box at her feet. She feels suddenly exhausted, emptied out of herself, looks up to find Jude leaning against the doorframe and looking in at her so kindly that Irene almost starts to cry.

'I can make you a tea,' Jude says, sleepy still. 'Or I can leave you alone and come back later.'

Irene shakes her head; thinks, for an instant, of the first time she told Jude she loved them, the moment that marked the end of waiting, of hanging around wondering what the big event of her life might be.

'I'll have tea,' she says, and abruptly puts her head in her hands. She feels, rather than sees, Jude pick their way around the boxes to join her in the armchair, allows herself to be shifted sideways and then curled around, one arm across both of hers, holding her tight.

'Are you crying because of your dad or are you just crying?'

'I'm just crying,' she says, and goes on doing so. Jude moves one hand to the back of her head and says nothing, cups her skull like something small and easily stowed. It is easier, she thinks, to cry like this, with someone holding all her vital parts in place.

'Did you know *Irene* means *peace*?' she asks after a little while, wipes her nose on the back of her hand. 'That's funny, isn't it? I always thought they should have called me something else. Called me *Great Big Spike*, or something similar. I think it would have made more sense.'

Jude huffs a laugh, squeezes her for a moment and then releases. An unspoken thought between them: the essential fact of Irene as a creature akin to a hermit crab, whose outer shell seems ostensibly tough but is only the home to a very soft animal, and the secondary fact of Jude as the only person who really knows this.

Somewhere away in the rear of the flat, a phone starts ringing.

'It'll be your sister,' Jude says. 'No one else ever calls this early.'

'I'm sure you're right,' Irene says, and remains where she is.

* * *

Irene met Jude at the coin wash launderette near a flat she was, at the time, subletting from a colleague. Close to midnight, sticky-hot and uncomfortable, she'd bled into the sheets, taken by surprise by a bad period that stained the mattress. Unable to go back to sleep in the mess she'd made, she dragged herself out in her sweatshirt and jeans to force everything into a rented washing machine. Still in her slippers, wet from the rain and cramping horribly, she stood with her head against the coin slot until someone tapped her on the back and asked if she knew that she hadn't set the cycle to *start*. Important to explain here how attractive Jude was, which is to say too attractive for one in the morning. Extremely tall and slightly stooped the way tall people often are, they rocked back half a step when Irene turned around and pulled a concerned face which she took a moment to realise was probably connected to how exhausted she looked and how wild in the eyes at the thought that the wash hadn't even begun. *No, it's fine, look* – Jude said, and leaned around her with a chivalrous motion – *I've turned it on now, there.* Irene nodded, shook her head, thought idly that both this stranger's eyes and mouth seemed to be trying very hard to be the most important feature in their face, and then passed out. Which is to say that Jude caught her, which was pretty romantic as first meetings go.

A while later, ensconced on the long wooden bench which ran up the centre of the launderette, Irene explained that this didn't happen often and Jude handed her a bottle of water and asked if she thought she was getting enough vitamin D. *Who's to say*, Irene said, with a dizzy sort of giggle that she would later look back on with embarrassment (what was funny about that? Why was she laughing?), and Jude smiled at her and put a hand on her shoulder. *Sorry, is that ok? I don't want you to go down again.* Irene let her back slip, felt some element of tension diffusing into Jude's hand, thought to herself *ok* and then drank half the bottle of water. They sat there for a while together, Jude telling her that they came here to do their laundry sometimes when their house-mate had a date over. *Not saying I mind, obviously, I mean good luck to him, but he does seem to spend a lot of time* **screaming** *when he's in there with whoever it is. Makes me feel like I ought to be elsewhere.* Irene laughed and Jude looked pleased, as though that had been the whole point of the anecdote. They talked for a while after this in the strange, open way one will do in the hours usually reserved for sleeping. Talked about work and about the state of things as the machines hummed softly around them, talked about how expensive it was to run non-essential appliances and whether either of them knew anyone who bothered with a dishwasher any more. Another person would occasionally shuffle past them, moving between the detergent stand and the dryers, one man bearing a basket containing a stack of baby bibs, one woman pushing a ketchup-covered blanket into a machine by the door. The rain hammered the glass shop frontage, misted over from the inside by steam from the washers and dryers, and Irene felt her cramps receding a little, felt the blood creeping back to her far-flung places: her ankles and fingers, the tip of her nose.

The second time they saw each other was at Jude's flat, Jude having first apparently ensured that the screaming housemate was absent. They had asked Irene round after more than a week of sustained texting during which Irene had at one point found herself typing *I basically think the one job you have as a parent is to give your kid a childhood they don't have to recover from* and then wondering why on earth she was saying this to someone she barely knew. Jude opened the door in a striped bowling shirt and Irene wanted them to fuck her and didn't know how to say this, so she held up the bottle of wine she'd brought and said something stupid about how she wasn't sure whether the grapes were naturally grown and Jude rolled their eyes and smiled and said *what even is any more?*

Crowded together into the galley kitchen, drinking wine that tasted like metal, they tried to find an ordinary way to look at one another. Jude pushed their hair back and cracked eggs into a pot of boiling water, talked about how they had a friend who had jerry-rigged a sort of covered run for the chickens she kept on the roof of her building; a sheltered pen that simulated sunlight and kept the chickens warm and dry and oxygenated, and producing eggs that she gave to her friends for free. *It's just too hard to manage it otherwise*, Jude said. *I don't know how people afford half the things they need.* Irene hopped up onto the counter, regretted the move and crossed her legs in an effort to look more nonchalant. *I know what you mean – my dad still buys red meat, still ships in olive oil and bananas and all the rest of it. You just want to say to him, 'Why? What makes you so deserving?'* Jude pulled out a loaf of bread. *Yeah, but then I guess he's older, isn't he? Stands to reason it's harder to give things up when you're more used to having them.* They talked about this for a while, the fact that it was still possible to get hold of most of what you wanted if you really tried, or really paid for it, the question of what was really worth it. *I miss really good coffee*, Jude said, and Irene said, *I miss pineapple*, and then Jude plated up two poached eggs on toast, the yolks soft and spilling, and it tasted so good that Irene wanted to cry. Pressed a hand to her mouth, grinned in a way that felt lascivious. Jude started to laugh and offered her black pepper. She took in their straight nose and slightly overcrowded teeth, dint of a smile in one cheek like something scored with a pencil. *You know*, they said, *this really isn't super-smooth of me but I think you're insanely beautiful. Like I saw you that first time and I was just like fuck.*

Later on, they took the end of the wine to the sofa and talked with the kind of incautious intimacy made possible by alcohol and the fact that one of them had already fainted on the other. *I'm a Scorpio*, Irene said, *which is weird because I think both of my sisters are Scorpios. Like my dad just wanted to make life as difficult as possible.* Jude told her about their work in social housing, about how they'd tried to go to university and then decided it was pointless, about how they weren't so sure about their hairstyle just now. *I look like I imagine JFK would have looked if he'd lived and got really into Elvis.* Irene finished the wine, accepted a glass of something stronger and explained that she was writing her thesis on Christianity and silence, on the concept of a God who said nothing. *God to me is something remote, a force which speaks through other people, and I think I'm starting to find that really depressing.* Jude looked at her and Irene felt a pleasurable sting of something, a vibration like a fingertip set against a string. *Why depressing?* Jude asked, and Irene shrugged, touched a knuckle to the rim of her glass and made a circle. *I think I'm just getting bogged down in how lonely it is, or how much I want to be spoken to, or something. In the Old Testament, God's constantly rabbiting on, you can't get through two verses without him giving orders to someone or setting up some ridiculous test or going on about himself. But then after the apocrypha he clams up and you don't really hear from him again. He retreats into this upper echelon of heaven like when a person gets really famous and it's impossible to get through to them any more. It makes everything more the job of an interpreter, and it makes us more reliant on angels and second-hand information and what people* **think** *it is God's saying. I think I've started finding that difficult, or sad, or something, I don't know why. And obviously that's before you even get onto the more crucial question of what's the point of further education, end time or no.* Jude nodded, looking at her in an even way. *So are you very into God then?* Irene shrugged. *No, not really. I don't even necessarily believe in God, it's just the idea of God, you know. Like someone telling you what you're supposed to be doing, how you're supposed to be spending your days.* Jude gave this a considering look and then took Irene's glass from her hand and kissed her and Irene thought *ok* and then *thank God* and then how ironic that was.

They fucked on the sofa in the deepening early-evening blue; blue like black with the lights turned on, hazy-blue, like the television caught between channels. Irene thought of warning Jude about the level of concentration it usually took for her to orgasm, about the darkened-room-blankets-to-the-chin-earplug-earphones commitment it could take just to get to a stage where it even felt possible. It wasn't, as she wanted to say, so much the issue of being unable as it was the relative breadth of distractions on offer. Too easy to think about something she'd seen on the train, at the supermarket, the jingle from a radio advert, and find herself running parallel to the moment, not unaroused but somehow abstracted, trying to work her way back to the point. She wanted to say this, but Jude kissed her neck, her jaw, pushed a hand between her legs, and Irene thought to herself *what if I were still bleeding* and then thought *Jesus Christ it's so easy, it's so fucking easy to be in love.*

* * *

Isla appears before the lawyer does, her face refracted on the laptop screen.

'Your signal's terrible,' Irene says, rests her chin on her palm and thinks about making a coffee. Isla says something unintelligible, makes a frustrated sound that blurs into something electronic and then the video cuts out, leaving Irene to stare at her own face on the screen. Irene sighs, clicks out of the call and navigates back to the website she was looking at before. It is a place she visits fairly often, a forum for people who have taken to expressing their anxiety at the state of the world by role-playing a very particular kind of normality. You can follow people's fantasy back-and-forths, request to participate in open narratives. *And after that*, runs one thread shared between two users, *we'll take the Underground and come up via the escalator and the light outside will be that particular kind of light you get when the sun has just burned off the morning and it's about to be a dry, hot day.* The tone of the website is vaguely romantic, if not to say sexual. People frequently role-play at dates but seldom the central fact of the date so much as its logistics. *I'd pick you up in my car because I have a car*, one post overexplains, *and after I've picked you up in my car I'll drive us both through the city because I have a car and we both love to drive.* Occasionally, narratives will take a turn for the cubist, if not to say outright surreal. *There's been a hosepipe ban*, one person posts, and another responds, *I'm mowing the lawn*, and another responds, *I'm bored at the airport*, and the thread continues on like that, a succession of random statements spooling out like free jazz, a curious dissonant music of yearning for the way things used to be. Irene is still scrolling when her laptop chirps and Isla's face fills the screen again, the image now a little less choppy and showing her scowling face in full.

'Moved rooms,' she says by way of greeting, and then, 'What's the matter with you?'

'Nothing is the matter with me,' Irene says stiffly, 'but thank you.'

'I didn't mean you looked *bad*, I just meant you were frowning,' Isla says. 'There's no need to start rolling your eyes because I asked how you were.'

'You didn't ask how I was,' Irene says, and Isla holds up her hand.

'The lawyer's in the waiting room,' she says, and Irene shuts her mouth, looks at her own face on the screen for a moment and wishes she'd thought to put on her glasses to cover the circles under her eyes. She had ignored Isla's first and second calls that morning but then picked up the third just as Jude left for work. *Dad's lawyer wants to speak as early as possible*, she had said, *if you want to be there when we do it. Good to do it now in case he made any stipulations about the funeral or whatever. I can't reach Agnes but what's new there.* Irene had nodded, realised that Isla couldn't see her nodding. *I'll come*, she had said, and thought of the Braque print her father had kept in his study and how much she had always hated it, because she hated Braque, hated his muddy colours and the way that looking at any of his work for too long began to feel like being trapped with your head between two stair rods with no way of moving forward or back.

'I'll let him in,' Isla says now. 'Please be nice.'

The lawyer is highly coloured in a way which might be to do with the contrast on his laptop or might be his face. He talks quickly, eschews pleasantries to first commiserate about their loss and then assure them this won't take long at all.

'Quick and dirty,' he says, and then apologises. 'I've been off for a week and you'd be astonished how quickly you forget how to talk to people.'

Their father's will, as it turns out, is succinct. The majority of his assets split between a number of design foundations, an architectural college, a scholarship endowment.

'The understanding,' notes the lawyer, 'appears to be that a settlement was reached four years previously with each of his daughters. He appears to have sought to endow a significant sum upon each daughter along with the agreement that no further financial endowment was to be sought after that.'

Irene's gaze slides to Isla's face on the screen – her curt little nod.

'That's correct,' Isla says. 'He offered us each a sum a few years ago and we didn't take it.'

Irene picks at a thread in the cuff of her sweater. Pictures the bathroom in her old flat, squirm of silverfish in the tile grouting and the space behind the pipes.

'I wondered,' Isla continues and then pauses, bites her lip. 'I wondered whether he was going to leave anything to Marie.' Her face stutters across the screen, her expression briefly pixelated and dragging to the left. 'That's Agnes's mother,' she adds, as the lawyer shifts through papers. 'She wasn't around for very long and we're not sure where she even is but I didn't know whether—'

'Nothing that I can see.' The lawyer shakes his head, flips forward in his papers. 'The only other thing of note is the

147

house, *White Horse*, and its contents, which he has left to his daughter Agnes. I'm presuming from what I've read that that would be your half-sister.'

Isla's connection sputters and cuts out. Irene looks at the space into which she has disappeared before turning to the lawyer and asking how he'd prefer to bill them for his time.

Agnes

Stephanie pulls her along towards the jetty, tall figure in her creased work shirt and cardigan. Agnes goes where she's bidden, chooses not to question how a hook-up transformed into a joint commute.

'Isn't it funny,' Stephanie muses, 'the way that everything's fucked but still patched up enough to let you get to work?'

She taps her card against the payment point, watches Agnes do the same. Wet-haired, neither one of them having thought to bring an umbrella, they wait together on the crowded lower pier. Companionable, to stand uncovered in a sea of black umbrellas and watch the inner-city clippers come and go. White lights on the water and a man intoning destinations over the tannoy. Wet wool smell of Stephanie's cardigan and a series of tidy thoughts: going down on her at 2 a.m. and the power coming back on midway through; curling close like things with tails wrapped tight in a nest. She doesn't want to hold Stephanie's hand, clutches loosely at her own wrist to avoid the implication that she's open to it. Easy to fuck someone twice and then say you don't hold hands but less rational to have breakfast and let them pour you coffee, accompany them to the jetty and then say you're not interested in getting involved. Always this; the nerves at the back of her neck pulled taut, the feeling that giving an inch will prove somehow on par with carving out a little piece of her face and handing it over. A section of cheek or cheekbone, the groove between nose and mouth – some part of her excised and relinquished, transferred by the willing surrender of her space.

The ferry arrives and they troop on, wet press of bodies around them. A man in thick pink plastic glasses is barking into a phone at Stephanie's elbow and she widens her eyes at Agnes, who starts to laugh and then covers her mouth. She looks around the covered deck as the boat leaves the jetty. A woman hanging on to an overhead strap and staring down at her phone with narrowed eyes, scrolling over a series of messages that Agnes can just about read: *i don't think i meant it the way you took it. you're always hearing me talk and then slinging your own translation over the top.* By the window, a man is reading a book on foundation repair and picking at a dry spot at the base of his temple. In the corner, a teenage girl gnaws hard at the cuticle on her left thumb, makes a little round *o* of dismay as it starts to bleed. The atmosphere is jangled, damp, soporific; at once sleepy and unsettled. It feels, Agnes can't help but think, like the kind of day where a person might quite easily start throwing their breakfast about. The kind of morning where someone might snap.

'Did you hear what I said?' She turns her head, realises Stephanie must have been speaking to her, shrugs one shoulder to indicate *no*. 'I said we could have lunch if you wanted,' Stephanie says, 'but also that I understand you might make that face you do if I go on suggesting things like that.'

Agnes feels uncomfortable, glances away and finds herself looking directly across at a woman whose gaze is already trained on her. Light eyes, light hair, as though she has been washed too hot and bleached of pigment, expression alert for the time of day. She could be thirty-five or fifty, strangely featureless in a chambray shirt, pale trousers, silver chain looped close around her throat. Unruffled, unlined. She is, Agnes thinks, an odd fit in this crush of work suits and swiftly creasing polyester. She doesn't drop her gaze when Agnes meets it, only tips her head a little in a manner that resembles deference. Her gaze throbs and Agnes holds it, feels a curious vibration and can't quite tell if it's the boat beneath her or the thrill of being caught in her usual act of looking. The woman moves her hand to take hold of an overhead strap, as if she might be about to make her way down the aisle to where Agnes is standing. But then Stephanie's hand is on her arm and Agnes looks back towards her, remembers that she has yet to respond to the question Stephanie has already asked her twice.

'I don't know,' she says, more or less at random, and then, 'Don't you think you'll get bored?'

'I mean,' Stephanie says, raises an eyebrow, 'it's lunch, I'm sure I'll manage.'

Agnes registers the particular shudder of the floor that indicates the boat is docking at its next regular stop. An interlude as the crowd retracts, people bunching up to allow others to squeeze along towards the doorway. Agnes looks back over her shoulder. The woman is no longer staring at her, is in fact nowhere to be seen. Stephanie clicks her tongue, shifts sideways to allow the man in pink glasses to elbow past her, still yammering into his phone. The route off the ferry involves a member of staff first securing a railed metal gangplank between the outer deck and the jetty before scuttling across to open the upper gate. Passengers make their way across one at a time, climbing up a steep set of stairs that lead them up off the jetty and away beyond the embankment wall. The tide is high today, and choppy, and Agnes watches through the smudged ferry window as passengers hurry across the gangplank, the swing and dip of the boat against the side of the wharf. A large number of passengers are disembarking and the wait is considerable. She blows up into her hair, shifts her gaze to watch the bland little line of people struggling up the narrow flight of stairs. The embankment is extremely high at this point, built upwards and reinforced in recent years to meet the overflow of what was originally a river and is now simply a long, deep stretch of open water. Stephanie appears to have given up her line of enquiry about lunch and is now looking down at her phone. Agnes tries to think of something to say, imagines telling her there's no point in having lunch because, once they do, they'll have simply had lunch and nothing will be different. *I don't think*, she wants to say, *that there's anything to be gained from keeping on getting to know one another. And I don't mean that about you or me personally, I just mean in general, you know?* She moves her hand, imagines patting Stephanie's arm in comradely fashion, but then a woman to her left and closer to the window starts to scream, and then several people are screaming – indiscernible noises, though one shout sounds very like *stop her* – and there is little enough time to make sense of what is happening before the figure of a light-haired woman in a chambray shirt comes crashing downwards from the upper embankment, cracks clean against the jetty's edge and slithers down into the water, feet below. The world rears back, a sound like humming close beside Agnes's ear. The moment holds for one second, two, as she stares out of the window, stares at the blank that has already reasserted itself – the woman's fall, the woman's landing and then nothing again but a stain on the jetty and the terrible gush of what is left behind.

Isla

You're not having a panic attack. You know what a panic attack looks like, and this isn't one so there's no point acting like you're having a panic attack. You're just breathing quickly, that's all this is. You're just upset. Get a grip.

She stays where she is (where she is being under the desk, where she put herself in fairly considered fashion after closing out of the videocall), and concentrates her energy on breathing normally. A stupid thing, really. A stupid fright, the lawyer's voice looping back on itself, twisting over as if to reveal her father's voice beneath it, or inside it. Her father's voice and the way she always knew it – mocking, impatient, hardly there at all. She had listened to the lawyer explaining – that the house was going not to none of them but to one of them – and felt her father in the doorway, in the corner, somewhere just behind her chair. *You're a silly little bitch*, she had thought (or known, or remembered), imagined a sensation like a hand around her wrist, *a silly little bitch who never thinks about anything*. Stupid thing, really. Just a house. Just an unpleasant shock. Just Agnes, just the whole wild unfairness of Agnes, her existence, and everything besides. Nothing to get upset about. She thinks, for a split second, about her mother and then stops before the thought can get up and walk around, start doing real damage. She stays where she is beneath the desk and holds herself, arms tight around her knees.

Agnes

You're not having a panic attack.

Stephanie's hand on her back. Her knees on the floor and the chaos of the boat around her. She can't breathe.

Don't look at it, she thinks.

You're not having a panic attack, you're fine.

Irene

Four years ago, they all sat together and considered the unfortunate fact of a dinner prepared by Irene; defrosted lettuce from a sketchy wholesale outfit drowned in its own meltwater, GM tomatoes split and oozing green across the plate. Jude hadn't been back in time to help, only to make encouraging sounds as Irene scooped most of a dropped head of chard off the floor and washed it. *That looks fine*, they'd said, *you're making this more of an issue than it needs to be.*

In the living room: Isla, Morven and Agnes, arranged as though tacked in position with pins. Isla by the window, Morven on the couch, Agnes chewing her nails and leaning back against the bookshelf.

'I wasn't expecting to cater,' Irene said, ferrying in plates with Jude's help and feeling defensive about the wet lettuce, the lack of a dining table. 'I didn't realise we'd be doing this here. So I guess if you want something else there's, like, sliced bread or I can get you some cheese or I can run out and try to find pasta or something.'

'This is just *lovely*, thank you,' Morven said, and Irene resisted the urge to roll her eyes, handed over her plate and stood awkwardly for a moment before Jude put a hand on her back.

'That one's yours,' they said, indicating the plate Irene was still holding, and she looked down at it, registered the limp arrangement of leaves and felt embarrassed, perched on the arm of the sofa while Jude passed cutlery around.

'That's fine, thanks,' Isla said, refusing a knife and just taking a fork when offered, stabbing at her plate while standing up as though attempting to eat at a university department mixer. *You can sit down*, Irene wanted to say, looked at the corner of the sofa where the stuffing was starting to poke through. 'So,' Isla continued, 'I thought it would be good if we spoke.'

'We can eat first, babe' – this from Morven. 'We can give it five minutes.'

'I wasn't hurrying us,' Isla replied, 'I just thought—'

'Five whole minutes!' Morven interrupted, smiling in a way that seemed to telegraph itself more than it needed to – *I'm **smiling**, we're all having a **nice time**.* 'Just while everybody eats. We can talk about *whatever we want* for five minutes, except what we've come here to talk about. It cannot possibly be that hard.'

155

There was a pause, people looking at their plates. Irene considered telling everyone that she had recently read a newspaper article about a new-fangled indoor method of farming cows and then thought better of it. It would have involved explaining that she had cried for forty-five minutes in her office cubicle at the thought of their never being allowed outside. The pause extended, unfurled itself into the beginnings of real discomfort. Irene opened her mouth, imagined saying that after she'd stopped crying she'd spent twenty minutes googling *veal farming, cows in the dark, do cows need sunlight to be happy* and so on until she realised it was time for lunch. Before she could start, however, Jude huffed a kind laugh, legs crossed in a chair they'd pulled in from the bedroom.

'I'll go, if you like.'

Morven pulled a face that might have been relief, waved a hand like someone ushering on a performer. 'Please!'

Jude tipped her a courteous nod, recrossed their legs and launched into a story about a woman they'd seen at work that afternoon whose family was requesting rehousing on the basis of diminished capacity. It was an anecdote Irene hadn't heard but that spoke to a theme with which she was generally familiar. Jude, home late from work and searching for silver linings, telling stories in an effort to unpick the stitches of a thankless day.

'Pretty early stages of dementia,' they explained. 'Her family was worried if they didn't try to sort assisted living for her they'd be on a waiting list forever and there's *so little*, now. So anyway, they brought her in and she explained the whole thing to me – really very lucid, you know, except she kept noting down what I said in response, even though she had her daughter with her. I guess it probably felt better to have her own record, not to just rely on being told what had happened at some later point.'

'That's interesting,' Morven said. 'Like maybe she didn't totally trust her daughter.'

'Yes, I mean, I don't think it was that so much,' Jude said, nodding in the way they often did when they disagreed with someone, like they could see the point being made, 'I'm not sure it was an issue of trust so much as translation. I think she just wanted to note down exactly what had happened so she didn't miss any of the nuance when her daughter recounted it later. I guess we have more control when we have all the details, don't we? Anyway, at one point she sort of explained her symptoms to me, or I guess explained how she experienced it. Sometimes everything would be normal except she couldn't find any of the right words, like someone had come along and wiped them. She said it could manifest as distortions in her vision, or like she was hallucinating different senses, hallucinating tastes and smells. She said once she thought she saw her own father, like he'd just wandered in from another timeline and was standing there, like she'd taken a wrong turn and ended up somewhere sidelong – a slightly different point in her own life. She said it was hard to tell what was real, she'd want to take a photo of a moment to check everything she was seeing in front of her was actually *there*. It was so strange, completely different from how I guess I've been taught to think about dementia? And she didn't seem particularly unsettled, actually. I think there was some comfort in being able to remember it well enough to recount it, even if what she was recounting was distressing in itself.'

'That's so *interesting*,' Morven said, nodding along.

'It was ok,' Jude said, looking towards Irene – the funny little line they often cast in group conversations, intended to reel her back towards them. 'Bore you to death with this kind of thing every day, don't I? It's a bad habit.'

'No, it's not,' Irene said at once, registered the fond little flare that was always so easy to pinpoint amongst however many other more abstruse emotions. 'I like to hear it.'

Isla, suppressing a sigh by the window, setting her plate down.

'So I wanted to talk about our dad for a second.'

Morven opened her mouth, closed it. Irene eyed her, wondering not for the first time just what it *was* about her, what it was about either of them. She had never liked Morven much but she had always had a marbling effect on Isla, like fat through meat, lending her a more palatable flavour. That element of things seemed off tonight, unfettered *Isla* coming through too strongly.

Irene shifted on the arm of the sofa. 'Ok,' she said, 'well, that's the small talk portion of the evening effectively over, I guess.' She looked at her sister, felt aware, for a moment, of the shape of her father around the corners of Isla's face – a suggestion, like something traced and then poorly erased. 'So what did you want to talk about?'

'I wanted,' Isla replied, 'to talk about what I have to assume he has said to all of us. Unless I'm wildly off the mark here, in which case I think we need to talk about that too. About him trying to give us all his money.'

'I don't think it's *all* his money,' Irene objected, and Isla sighed again.

'Ok, so a sizeable portion of his money in response to his recent heart attack, but thank you for confirming that he has indeed spoken to you too.'

'Why do we need to talk about it?'

This last from Agnes, edging into the conversation the way she often did, as though first coughing loudly outside a door to announce her presence.

Isla turned to look at her. 'Because I thought that for once it might be good for us to present a unified front.'

'Why?'

'I don't *know*, Agnes. Because I tried to get us all in line when we thought he was dying and it didn't work. Because sometimes I think that allowing someone to bully us and pit us against each other while maintaining the financial upper hand *isn't* the healthiest way for three sisters to relate to one another. And I think that in fact it is probably the key to a lot of our issues. I don't know.'

I think the key to a lot of our issues, Irene wanted to say, *is that we just don't like each other very much.*

'I guess,' Agnes said, 'that's fair as far as it goes, but I don't really know what you want to discuss, exactly. I've already told him I'm not taking anything.'

Isla nodded, seemed to digest this for a moment.

Irene looked at Agnes. 'You said that already?'

Agnes nodded, shifted her untouched plate from one hand to the other. *I don't know you*, Irene thought, more or less out of nowhere, *you're just some person in my house.*

'He called me and I told him.'

'Since when do you ever have your phone on?'

Agnes shrugged. 'I don't know. It was on, I answered it.'

'And what did you say, exactly?' Isla now, in her therapy voice, the voice that strove for moderation while surreptitiously checking its watch.

'I said *no thanks*,' Agnes said, and set her plate down on the table by the bookshelf. 'I said I don't want it, so no thanks.'

'And what did he say to you?'

'He said *fine*.'

'Well, that's very useful, Agnes, thank you.'

Irene glanced from Isla to Morven, watched as Morven pushed lettuce leaves around her plate and eventually set the plate aside. A funny impulse to look from her to Jude and find fault in the comparison, pinpoint all the ways in which her sister's partner was inferior to her own. Morven's hair was long and thin, as was the rest of her; the heavy pair of knees, the skin pulled taut at calf and neck and clavicle.

A strange, spent affect, like something chewed too long. She looked, Irene thought, somehow ersatz, or insubstantial, like a person who might quite easily rise in the middle of a conversation and excuse herself, never to return. She wondered if she and Isla were happy and then couldn't figure out what she'd do with this information if she had it. She looked back at Jude, still watching Isla and Agnes talking, and felt better for a moment.

'It's your prerogative, of course,' Isla was meanwhile saying to Agnes, 'and I'm glad you said what you felt you wanted to say. I suppose I just think it's a shame that we didn't all get to discuss before we responded. To present a unified front, I mean.'

'Yes, I know, you've said that already.' Agnes crossed to the sofa, slid down next to Morven and looked at Isla, as carefully blank as a Flemish angel. 'But it doesn't matter that much, does it? Whether you want to take the money or not, you just say so and that's it over with. I don't see why it has to come from all of us like we're the United Nations negotiating with a terrorist.'

'Well, I wasn't planning on accepting it, now you ask,' Isla replied, 'I just *thought* it would have been nice to show him that he couldn't separate us out like he used to, offer us money separately, speak to us separately, that we wouldn't make decisions without speaking to each other first.'

'But why is that important?' Agnes asked, still impassive. 'Do you think he cares whether we all say no together or separately? *I* don't want it. I hate to be all *people in the world are dying* but people *are* dying, you know? I don't want his money, I never wanted it, so there you go.'

'Yes, well, I appreciate that,' Isla replied, 'but if you'll pardon the characterisation it is also possible to respond to things outside of the strict bounds of teenage nihilism.'

'It's not teenage nihilism to say you don't want money if you don't like where it's come from,' Agnes said. Irene shifted, considered the way that sentence would have sounded coming out of her own mouth, once upon a time. Isla pinched the bridge of her nose.

'Ok, well, there's no point doing this. You've told him where you stand already, as is your right. So I suppose Irene and I can give him our responses whenever we want to. He can hear from all three of us as and when.'

'King Lear and his dyke daughters,' Irene said, and then wished she hadn't.

'Yes, well.' Isla shook her head and Irene wondered briefly whether her sister was going to cry, squinted at her for a moment. She sometimes tried to imagine Isla speaking to her openly, revealing her cut-off secret heart. The problem was that, when this imaginary Isla spoke, all that came out were greeting card sentiments: *to a wonderful sister, with deepest sympathy, to a true friend on her wedding day.*

'I don't think,' Agnes now said, slowly and with the slightest inkling of a frown between the dark brows that were so like their father's, 'that you can fix however many years of him playing us off against each other by just having a little three-way chat and hoping he feels our combined wrath, or whatever. You know?' And here she looked to Irene, the first indication so far that she cared about Irene's opinion. 'I mean, we are what we are by now, aren't we?'

Irene considered the fact of the three of them. Their father, expert at elevating one and then the other, referring to Irene as *nasty Irene* and making her sisters laugh with imitations of her voice and expressions. Their father, giving pocket money only to Irene and telling her not to tell Isla. Their father, confiscating all of Isla's books for using his computer and giving them to the others. Their father, making a four-year-old Agnes stand out in the corridor when she screamed, refusing to let anyone go to her as she howled into insensibility and finally wet herself. *At what point*, she wanted to say, *do we stop being the direct product of our parents? At what point does it start being our fault?*

Funny to think about Isla, the only one who ever actually came out to him, now demanding solidarity. Isla, who had told him what Irene and Agnes never could and had absorbed what she later referred to as his *feedback*, while he went on knowing nothing about what Irene did with her days or who she lived her life with, went on knowing nothing about Agnes at all.

Funny too, despite this, to recognise their weak moments of alliance, of affection, the way Isla had tried to take care of Irene when their mother died, the way Irene had done her best in return when left in the house with Agnes. The three of them, trying to be less isolated and frequently failing, trying to be less conclusively the product of their past. It was impossible, Irene often felt, to be more generous, less impatient, impossible not to go on living their lives as if he were just in the next room. Death, or the near miss of his death, like a promise, the possibility of a better way, the three of them blinking into the thought of a life without their father, uncertain of the rules.

6.

Isla

The night before the funeral, she makes a cup of tea and sits on the floor of her father's kitchen to drink it. Irene has texted to tell her they're heading over, have just left, will be there when they're there. Rain streaking down the windows. Tail end of a long, thin day.

They're staying in the house because it's closer to the crematorium. *I thought*, Isla had texted Irene, *that it might be easier*. Didn't say that she felt like she needed to be on the ground, close by, in case. (*In case of disasters, in case the house blows away before we can burn him, in case someone tries to get inside.*) She has no idea what she's really expecting to happen, only that being here makes her feel more ready to prevent it. She is feeling, she thinks, ok. Or better, anyway. More able, again, to be the version of herself who keeps things running to time. She's not entirely clear how long she stayed under her desk, after the call with the lawyer over a week ago. Is not entirely clear, in fact, when she started feeling able to move about again, to plan and work and speak in complete sentences. She's booked the venue for the wake, invited the guests, found a caterer who claimed access to all sorts of foods she hadn't imagined possible. She's made lists and ticked those lists off and made new ones. She's fine.

She runs her thumb around the rim of her mug and thinks about nothing. Imagines, then dismisses, any number of things, but still in principle thinks about nothing. The night feels poised on the tip of a finger. She sips her tea, sets one hand against the floor.

Her mother, once, leaned close to her ear in the darkness and told her to go to sleep, the corners of her mouth wet with blood as if torn at the edges. Afterwards, Isla would be unable to tell whether or not she had dreamed this, would sit upright in her bed and try to find traces of blood in her hair. Sometimes she recollects a series of events she's fairly sure she didn't witness – a rainy night and voices downstairs, one woman and another. She thinks of this now, and before too long she hears Irene's key in the door.

Irene

She goes about the ground floor turning lights off and ignores Isla telling her to leave them on.

'It's blinding in here,' she says, 'it's ridiculous.' She pauses in the kitchen doorway to watch Jude dumping bags on the counter.

'That's all I brought,' they say. 'I figured there would still be some actually fancy stuff in the cupboards. I was going to just do a pasta thing, if anyone feels like eating. This house is *insane*, by the way.'

Isla, on the floor for some reason, nodding, rolling her head back to look up at Jude.

'You're very thoughtful,' she says, and Irene wonders whether she'd been drinking something else before she decided to make herself tea. 'I forgot you've never been here before.'

Irene goes out into the main room and looks around, trying to assess whether or not anything has changed since her previous visit. They don't own this place any more – not that they really did before he left it to Agnes, but still, the certainty is different. She can not want the place and still feel cheated out of it.

'Is Agnes coming?' she calls into the kitchen, where Jude is now filling a glass of water from the sink and handing it down to Isla.

'I invited her,' Isla replies, 'so who knows.'

Irene nods, cracks her knuckles, tries to remember what it is she's agreed to say at the funeral tomorrow. *It doesn't seem to me*, Isla had said, *that we're obliged to say anything, but people are going to be expecting it and if we don't then I don't know who will.* Irene pictures herself standing up in front of countless of her father's friends, contemporaries, associates. Pictures herself saying *well, I used to eat chalk and vomit because I wanted to be a Christian mystic and I think a different sort of dad would have dealt with that differently.*

Isla

Jude leaning down, asking if she wants another glass of water. Isla considers telling them to fuck off and then remembers that it isn't Jude's fault that Irene is here or that Morven isn't or that everything related to the organisation of a funeral seems precision-tooled to make a person feel studded with tiny little pieces of glass.

'I'm fine,' she says, wants to say *I'm actually not fine but I don't think water is what's going to help me.* Before Irene and Jude arrived, she necked two glasses of her father's vodka and the after-effects now appear to be manifesting in a bleary kind of stop-motion: Jude's hand moving down towards her as though in stages, one little movement and another, and again. She picks up her tea and finds she's let it go cold.

'I'm feeling fine,' she repeats, and then Irene appears from the other room, still wearing the ridiculous heavy coat she arrived in. 'You look,' Isla says, 'like a female Rasputin.' Somewhere over towards the sink, Jude makes a noise that might be a laugh.

'You got shitfaced, didn't you,' Irene says, and Isla considers telling her to fuck off too, that she can do what she wants when she wants to, that she's the oldest child.

'I'm fine,' she says for a third time, and remembers their mother scrunching nit shampoo into Irene's hair after washing it over the edge of the bath. Their father used to joke that they should shave the girls' heads if they couldn't be trusted to come home from school uninfested. She pictures this: their mother, on her knees beside the bath, holding the back of Irene's neck so she wouldn't scream when the comb met a tangle. So too, she pictures later: their mother, holding on to Irene's face in the kitchen and telling her to listen, that there was a dangerous spirit somewhere near her, somewhere over her, that she needed to help her get it out.

'I think pasta's a good idea,' Irene says to Jude, who hums assent and starts pouring water into a pan to boil. Irene turns away towards the island, shrugging off her coat and reaching for a chopping board. Isla stays where she is, watches the two of them moving around her and tries to summon the words to best communicate how she feels about this attitude, this swanning in and setting to. She could, she supposes, tell them both to take their pasta and fuck off back to where they came from, since actually it was she, not them, who organised this funeral, and she, not them, who sorted the housekeeper and the bill and the invoices, who has done anything at all. The scrape of her sister like nails down a blackboard, somehow engineered to always be pissing her off. *I don't care for you to come in and organise me when I've organised everything for you. I don't care to look at you*, Isla thinks, *when someone loves you the way Jude loves you.*

As it is, she simply pushes herself up off the floor, steadies herself against the worktop with one hand and then reaches for the vodka bottle which she had previously stoppered and stowed beside the hob. Irene eyes her as she swipes a fresh glass down from the shelf and pours a drink, nudges past her to get to the larder.

Irene

Hard to tell if the noise is approaching thunder, hard to hear over the hum of the air conditioning and the rattle of the wind without. Isla has drifted off into the next room with her drink and Irene leans up against the counter and wonders how best to handle the situation. Jude pours pasta, chops garlic, gives her a look.

'You can go in there, I don't need you for anything.'

'I feel like she's going to fucking bite me.'

'She isn't a Venus flytrap.'

'She's a menace.'

Jude sighs, rests the tip of a paring knife against the chopping block for a second and looks at her.

'You don't like her either,' Irene scowls.

'I don't like or dislike anyone,' Jude says. 'I'm just trying to make dinner.'

Irene shakes her head, feels irritated and then ashamed of being irritated. Pictures Jude: black and white and exhausted in the 6 a.m. half-light, getting dressed and promising they'll buy food on the way home from work.

'Ok, fine,' Irene says, 'I'm sorry.'

Jude quirks a smile. 'You're not very nice, are you?'

'No, I'm not.'

'That's ok.'

Irene leans up on tiptoe, tucks her face very briefly into their neck and then withdraws, waving her hand a little tragically as she moves towards the doorway. Jude watches her go, seemingly amused by the pantomime.

'Courage.'

'I don't have any of that.'

She finds Isla in the main room, sitting like a spilled drink and staring at her phone.

The room seems to sit at a tilt, pitching low at one end like a ship slowly taking on water, though this is only because the light from the assorted standard lamps pools in such a way that one end of the room is far brighter than the other. Irene stands where she is for a second, imagines all her father's artfully mismatched furniture sliding down into the water; plates pitching forward out of glass-fronted cabinets on the upper decks of the *Titanic* and so on, people wandering around rearranging the chairs.

'You should stop drinking,' she says, and Isla slumps back further into the cushions as she does so.

'You should stop wearing stupid coats.'

'Right.'

She comes around the sofa, sits herself down on the edge furthest from Isla. Her sister, she reflects, looks more like their mother in this light than usual. Shades of their father, of course, but still – the sharp nose, the hands and neck, the way she holds herself. She feels uncomfortable, wants to tell Isla to snap back to her usual self. She remembers tossing back a drink in front of her the last time they were in the house together and the memory is prickly, embarrassing.

'We need to tell Agnes about the house,' Irene says. 'That he left it to her. I mean, we can if she comes tonight, or if she comes tomorrow, but either way it's a legal obligation.'

Isla shrugs, takes a sip of her drink. 'That's fine.'

Irene crosses one leg over the other, feels uncomfortable, uncrosses them.

'I don't imagine she's going to want to live here, is she? I mean, I can't picture it. I guess she might sell it.'

'I really don't care what she does.'

'I don't think that's true.'

Isla runs a hand through her hair in a way that makes it stick up.

'Well, fine, it's not. I just think it's ridiculous we haven't been able to get hold of her since we found out. It makes me feel insane – like, physically insane. If she comes tonight and we can tell her normally that'll be fine but even then … I'm just so sick of her never confirming and never getting in touch and never saying where she'll be or what her plans are. It's like we don't figure with her at all.'

Isla leans backwards, fumbles around on the side table next to the arm of the sofa and picks up a hexagonal agate coaster which she squints at and then sets down again.

'Do you ever think about all the stupid incidental shit in this house that probably costs more than your rent?'

'I try not to.'

'Well, whatever. Point is I'll be glad when it's all gone, whatever she chooses to do with it.'

Irene looks at her, scuffs one toe against the floor. 'You really think that?'

'I really fucking do.'

Irene nods, looks away towards the window, her own face reflected back.

'I've been wondering why he left it to her,' she says. 'I keep going round and round. First I think maybe he did it because of her mother, then I think maybe he did it because he saw her as more of a mess and in need of help, and then I think maybe he just did it to fuck with us, and then I'm back at Marie and I start going round again.'

Isla blinks, appears to be having some trouble focusing, and Irene realises she keeps talking in hopes of her sister

173

responding with something useful, sitting up and replying in characteristically officious tones that she already has a theory and Irene is being terribly slow. *Be Isla, please*, she thinks, *so I can tell you to shut up.*

'Do we suppose,' Irene continues, 'that her mother might come tomorrow? To the funeral?'

Isla necks the rest of her drink and sets the glass down on the floor. 'Why would I know that?'

'I don't know. I guess because you invited people.'

'Yes, I did, I invited all the people whose locations I actually knew.'

Irene can't quite access the words for what she's thinking, which is that she had assumed Isla was at some point just going to turn to her and say that she'd discovered what became of Agnes's mother, just as a point of admin, in between her many other tasks.

'I had a good one the other day,' Isla continues, apparently indifferent, fishing her phone out from beneath her and opening up an email. '*Re the funeral*,' she reads aloud, '*I won't be there but tell your lovely mother I said hi.* This is from someone calling himself "Uncle Ned" – I can't remember who he is or why I invited him or which mother he's referring to.'

She lowers her phone, fixes Irene with a look that seems both amused and ill-tempered.

'I ask you,' she says, 'who *are* any of these people?'

'I don't know.'

'Who do they think they *are*.'

'I really don't know, Isla.'

'Well, they're all coming tomorrow.'

'Yes, they are.'

'Except for Uncle Ned.'

'So you say.'

'So that'll be fun.'

Irene thinks of asking whether Morven is planning on coming, notes that her sister is now scrubbing at one eye with the palm of her hand and thinks better of it. She remembers Isla, aged seventeen, slicing three or four times at the curve of her own waist with a pair of kitchen scissors before applying antiseptic cream, disconnected as a school nurse. *I think we should be on the same team tomorrow*, she wants to say, but before she can do so there comes a rapping at the front door, and Jude emerges from the corridor to say that Agnes is here and appears to have brought someone with her.

Agnes

It occurs to her that there has always been one shitty witch in *Macbeth*, the one that never says anything useful and always just seems to be filling in space between the other two. Most of the time she feels like this witch is Irene, although sometimes it's Agnes and sometimes it's all of them, which doesn't really make sense but still feels fundamentally accurate.

Her sisters are looking at her like maybe she has chosen the wrong day for this visit, like when they said *come to our father's funeral* they actually meant a different father, at a different time of the month. Jude is standing in the doorway looking the way Jude tends to look: kind of hot and kind of like they've been airlifted in from another genre of TV show. Agnes considers saying something to them about this – *hi Jude, it's really cool how you're a casual afternoon cooking show and you're functionally married to my sister who's like one of those unethical TV documentaries about a woman who went mad and murdered her entire family* – but then remembers that Stephanie is standing next to her.

'Ok, so, Stephanie Muradyan, these are my sisters, Irene and Isla Carmichael. You don't actually need to know their surnames because their surnames are the same as my surname. And also this is Jude, whose surname I now cannot remember.' She pulls a face, turning towards Jude, who looks like they might be about to laugh. 'I'm sorry,' Agnes says, 'I always just say *Jude*.'

'What's going on here?' Isla says before Jude can clear up the mystery. She is slumped at one end of the sofa and seems drunk in a way that doesn't suit her, like someone is impersonating her more or less accurately but with crucially fewer bones. Agnes looks at her, then at Irene, who meanwhile is sitting up looking like she can't decide exactly which type of irritating bitch to be.

'I'm surprised you made it,' Irene says at last, which feels oddly feeble. Agnes meets her eyes for a second, then watches her gaze pass over to Stephanie, who continues to stand impassively to her right. Agnes sighs, thinks for a second about explaining but finds she cannot summon the energy. The image of herself as she was last week: on her hands and knees on the deck of the ferry and gasping at what she'd seen, her breathing too fast and hysterical and chaos everywhere as the teenager tasked with mooring the boat tried to stop people swarming the jetty to see what had happened. The woman who'd stared at her before she disembarked. A body falls fast – too fast, in fact, to make much of the fall, only the impact. Agnes had seen the way she landed, the body disconnecting from itself, the crack and opening, the head like an egg.

She imagines explaining this to her sisters; explaining Stephanie's hands on her back, on her neck, and everyone screaming around them. Stephanie telling her it was ok, telling her not to look at it, and hours afterwards finding herself back in Stephanie's flat and with no memory of how she had got there, buried under the duvet and Stephanie bringing her a cup of tea and a biscuit wrapped in purple foil. *I stole this from Casper's private stash. I think sugar's good for shock, isn't it? Or stress or something. I don't know. It's a biscuit.* They had stayed like that, Stephanie sitting on the bed beside her, and Agnes had gone to sleep and woken up again and thought about the way a body can break, the shudder and roll, the laughable ease of it. She had cracked her knuckles and imagined wrenching her fingers further backwards, noting that nothing stood between her and this bending and breaking beyond the anticipation of pain.

'This is Stephanie,' she says again, and Stephanie raises a hand as if being newly introduced. 'We've been hanging out.'

Her sisters stare at them both.

'It's nice to meet you,' Stephanie says, as smoothly as if this weren't frankly the weirdest possible social situation to have signed up for.

'Sorry, are you seeing this person?' Isla asks Agnes, with an *s* that requires a tactical chin-wipe.

'Is that relevant?' Agnes replies.

'I mean who is she?'

'I told you her name already.'

'And you've brought her here tonight of all nights and we all just have to pretend like it's appropriate?'

Agnes narrows her eyes, tries to remember the last time she saw her oldest sister drunk. A flash like a face seen through the window of a passing car: Isla eighteen and dancing in the living room on a night not long before she left for university, leaning down to kiss Agnes sloppy and hot on the top of her head and then shimmying away again.

'What's inappropriate?' Agnes says now. 'I thought it would be better for me if I brought someone, so I brought someone. Jude's here too.'

'You're asking me *what's inappropriate.*'

'Yes, I am.'

'Well, I don't know what you think is inappropriate, Agnes' – another soggy *s*, whole body listing sideways – 'I frankly cannot claim to have the *faintest idea* what goes on in your head, but I guess you'd think it was *inappropriate* if we told you in front of a perfect fucking stranger that our father decided to leave his entire house and its contents to *you*.'

Sitting next to Isla, Irene opens her mouth, leaves it open as though hoping words will come out if she gives it a moment. Agnes reels, stares at the two of them, Isla now sliding down to a near-supine position and picking up her empty glass.

'I don't have a drink,' she says.

'I don't—' Irene says, and then stops talking.

Thunder outside, or something quite like thunder. Either way, a low and terrible sound.

Irene

The evening swings like a pendant light pulled back and then released. Isla pushes herself up from the sofa as though nothing has happened and wanders unsteadily off into the kitchen with her glass.

'I'll just …' Jude says, and gestures towards the kitchen, following her without pausing to explain.

Agnes and whatever-her-name-is stand together in the doorway and Irene registers a ridiculous impulse to play host, all her usual less helpful tendencies thrown off by whatever Isla is doing.

'Um, well, you should probably take your coats off.'

The girl her sister invited to their father's funeral nods at this, shrugging off her rucksack and bomber jacket in one go. She doesn't apologise for her presence, only hands over both items to Irene. Irene holds the jacket and bag a little stupidly for a second, wondering why on earth she offered to take them. Agnes, meanwhile, is still wearing her jacket and doesn't move as Irene holds out an arm to suggest she take it off.

'Is she drunk or is she serious?'

'Um' – Irene shrugs – 'both?'

'About the house?'

'Yeah, about the house. The lawyer told us he left it to you. We couldn't get hold of you to say but he did.'

'So you were just ... what ... not going to tell me?'

Irene rolls her eyes. 'No, Agnes, I think it's pretty obvious that we were going to tell you this evening, assuming you came.'

'And what if I didn't come?'

'Why is that relevant?'

'Fuck's sake.' Agnes exhales sharply through her nose and crosses to the fireplace, still in her jacket and folding her arms over her chest. As a child, Irene had imagined Agnes as something opaque, edgeless, like a pottery cup, filled with things she couldn't see. She had snuck into the nursery and imagined smothering her in the throwaway fashion young girls often picture great acts of terrible violence. She looks down at the jacket and bag in her arms, wishes in a pathetic sort of way that Isla could gather herself enough to take charge of the situation because she isn't equipped to do this herself. Sisterhood, she thinks, is a trap. You all get stuck in certain roles forever.

'Well, I don't know what to tell you,' she says. 'I'm going to go and hang these up if you want to give me your jacket.'

Agnes

Irene disappears with Stephanie's things and Agnes turns around to look at the room. She takes in the long strip of window, the cold press of the poured-concrete floor, the large Persian rug that she doesn't recognise and which does little to alleviate the chill that bleeds up into unsocked feet. *Who bought that*, she wonders, *and why did they bother.*

'So' – and this from Stephanie, who has meanwhile wandered over to a straight-backed chair near the bookcase and settled down, apparently unconcerned by what just happened – 'which is the drunk one and which is the other one?'

Agnes snorts, leans back against the mantelpiece to look at her.

'Isla's drunk, Irene's other. Isla isn't usually like that, she's more sort of …' She thinks for a moment, then assumes a pose reminiscent of Count Orlok, elbows glued to her sides, hands curled into claws, eyes darting. 'Like … she's sort of trying so hard to be well behaved and normal that it goes round the other side and comes out completely unhinged. Sometimes I imagine she sleeps hanging upside down in a wardrobe like a fucking bat.' She laughs for a second and then shakes her head. 'Sorry. This all feels incredibly weird.'

'Well, you said it would be.'

'Yeah. I mean I don't think I've really taken in …' She gestures around her, trying to indicate the concept of the house at large or her father at large or something, somehow.

She hadn't intended to invite Stephanie, although when she did and when Stephanie said yes, she registered such an intense wave of relief that it felt briefly quite nauseating. They've been almost exclusively in each other's company ever since the incident at the jetty. Accidental, in the main – Agnes simply came back to herself in Stephanie's bed and then never meaningfully left again. Stephanie had explained a few things that Agnes appeared to have blacked out: the police who had made everyone stay on the boat for upwards of three hours until the water took a turn for the choppy and everyone started being sick; the calls made to work to explain both their absences; the disembarkation and the long trip home again. In the flat, Agnes slept fitfully and dreamed about falling, dreamed about taking water into her lungs. On waking, she lay for a long time and imagined being sawn open to find her insides were brindled with sea anemones, or possibly tumours. *Don't cry*, she thought to herself – her own voice but different, as if from early childhood – *whatever you do, don't cry*. She listened to the rain and watched

Stephanie reading a book by the light of an Anglepoise lamp and wondered what Jason was playing on the work sound system and whether Svetlana had agreed to cover her shift. They didn't discuss her staying, only avoided the topic of when she might leave. She felt embarrassed, aware of how recently she had baulked at the simple prospect of lunch together. Too like being caught out, to change her tune so dramatically, too like being seen for the fraud she was.

Stephanie, for the most part, was bizarrely calm about it, called in sick three days on the trot before suggesting they both go back to work again. In the intervening period, they spent a lot of time fucking, and a lot of time talking, and most of the time they weren't fucking or talking either sleeping or trying to make dinner in the warzone of Stephanie's shared kitchenette. Agnes mostly wore Stephanie's clothes and mostly didn't think too much about it. She learned that Stephanie had no father and a tricky but functional relationship with her mother. *Functional in that we're both sort of performing CPR on it all the time,* Stephanie said. *She's Armenian Orthodox and I'm a dyke, which keeps things spicy, but I still feel like it's comforting to have a mum in terrible times, even if she is a twat.* Agnes nodded and decided not to chip in with a story about her own mother. On occasion, she would note the impulse to run away and would instead do something rational like make the bed. On occasion, she would picture the woman who had stared at her, picture her snapping sharp across the jetty, the shift from solid to liquid as she spilled into the

183

water. When this happened, she would turn her face into Stephanie's neck and find that she liked it there; her smell and the unshaven warmth of her underarms, the way she talked like things weren't as hard as Agnes was always making them, the long, soft line of her body whenever she came. She had asked Stephanie to come to the funeral without really thinking about it and thanked her sincerely when she said yes. One of Stephanie's housemates, Beck – a hot butch with a number of worthy causes – looked at the two of them when Stephanie explained where they were going that weekend and rolled her eyes. *So you got serious because someone died in front of you and now you're going on minibreak to a funeral. That's the gayest thing I've ever heard.*

Now, she looks at Stephanie and wants to say something reassuring, something that will make this whole trip seem like less of a terrible error in one or both of their judgements. Stephanie, however, is focused on a framed photo she has found on an end table, picking it up and scrutinising it for a second before smiling.

'Is this you?'

Agnes crosses to take the photo from her and looks at it. Small girl half-turned towards the lens, dark hair apparently chewed at the edges so that it curls rather wetly around her chin.

'That's pretty weird.'

'Why is that weird?'

'I mean, I've told you about my dad. It's pretty weird that he would frame a photo of me and put it out like this. Feels like something someone might do in a show home.'

She looks away from the photo, eyes something she has hitherto been avoiding: the wheelchair tidied unobtrusively away into one corner of the room, the oxygen canister beside it. Thinks about her father and then tries to elude it, imagines folding herself up so thin that the thought can't find her and has no choice but to glide right past. *Don't cry, keep quiet and for God's sake don't cry.* Looks towards the wall and notes the shape of something scratched there. A face, she thinks, or something similar, barely the size of her thumbnail, a round mouth and pinpoint eyes, something clawed as if with the tines of a fork. *Did I do that?* she thinks. *Did Irene?* She half-turns towards Stephanie to point this out, but at that moment there is a sound of breaking glass from the kitchen and then the muffled sounds of Jude demanding Isla get out of the way so she doesn't cut herself.

Isla

Difficult to tell when the evening slipped. Glass gouged into the soft part of her palm after trying to pour a new drink and dropping it, eyeing the cut – the shape and consistency of a mouth when it's wet, stretching up from the pad of her hand to the webbing between thumb and index finger.

Out of the kitchen again before Jude can stop her, tilting slightly, holding on to the doorframe. She finds Agnes and the stranger where she left them, looking up as she kicks the door shut behind her.

'For God's sake' – and that's Jude, pushing the door open again and following her out with a tea towel – 'you're going to bleed everywhere.' Trying to press the tea towel to her hand but it stings and she pulls away, staggers, draws herself up. *You're a **therapist**,* a voice in her head says, as if this statement ought to mean something concrete. She looks at her hand again and thinks about the patient whose father set himself on fire, thinks that all through their most recent session she couldn't stop noticing how much this patient resembled someone she'd seen on TV. *You're a terrible therapist,* she thinks, and holds her bleeding hand aloft the way you're supposed to.

'You're so fucking *selfish,*' she says, and realises she is speaking to Agnes apparently around the same time Agnes does. 'You are,' she continues. 'This whole thing, it's just completely classic You.'

Agnes stares at her. The stare is so rude that Isla finds herself talking again before she can help herself.

'It is, it's you all over. You do something first without talking to either of us or you don't do anything at all. You completely drop off the face of the earth or you turn up but with some total stranger who you didn't ask to bring. It's exhausting. It's completely exhausting to have to keep caring about you when you plainly do not give a fuck about us.'

Agnes's posture goes tight. The girl she's brought with her puts a steadying hand on her shoulder and Isla registers a sudden and powerful desire to put her fist through a wall.

'It is not my fault,' Agnes says after a moment and in an infuriatingly measured voice, 'if you have certain expectations of our relationship that I never invited you to have. It is not my fault,' she adds, 'that you insist on pretending that being sisters means anything to any of us.'

'Well it *should* do,' Isla snaps, and notes that the blood from her hand is now dripping down into the sleeve of her sweater. Morven's voice: *you never think that anybody likes you.*

'Well, it doesn't,' Agnes replies, and then Irene is back, looking between them in apparent bewilderment, and Isla resists the urge to tell her that for all her academics she has the brain of a tin monkey clapping cymbals together.

'What's going on?'

'Isla was just expressing herself,' Agnes says calmly.

'I was just telling Agnes that it's good to know she can always be relied upon to make everyone around her feel foolish for trying to be a grown-up while she swans around doing whatever she wants.'

'What?' Irene blinks, looks over at Jude, who takes advantage of the moment to try to reach for Isla's hand with the tea towel again. She wriggles away and they throw their hands up.

'I'm literally just trying to stop you bleeding all over yourself.'

'When did you start bleeding?' Irene asks.

'It's all *fine* anyway,' Isla continues, still with her hand aloft and feeling, briefly, like she might be about to faint. Looks from one sister to the other. *Why can't you both just be nice to me?* 'It's all *fine* to behave however you want your whole life and then swan in and inherit a whole house after saying you were *morally opposed* to it all for years. It's *fine* to wander into a private family occasion with someone none of us have ever even met and then inherit a house when you never even had to put up with half of what we put up with. It's all fine, honestly. I think it's really wonderful.'

'Half of what you put up with?' Agnes stares at her.

'Not even *half*,' Isla snaps. Imagines her voice overlapped by their father's – the viciousness to him, brittle trace at the tops of his teeth. The way he could be funny, genial, then breathtakingly cruel. He would get irrationally angry when you weren't having a good time, when you couldn't just get on with it. *Can't you just not be*, he said to Isla when she told him she was gay. She feels furious in a way that is like being possessed, an emotion not entirely her own infesting her. 'And that's *good*,' she says, 'it's *fine* that you had an easier time of it and it's *fine* that you never had to cope with our mother before he fucked off with your mother and—'

'That is an absolute fucking *laugh* if you think that's true,' Agnes replies, revealing more of something like a snarl. 'That is an absolute *delight* if you really think it was all smooth sailing when I was here with him all by myself for longer than you ever—'

'Well, it doesn't matter anyway,' Isla interrupts, 'because now you have the house and you can do whatever you want with it.'

'Is it that you want the *house*?' Agnes responds in a shrill voice. 'After all that chat about not wanting to take his money or be beholden and *unified front* blah blah blah, you're pissed off because for whatever twisted reason he decided to leave the house to me and not you?'

'I don't *want* the house—'

'Well, neither do *I*!'

Isla lifts her hand in the air to cut her off, pauses for a second, tries to decide whether the specific sick feeling in her stomach is directly related to anger or blood loss. 'It's about … it's about being exhausted. I'm so *exhausted* of everything. I'm exhausted that he fucked your mother and drove our mother insane, I'm exhausted that I had to deal with everything. I'm exhausted by all of it, I'm sick of it. I'm done.'

'Isla …' Irene, out of nowhere, raising a hand as if in class.

'Well, I can't *help* that even though we all said no to his money, he still did this,' Agnes replies, and her face is pale now. 'I thought the whole point was that none of us wanted it. You can *have* the house, I don't care—'

'It's not about that, Agnes. It's just hard to accept that basically the last thing our father did was choose to make a

189

fool out of me and Irene for not taking his money and reward you for the same thing.'

'Isla …' Irene again.

'Well, I get that' – and Agnes is speaking more slowly, a voice that reminds Isla, bizarrely, of the kind of painfully rational tone she takes with patients who are spinning out in front of her – 'but that isn't something I did to you.'

'Isla!'

'Oh, for God's sake, Irene' – and Isla swings around to Irene, who has moved across the room to stand by the sofa – '*what* is it?'

'We took the money.'

A pause. Isla can't absorb it, thinks, in a faraway manner, that it's ridiculous, it's all ridiculous. Why on earth are they all standing around here acting like a cult whose leader has died and they don't know how to plug the power vacuum?

'What?'

'When he offered it. Jude and me. We took Dad's money.'

Isla lowers her bloody hand, looks at it a moment. Then she crosses to the sofa and smacks Irene in the face.

Part Two

City

It is an accepted belief that things fall apart. The question of whether or not the falling apart is necessary is separate and usually secondary. People still discuss this, of course: the fact of the turn, the moment a warning mutated into the only possible outcome. When, people ask, was the last time you remember thinking *oh it's raining again*. When was your last real sunburn, your last flying ant day, your last good look at the stars. It is easy to think about these things, recollections of things passing fast from your grip, and decide they are simply too much to acknowledge. Easy to imagine inevitability when in fact there might once have been any number of options. *It was always going to turn out this way,* spoken like a charm against pain, against memory. Sweat and sun feel like virtue, like expiation, so now damp and rain feel like failure, like an opportunity for some great act of heroism missed. Better, all things considered, to turn away from the fact of before until the thought fades again, the way a headache can suddenly cease, and all that exists is the now. The great washout of the world and no sense that it might have been otherwise.

1.

Jude

Forty-five minutes until lunch and the waiting room is already chaotic – windows steamed and standing room only, children shrieking and a woman by the water cooler repeating loudly and to anyone who will listen that there's actually plenty they can do to help and they just don't want to, that the whole thing's a set-up, that the place is staffed by Nazis anyway. The radiator, for whatever reason, is stuck on subtropical and the automatic doors aren't working properly, opening and shutting with wholly random regard for whoever happens to be in their path. *Fucking Indiana Jones motherfucking bullshit*, as Cathy said first thing this morning, having hopped past the doors and dropped her beret in the process. The social housing place two miles away had to close overnight due to flooding, which isn't helping matters, nor is the fact that seventeen local authority blocks in the area were recently declared unsafe. Something in the air like bedlam – chemical taste, metallic on the tip of the tongue. Jude fists a hand in their hair and releases, checks their phone and sets it down. Five more families to see before lunch, then lunch, then whatever they can manage until closing. Swivelling off their chair in the back office, they swing around the door to find Cathy at the vending machine.

'Can you get me some crisps?'

Cathy waves a hand. 'What d'you want?'

'Nothing prawn-flavoured.'

'Wow, accusations.'

Cathy inserts her money, chucks a packet of something ready-salted to Jude.

'How are you doing?' she asks, leaning back against the machine to open a KitKat.

Jude shrugs, wonders exactly how much time they all spend asking each other this question.

'No complaints.'

'I heard a little old lady called you a pencil-pushing capitalist cunt this morning.'

'She was having a bad day.'

Cathy snorts. 'I suppose we all make a bargain when we decide to become faceless bureaucrats.'

'I thought we were social workers.'

'We're whatever anyone needs to be able to blame for everything.'

'I don't think that's fair.'

'Whatever you say, Jude.'

Cathy has already had a plastic cup of water upended over her lap today and it isn't even twelve thirty. Jude caught her in the bathroom earlier, standing in her tights and holding her skirt under the hand dryer, muttering about pay and it not being worth getting out of bed. The problem, of course, is the general worsening of things – things being housing, and the weather, and The State Of It All. The problem is private companies springing up every other week to mishandle the business of dealing with it and siphon off funding in the process. The problem is the fact that there's no money, and nowhere to put people, and the fact that they're working on a skeleton staff with no time and no way to do more than they're already doing. The problem is all of this, but also a recent and much sharper decline. They are, as Jude reflects, a ship being mended as it sails, except that they aren't really being mended and their sailing has become less a smooth progression and more the basic act of staying afloat. It's been a strange period, desperation like something over-turned and spreading everywhere. Widespread power cuts, rising water levels – none of this so unusual in itself but that the system seems to be overloading, the infrastructure caving. Everywhere Jude looks, these days, there seem to be problems that used to come with workarounds but no longer feel solvable.

Someone, a couple of weeks ago, brought a sharpened wooden stake into the waiting area, only to do very little with it. He waved it around a few times until Cathy ducked behind the triage desk and Jude came towards him, palms up, and asked him to hand it over, which he did with very little fuss. This is more or less just how it goes. Jude comes to work, deals with people increasingly likely to call them a cunt out of panic or exhaustion or simply because they want to call someone a cunt. Goes home again. Sleeps it off. Tries to remember what it was that they did, or liked, or expected, before all of this became so all-consuming. Comes back to work again.

They are screwing up their empty crisp packet as Luke slides around the door into the corridor. Luke started in Housing and Advice about three months after Jude did and has a habit of arriving in rooms as though having only narrowly avoided being set alight.

'Are you both on break? It's getting too psychotic out there.'

Jude nods, lobs the packet into the bin. For a brief second, two, they experience a wave of such exquisite exhaustion that it almost seems to register as flavour. They look up, try to focus on something concrete. They think about last week, when water started coming through the ground-floor office windows and everyone was forced to move to the upper storey until they could call in maintenance. They fished a husk of petrified crab from the corner of the overflowing gutter; the rose pink shell of a sea crab, hollowed out along its underside, the white meat eaten or otherwise hacked away. They set it down in an empty tissue box in the back office and wondered where it had come from, how far it must have had to swim off course to find itself stranded here.

Above Luke's head, the advisory sign which someone from management tacked up a year or so previously: *Do **not** overstep professional boundaries. Do **not** become emotionally involved. **Do** practise empathy within stated guidelines. Do **not** make promises you can't keep.*

Jude straightens their shoulders, raises a placating hand at Luke.

'I'll go.'

They check their phone again briefly, note a message from Irene: *I'm going to try to cook again tonight – a woman should cook, so I'm hearing.* Yesterday evening, Irene tried to make a casserole and instead ended up burning the bottom out of a saucepan and setting off the smoke alarm. Prior to this disaster, Jude had leaned up against the kitchen counter to watch her; orange light from the overheads ringing her head like a corona and the way she clattered pots and pans, doing everything all wrong. It is easy, Jude has always reflected, to love a difficult woman. Easy to become the solid place around which she gathers herself, all her insecurities and rages and vendettas, the mooring from which she hangs. Irene is a fucking nightmare, and lovable for it. Lovable because she asks consistently to be loved; a desire that streams from her spiteful, sparkling face, from the way she kisses, from the way she'll sometimes jerk awake at night and stare around in panic. She expresses a constant desire to be better – tries hopelessly to cook, tries to let go of grudges – yet Jude loves the specific truth of what she is prior to trying as much as the fact that she always tries again. *But just assuming my efforts are not successful,* Irene texts as follow-up, *I'll also buy a microwave dinner. Just covering all bases. I love you,* she adds, *I just think you're really fucking neat.*

Jude pockets their phone, squares their shoulders and strides back through the doors into the waiting area. A family whose landlord has told them ankle-deep water in the living room isn't a springtime priority. Two women, one translating for the other, who are being rehoused ninety miles away from their current postcode. A man who spends the duration of his time slot complaining to Jude that he can't get his mobile phone working. Yet another pylon from one of the abandoned city cable cars has come down in a storm and cratered a building and none of the tenants has anywhere to go. Worse than it was – intangible down-turn, things hanging by a thread.

It's easy to get caught up in things, someone had said to Jude at Irene's father's funeral, nearly five months ago now – large man, face the consistency of something left to cool and grow a skin. *It's easy to get caught up in hysterics and forget the bigger picture.* Not entirely clear what Jude had said to invite this, only that the man had introduced himself as an erstwhile colleague of Irene's father and then asked Jude to repeat their name three times. *Loud in here,* he had said the third time, despite the fact that it was demonstrably quite subdued. *People are queasy about progress when it seems not to immediately benefit **everyone**,* he continued, *this counterintuitive sense that we ought to be spending our time bringing everyone **down** to the same level when we should be bringing everyone **up** to the same level. People don't know what there is to aspire to if you don't show them, you know?*

Jude nodded, considered asking what any of this was regarding and decided not to bother. The reception was muted, prickled over with something like dread, though that may simply have been the air conditioning. Tasteful canapés, Isla circulating in chic black crêpe and her hand discreetly bandaged, no hangover apparent aside from a certain tightness around the base of her neck. Jude glanced away from their current assailant towards Irene, halfway across the room and talking to a circle of middle-aged men, including one whom she had earlier identified as one of her father's two biographers. *The good one,* she had noted, as though this distinction were obvious. *Every so often he'd actually suggest that Dad's buildings were, say, incredibly elitist and pointless and a waste of public and donor funding. The other guy was just a simp.* Jude cocked their head, caught Irene's eye and noted the usual little drag of a ripcord, a line to be pulled in emergencies. Irene's face was still unnaturally pink on one side, the underside of one eye ringed a colour that threatened a bruise. No one at the funeral knew that none of the Carmichael sisters were speaking to each other.

This is probably a hiding to nothing, said a voice at Jude's elbow, and they turned away from the man now asking them to repeat their name for a fourth time to find Stephanie standing directly behind them, *but you do not by any chance happen to smoke, do you?*

They went out onto the covered veranda and Jude pulled two emergency cigarettes from a pack in their back pocket, lighting one for Stephanie with a gesture which leaned towards chivalry in a way they couldn't entirely help. Jude has always found it difficult not to hold doors, not to metaphorically doff a cap in a manner which feels increasingly like pantomiming gender at women who haven't actually asked for it. Stephanie took the cigarette without comment and leaned back, fixing her hair with one hand and looking vaguely put-upon. The venue was a curious municipal structure, built to accommodate both crematorium and reception space, hovering high above a largely residential area and sheltered enough to still be just about accessible by road. The cars clustered round the small circle of parking below the veranda were mainly large and uniformly ridiculous. Jude watched a parking attendant circling in a boxy red Mercedes, rain-washed windows tinted black, and looked away again. Glanced at Stephanie, who meanwhile had abandoned her hair to readjust the front of her dress.

I didn't think about funeral etiquette when I picked this outfit, she said, *or I did but I didn't think about the kind of funeral that's got old men crawling everywhere.*

Jude snorted, tried to blow smoke away from her.

If it helps, I think this would still be a terrible day out no matter what you were wearing.

Stephanie hoiked at the neckline of her dress again and Jude thought about Irene, who had spent upwards of forty-five minutes that morning scrutinising her funeral dress unhappily in the bathroom mirror. *It looked ok on the hanger, I don't know what happened. I look like someone who's knocked on your door to tell you all about God.*

Weird, Stephanie continued, *to be at a funeral where no one cries.*

Not unexpected, I would say.

Mm. You've been doing this a while then?

Jude looked at her oddly for a second, then nodded.

I've known the family a while, yeah, though I never met their father. We've been together eight years, Irene and me, give or take?

Stephanie nodded, ground a heel into the deck for a second and looked pensive.

Do you – Jude thought about saying something, tried to imagine how best to put it across – *did you know what it would be like? When you said you'd come with Agnes?*

Yeah, it's not that, Stephanie shrugged, *I pretty much knew everyone was going to suck. All that stuff with Isla, I mean. No offence to your girlfriend, or whatever. I think I just didn't realise how depressing I'd find it all, you know? Like … everyone here is completely divorced from reality, all those eulogies about their dad bringing a liveable future* *to the masses or whatever when it benefited no one … It's not like he designed innovative structures which recycled greywater or whatever. I've seen the pictures – all these mad glass boxes for rich people, all this excess. And I **knew** all that, but I didn't realise how deeply fucking lowering I'd find it. I mean, combined with the fact that the three of them hate each other.*

Oh, I don't think they do. Jude shook their head, shifted from one foot to the other. *I mean, I think they do right now but I don't think it's possible to hate someone you don't also fundamentally love.*

Stephanie eyeballed them. *Right.*

I've known them longer than you have, Jude said peaceably enough, although noting as they did so a vague realisation that they really didn't know an awful lot about Agnes. *I've seen them in different contexts to this.*

Mm. Stephanie ashed her cigarette over the veranda's edge, looked idly out into the rain. *Well, maybe. Do you find it weird, ever?*

How do you mean?

Sometimes I want to tell Agnes that my mum and her sister and her sister's husband and my nan all live together in like four rooms and it isn't my job to make her feel better about the fact that her dad was rich and she hated him, or whatever. Or that she's inherited a whole fucking house that she doesn't want.

Jude nodded. *I know what you mean.*

Buffet was good though.

Jude laughed, flicked the end of their own cigarette into the gravel below the veranda. The rain was heavy, monotonous. Stephanie blew out a fresh cloud of smoke and seemed to consider for a second.

Sometimes, she said, *I fantasise about being a nineteen-fifties housewife and then I realise that all I'm actually getting off on is the idea of having enough money that I don't have to work or worry about working.*

Jude tried to find something to say to this, although Stephanie seemed happy to keep talking. *I said this to Agnes,* she continued, *and she said she'd already assumed that was what I was into. I can't always figure her out and then it's like there's all this stuff she's already twigged about me. She doesn't give very much. She makes me think of an egg – this weird thing with no corners.*

Jude nodded, felt fond in a way they couldn't quite place. *Irene's all corners, I think.*

They were quiet for a moment, then Stephanie sneezed and Jude offered her their jacket. She shook her head, threw away her half-smoked cigarette. The building hunkered up around itself in an L-shape, one long glass wall of the reception area visible from the veranda, people milling around the buffet table and talking in twos and threes. Jude peered across now, watched a group of unfamiliar black-clad men and women huddled together, caught a figure that might have been Isla – although difficult to tell at this distance – cruising across the room at high speed. Strange sight, from afar: these clumps of anonymous, well-groomed people. All in black, it was hard to tell one from another, figures seeming to merge like droplets of oil collecting on a surface, converging to produce a larger spill.

It was as they were staring distractedly at the guests that the commotion started: a sharp shift in frequency, bodies turning towards something too deep inside the room to be seen from the veranda. Jude stood up straighter. They heard muffled shouting, saw several people muscling back towards the window as though trying to get away from something.

Do you see that? Jude said, nudging Stephanie, who turned around, leaning forward and squinting towards the window.

Is someone making a speech?

Jude shook their head, registered a brief stab of concern for Irene.

Another shout and the crowd against the window shifted. Stephanie glanced at Jude, opened her mouth to say something, but before she could an object appeared to sail through the air from the centre of the room. Thrown by an unseen hand, it arched upwards and collided directly with the window.

Stephanie

She has been trying and failing to teach herself Crow pose. She tips forward on her hands, tries to wedge her knees into her armpits and immediately overbalances, ducks her head and collapses on the floor. She isn't very good at yoga but persists with a sort of dogged belief that she may one day conceive a talent for it. She sits on the rug beside her bed for a second, listens to the sound of her body turning itself right side up again. Listens for the sound of her stomach, the mild tinnitus buzz in her ears. No heartbeat, she thinks. Presses two fingers to the side of her neck, thinks *quick, check you're not dead.* Sitting with her fingers against her throat, she locates her heartbeat after a couple of seconds, then wonders how she managed to misplace it.

'Knock-knock.' Agnes slides into the room with two mugs of tea, takes in Stephanie in her yoga clothes and smiles.

Peculiar, still, to have Agnes in her space. (Agnes who, as of four months ago, has given up the lease on her own flat, who sleeps or pretends to sleep every night packed tight towards Stephanie's bedroom wall.) Peculiar to look up and find her washing dishes, or coming in from a swim, or moving about the flat in the way she does, like she's hoping not to disturb some delicately sleeping creature. She has become part of the flat's daily squalor and even helped

Stephanie, Casper and Beck interview for a new housemate when the last brand-new fixture took off with Casper's weed and the petty cash tin. The new flatmate is quiet, tired, keeps to herself. Stephanie has peered around the corner of her bedroom to see her painting out stains on the wall. Agnes has even made an attempt to befriend her, only to come away afterwards claiming that the whole time they were talking it felt like she'd just caught her in the middle of a crime.

Agnes in general is so strange to Stephanie, such a palpably dissonant mix of tender and stand-offish, given to flinching away from affectionate gestures and returning half an hour later to ask for a kiss. She is good at housework, good at being quiet, good at fucking, terrible at listening to the tail ends of sentences and always asking to have things explained to her twice. Her moods are unreliable, sudden spells of bad temper whipping up into snappishness that abates almost as soon as it manifests. Things that appear to upset her: being asked to share her thoughts when she doesn't feel like it, being looked at affectionately for too long, loud noises, cold nights, her father's house, the suggestion that she might want to talk to a professional about her relationship with her family.

Sitting down on the rug, she hands Stephanie a cup of tea and kisses her shoulder – gruff little motion, like the clearing of a throat. Stephanie looks at her, feels a throb of affection at the way her formerly choppy haircut is growing out on both sides. Once upon a time, she watched a movie in which a man looked at a woman with whom he would never be allowed to live happily, surveyed her face as if surprised by every minute detail. *Each time*, he said, *you happen to me all over again.*

'I was going to start making dinner but Casper's in there doing one of his soups,' Agnes explains, 'so I thought I'd give it half an hour.' Stephanie nods, takes a sip of her tea. 'I forgot I said I'd cover Svetlana's shift tomorrow,' Agnes adds. 'It just occurred to me out of nowhere when I stuck the kettle on.'

'Oh, rubbish,' Stephanie frowns, 'I thought we were going to do lying in bed all day.'

'In fairness, that's mainly what we've done all day today.'

'Well, I thought we were going to make it a double-header.'

Agnes huffs a laugh and looks at her knees, humped up close to her chest, sets her tea down on the floor beside her.

'I'd prefer to stay here with you.'

Small victories, Stephanie thinks. Agnes allowing her to touch the sides of her face during sex, Agnes agreeing to lie with her for a whole minute afterwards, rather than getting straight up and asking if she's ever seen *The Last Days of Disco*. It's difficult to explain the appeal of such a painstaking act of acclimatisation, except to say that every small step forward feels gently monumental. A few nights ago, Agnes rolled over in bed and fixed Stephanie with the sort of quiet, unworried look she only ever seems to take on during periods of darkness. *The real Agnes*, as Stephanie has come to think of this look, only visible when the light's too bad to see it. *I feel*, Agnes said that night, apropos of nothing very much, *like I've known you for years*, and Stephanie smiled at this. *Isn't it odd that we never say that to the people we've actually known for years?*

'Have you spoken to your sisters?' Stephanie says now, out of nowhere, half-wishing she hadn't but likewise relieved that she did. She wrote it down on the palm of her hand earlier today and then proceeded to sweat it away again – humid day, steam rising off the impacted concrete even as the rain continued to fall – a quick note to remind herself: *ask A abt I + I*. Stephanie isn't particularly invested in the relationship or lack thereof between the Carmichael sisters, but likewise believes that Agnes's purported lack of interest in the subject is less genuine than it might be. They haven't, to Stephanie's knowledge, spoken once in the months that have passed since the funeral. She has occasionally caught Agnes turning her phone on to look at it quickly, then snapping it off again. Sometimes she mumbles in her sleep.

'No, I haven't,' Agnes says. Sudden bolt of bad feeling. 'Why are you asking me that?'

'I didn't mean anything by it,' Stephanie replies, tries to keep her voice even. 'I'm just asking.'

'Well, why is it any of your business?' Moray eel, sharp sting replaced almost at once by an awkward expression. 'Sorry.'

'It's fine.'

'No, I'm sorry. I mean, that was a stupid way to react. I haven't talked to them. I don't want to. I don't know.'

The aftermath of the funeral has been odd; long weeks, time unsticking from itself, Agnes first unwilling to tell her what happened and then telling her everything at once. By the bar at the reception, Agnes had watched Isla walking from group to group in ever-diminishing circles, her tall heels appearing to razor through the muffling pile of the carpet, leaving twin tracks in her wake. Agnes had been watching with such concentration that she failed to notice the woman appearing beside her, a woman whose presence she only became aware of when she took hold of a strand of Agnes's hair and brushed it behind her ear. Agnes had jumped, jerked around to see who had touched her. Impossible, as she later explained to Stephanie, to hold the face in her head. *A woman's face*, she said, *an older woman*, but the finer details had slid from her mind like something scraped from a plate. *Purple dress*, she said, *I remember that*. She had asked the woman what she thought she was doing and registered no embarrassment in her manner or expression, only a curious gentleness as the woman retracted her hand and told her that she looked very much like her mother. *Which is weird*, as Agnes said to Stephanie later, *since everyone always says I look like my dad. I mean, not that that's really the point, but still*. The point, of course, is that no one knows very much about Agnes's mother. Are not even certain if she is still alive. This is information that Stephanie has now, but did not have when Agnes first explained the encounter at the funeral. The story of her mother came later and out of necessity.

The woman, having said this, had reached to touch Agnes's hair again and Agnes had slapped her hand away. *Don't do that*, she had said, and the woman had continued to stare, and she had wanted to tell her *don't do that* about this as well. *I don't mean any harm by it*, the woman had said, reaching out for a third time, catching hold of Agnes's hair, pulling, pulling hard, and Agnes had twisted away, turning all the way around with her back to the bar and elbowing the woman. *Stop it*, she had said – had wondered, as she told Stephanie later, why no one seemed to notice what was happening, why groups of people on either side continued with their low-toned and respectful funeral conversations. *Please stop touching me.* The woman had stumbled back a step or two, looked confused for a moment and then started to make for her again. *I'm sorry, it's so good to see you here*, she had said – although the chatter rising on both sides made it difficult to hear her clearly – and as the woman had raised her hand, caught her hair again, Agnes had done all she could think to do, which was to grab an empty glass ashtray from the bar behind her and lob it directly at the woman's head. The throw was wide, and the ashtray had sailed past the woman and embedded itself in the long window overlooking the car park with a crack.

That's not right though, Stephanie said when Agnes had finished this story. *We heard shouting. Jude and me. We were out on the veranda and it looked like a commotion, people trying to get away from something.* Agnes frowned for a second as though in serious thought.

I didn't think I made a scene, she said after a moment. *When she came for me that third time she grabbed my hair so hard I thought she was going to pull it out. But I don't remember people looking. I just pushed her off me. That's what I remember.*

I don't think that's what happened, Stephanie said. *Baby, I think what happened is you screamed when she pulled your hair. I think what happened was everyone was looking when you threw the ashtray.*

I don't know, Agnes said, picking at the skin around her thumb for a moment and then looking away. *I don't know how that could be true if it isn't what I remember.* She laid her hands flat on the kitchen table, seemed to inspect each fingernail in turn. *When I was little,* she continued, *I used to think I was being quiet but then my dad would get angry anyway, so I guess it's possible to be wrong about things.* She added, in a low voice: *I hate being touched when I'm not expecting it.*

After the scene-that-was-not-a-scene, Stephanie had gone to Agnes and hurried her out of the function room and into the foyer. A confused impression as they left: Jude crossing the room in the other direction and making for Irene; Isla's face, her bandaged hand raised to her head; people everywhere, older men and women staring at them, at Agnes – strange, carved faces of people upon whom wealth conferred a certain kind of density, a solid force. In the foyer, then – Agnes cupping two hands across her mouth and breathing, squeezing her eyes shut. *Baby* – Stephanie had tried, and not known what else to say. A lunatic sensation of being trapped. How to call a cab when she wasn't exactly sure where they were, or the address of the house they had come from, or anything useful? Stupid sense that she should have been paying better attention. Touching Agnes's arm – *baby, where's your bag?* A noise to her left and she turned her head, caught a glimpse of two women in the half-open doorway of a room just up the hall. *You mustn't* – an unfamiliar voice, the sound of heavy breathing – *you have to control yourself better than this. It will be alright, in time, but you have to control yourself.* Stephanie tilted her head to try to see more clearly but only caught an inch of black plisse material. *I can't* – and that was Agnes – *I can't get my breath.* Stephanie had put her arms around her, held her tightly. After a little while, she had noted a petite woman in a plisse dress slipping out of the room down the hall and back into the main function room. A shape behind the still-open door had shifted – brief glimpse of purple.

'We could watch a movie,' Agnes says now, 'if you wanted to.'

Stephanie looks at her – Agnes, her girlfriend, closed like curtains, shaft of light through an incautious gap.

'I could watch a movie,' she says, and shifts closer, feels Agnes reaching out to squeeze her leg.

2.

Agnes

Some things Agnes knows about her mother:

1. Her name, which is Marie, though her surname prior to her brief marriage is a mystery and the marriage certificate never something that Agnes has thought to locate.

2. The fact of her existence, inasmuch as that Agnes also exists – proof positive, litmus paper turning pink. No one knows very much beyond this, except to say that she married their father, gave birth and then almost immediately departed. *I don't think she was cut out for it*, Irene once said in a rare moment of something like kindness, *but you simply can't dwell on stuff like that.*

3. Her belongings, in the form of two bottles of coral-pink nail polish, one labelled *Rattlesnake* and the other *Cinnamon Fizz*, despite being virtually identical. These, indicative of nothing very much in themselves, assume a totemic quality whenever Agnes chooses to look at them, although in truth she is aware that they may not be genuine relics at all. What little Agnes knew of her mother came from the reasonably unreliable sources of both her sisters. At the age of six or seven, seized by a brief frenzy for knowledge in the way that six- or seven-year-olds will be, she had made such a concerted fuss demanding information that Isla had eventually handed the nail polishes over, explaining in a neutral voice that they were all her mother had left behind. In point of fact, they were almost certainly Isla's, but Agnes keeps hold of them anyway and draws what she wants from their heavy glass bottoms and neat little screw-top lids. Her mother as glamorous, well groomed, forgetful, her mother smelling of acetone, her mother going out and coming in again, her mother covered in coral-pink paint.

4. Her absence – itself like a presence, the sensation of something just over the curve of a hill, perhaps approaching, perhaps moving further away. No one knows where she ended up, if she is even still alive. Their father behaved, for the most part, as if she had never existed, explaining once that she had been dead to him from the minute she left.

All of which is to say that Agnes knows very little. The idea of her mother, save a brief flowering of curiosity prior to her teens, has seldom exercised much power over her imagination. Too easy, instead, to imagine herself distinct in the landscape, a creature not born but hatched or otherwise independently brought to being. Too easy, in turn, to imagine that the absence of a mother might indicate a corresponding lack of significance on her father's side, that perhaps neither of them ever had much to do with her at all. The idea of looking like her mother is something she has never considered. Having no recourse to photographs and no reliable accounts, she has imagined her mother only as a kind of blank, like the thumb planted square over the lens of a camera. Impossible to imagine herself resembling someone without features, without the eyes or mouth required to make up a face. The encounter at the funeral had been unpleasant for a number of reasons – the stranger leaning close, the grasping hands, the curious nothingness of after – but the most unsettling thing had been a simple statement: *you look so like her, I never thought you'd be so similar.* If Agnes did scream, as Stephanie claims she did – as Jude also seemed to think she had when they came over to ask if she was ok – then it would have been because of this. Not the hands or the fright of a stranger who apparently knew her mother but the thought of her mother's face held up to her own.

She takes no comfort in the thought of looking like her mother. She knows that some people seem to find it helpful, like a bridge of connection, a point of shared grace or shared pain to link them to people long dead. She has heard Svetlana talking at work about all the women in her family having identical noses and, subsequently, identical nose jobs. She has heard Jason talking about how he has his father's stance, whatever that's supposed to mean. But Agnes has no interest in looking like her mother, no interest in the idea of commonality, any quirks or expressions or features they might have shared. Looking like her father is, frankly, bad enough. She can't quite articulate the discomfort at the root of all this, the fact that it sometimes feels less like discomfort and more like out-and-out fear. She can't explain it, except to say that the thought of looking like someone seems only a prelude to the thought of acting like them. How long, if you really resemble a person, can you stop yourself falling in step with them? How long until it turns out you are where they were hiding all along?

She imagines going back to her father's house – *her* house, as she is still unwilling to think of it. She imagines looking for evidence of her mother, rooting around in her father's study for a marriage certificate, a photograph, a note scribbled on a piece of paper, perhaps, when he was in the midst of the affair that would see off his first marriage and usher in his second. She imagines finding some crucial item or other, some key to the blank of her mother, then wonders what use this would be. *Throw it away*, she thinks, imagining turning over some seemingly innocuous document and finding the truth of herself staring back. *I won't be fucking dictated to*, she thinks, and then wonders why exactly she thought this. The stranger at the funeral had been taken in hand by someone Agnes didn't know, had been ushered away, and Agnes hadn't gone after her. She hadn't thought to ask how she knew her mother, who she was, what she was doing there. *Throw it away*, she thinks again, and turns away from the thought of her mother somewhere, just to the left of her, pulling back a curtain, stepping into view.

Isla

She has a patient crying in her office, which is aggravating as she really needs to use the bathroom. It is twenty to one, which means the session has already overrun by ten minutes, and the patient is talking about a dream they keep having where a rogue planet collides with the earth and everyone bursts into flame. Isla has considered telling the patient that this is the plot of a movie she saw fairly recently and then dismissed this as therapeutically irrelevant. The patient has a long, wide chin which hangs down some distance over their collar and Isla keeps wondering whether it gets in the way when they're kissing, or trying to get dressed.

She tries to focus, rubs her hands together and wonders about the exact ethics of interrupting to note the time. On her desk, the basket of plastic geraniums Jenny from reception gave her after her father's funeral sits as if marooned, inappropriate amidst the stark dark lines of her furniture, the Barcelona chair. Jenny had presented it to her along with a copy of *Stephen Carmichael: A Retrospective*, which Isla of course already owned. She had thanked her for it anyway and felt pathetically grateful when Jenny enquired after her bandaged hand and asked about the funeral more generally. *You know how those things can be*, she had offered in response, *all blah blah blah, relatives relatives relatives*. Jenny had nodded, pulled a sympathetic expression. *I'm surprised you're back to work so soon, don't want you to overdo it.*

The patient tapers off, blows their nose with an alarming honk and then shakes their head.

'It's silly, I know,' they say, and Isla registers the urge to reply *well, yes*, 'I suppose it's just my subconscious trying to cope with what's going on. The way things are, I mean, the hopelessness.'

Isla nods and looks discreetly at the clock. People, she often feels, are far too literate in therapy-speak. She supposes it comes from television, from books or magazines – media suffused with the smooth dialectics of trauma. Patients come to her to talk about *feelings of inadequacy stemming from an unsatisfactory homelife*, about *generational trauma* and *buried emotions* and *displaced panic at the thought of the end of the world*. None of it incorrect, exactly, but it can sometimes be difficult to tell what they need her for, if they've already figured this out.

'I should leave you in peace,' the patient says now, and Isla nods, tries to appear regretful. She sees the patient out and closes the door, glances again at the clock and tries to remember who she has scheduled next and for when. The day has been unpleasant, if not to say actively terrible; two cancellations and a burst pipe in the offices directly above theirs, flooding the reception for several minutes until someone ran out into the corridor to shut the water off at the mains. The weather is bad, hectic, scream of wind in the power lines. It feels worse, just recently, although perhaps this is just because Isla feels worse. Someone in the office across from her has been talking loudly to somebody else about St Elmo's Fire, which they claim to have witnessed from their bathroom window at some point during the night. *I read about it once, I can't remember when exactly. It's a sort of glow in the sky – usually blue or violet – something to do with plasma or electrical discharge in the atmosphere or something. It's meant to warn of imminent lightning, which I think must be right because when I came out this morning all the satellite dishes had been toasted off the side of my building. I must have slept through the storm.*

Isla listened to this exchange while sharpening pencils earlier and thought, in the all-at-once way that unwelcome thoughts will usually appear, that Irene would probably know who St Elmo was and what he had to do with lightning or with fire. She hasn't spoken to Irene in nearly five months, not since the night before the funeral, and it is difficult, now, to imagine asking her a question, to imagine switching on her phone and typing out an ordinary sentence, to know how that sentence ought to start. *You let me believe that neither of us took that money, you made me look like a fucking idiot, like I thought we were on the same page. Also what is St Elmo's Fire, please.*

She still needs to go to the bathroom but pauses where she is for a moment, looking around her office and feeling unaccountably weary, despite the fact that she slept well last night and has barely had to see two patients all day. She eyes the copy of *Stephen Carmichael: A Retrospective*, which she had wedged into the topmost shelf of her bookcase to keep Jenny happy. Looking through the new copy on first receiving it, she had tried to remember how many of the featured buildings she had actually seen in person, flicking from a high-rise glass-fronted penthouse complex to a building that staggered up a hillside like a series of wide, white steps. *The Substratum project*, a caption notes beside one building, *though a relatively early work, nonetheless marked a significant step forward in Carmichael's preoccupation with weather-proofing and otherwise 'levitating' structures out of increasingly unstable foundations.* The building pictured appears to hang in the air, some four feet above a nondescript stretch of water and apparently unsupported by either struts or wires, although Isla knows the solution to this seeming magic trick lies somewhere in the fact of concrete's tensile strength and a set of metal rods looped tight around the building's inner structure and connecting it to the adjoining cliffside. She thinks about this picture now, imagines a room hung in space, unsupported, the clasp of some antediluvian creature rearing up from below, from the water, to pluck it out of the air.

Her desk phone starts to ring and she startles, crosses to answer it and finds Jenny on the line, calling to tell her another patient has cancelled.

'Time of year,' she says, nonsensically, because it really isn't any time of year to speak of and what does *time of year* even mean now that seasons and weather patterns blur into one, 'or maybe it's the weather. I haven't been able to get over to see my mother in weeks now. All flooding and electrical storms, then that time the foundations of that building near mine collapsed and we were all stuck inside for two days. It'll be something like that, I'd imagine.'

Isla nods, thanks Jenny and puts the phone down. The afternoon stretches ahead of her, uncomfortably empty until her three thirty session – too much time to adequately fill with paperwork, not enough time to nip out and come back. She sits down, flips through her planner, finds a note scribbled on yesterday's page: *check in with Caroline*. A task forgotten in the mess of untold larger tasks. Her father's housekeeper had been at the funeral, had materialised at Isla's elbow just before Agnes made a spectacle of herself by the bar.

It had been a strange scene, coloured by the unpleasant shimmer of a hangover, unfamiliar voices too loud and Irene somewhere across the room saying *yes, all three of us* to someone Isla didn't know. *I've actually heard that on rare occasions people even have multiple* straight *daughters, if you can imagine that.* Isla touched her forehead and found she was sweating, wondered dully where her glass had got to. *Who are any of these people?* she thought, looking from one stranger's face to another. *Why don't I know who they are?* Then, a brief, unfocused image – a small woman in a black plisse dress who could have been almost any age, pale eyes, the weight of a hand on her shoulder. She recognised her, struggled to place her, failing at first to pull up the appropriate memory of a woman assessing her father's house, kneeling down to pass a hand over the bare concrete floor and noting that the wheelchair might make scuff marks. *Hello?* Isla started to say, only to be interrupted by chaos as Agnes shouted, shoved at someone and shouted again, then threw an ashtray hard across the room. The woman at Isla's elbow dematerialised, appeared again a moment later beside the bar and apparently ushered away the purple-clad stranger with whom Agnes had had the altercation, speaking very close to her ear. A moment of confusion, Agnes ducking away and several erstwhile colleagues of their father's clustering around where the ashtray had wedged in the thick glass of the window, cracks spreading around it like the lid of an egg half-shattered by the back of a spoon. Isla stood for several seconds, her bandaged hand throbbing, noted Jude and the girl Agnes had brought with her appearing in the doorway. Hum of consternation; strange, unpleasant ringing like a finger drawn round the rim of a glass. Isla put her hand to her head again, felt sick and frustrated and quite like biting someone, or biting her own arm, wondered what Morven was doing and where she was and why everyone seemed to have someone along for the ride except her. Shifting around, she looked vainly for her glass on a nearby table and saw Agnes's girlfriend slipping from the room. She breathed in and out several times, tried to remember the name of the man now inspecting the cracks in the window, or the woman next to him, wondering who any of these people actually were.

It was at this point that the woman in plisse appeared again, reaching out to touch her elbow as though she had simply stepped out of the air. *I'm so sorry*, she said, and then, *I hope that didn't make things uncomfortable for you.* Isla flinched and then tried to refocus her gaze. Large eyes, sharp nose, wide, capable hands a little at odds with her otherwise delicate frame, good posture. *I don't think* — Isla started, but the woman nodded and smiled and interrupted. *I know*, she said, *it's been a long time since we saw each other. I hope you don't mind my saying hello. It's Caroline – we only met once, of course, but we've corresponded. I thought you spoke beautifully at the ceremony.* Isla nodded, tried to remember what meaningful reflection she'd shared at her father's funeral – something about gratitude? Something about family? She nodded again anyway, turned her mouth up at the corners in what she hoped was a smile. *Oh yes ... yes, of course* – and then, standing up straighter, *I've been trying to get hold of you. I called several times.*

The woman, Caroline, tilted her head, nodded gently, produced a clean tissue from inside her sleeve. Isla had no particular use for it but accepted it anyway, registering as she did so a brief squeeze of gratitude, looking up to find Caroline still looking at her. *That's why I wanted to come over*, Caroline said, *to apologise. After what happened – when I found your father – I felt very shaken. I've worked with ill clients before but it wasn't ... I found it very upsetting. After I took him to the hospital I had to take a little time off work to recover. As soon as I was myself again I felt dreadful that I could have been so thoughtless about you. I knew I had to come to say that to you.* Isla stared at her, nodded dumbly for a moment, felt a twinge of embarrassment creeping amidst her more righteous anger. Why, after all, would Caroline ever have thought to contact her when in all the years she worked for her father, Isla barely ever got in touch herself? *I'm sorry about the commotion*, Caroline continued kindly. *I believe that was your sister? I'm not sure what any of that was about although I feel almost certain I've seen the woman with whom she was – ah – chatting before. Perhaps they upset each other. I do hope you don't mind that I involved myself, it just felt more sensible to ask her to step away from your sister and collect herself.* Her voice was oddly formal, as though she were writing a letter rather than speaking directly to someone. Isla registered a sensation of relief at this woman's matter-of-factness. Glancing over towards the door, she wondered briefly whether she ought to go after Agnes, to check that she was alright. *You've met that woman before?* she asked instead, looking back at Caroline. *The one Agnes yelled at.*

Caroline nodded. *I'm not entirely sure, but at the house, I think? A friend of your father's, perhaps, or an old associate.* Her voice was smooth, a little soporific. Isla closed her eyes briefly and felt the impulse to further involve herself fading. Agnes's girlfriend probably had her. Irene was nowhere to be seen. Why bother, really. All just something silly, Agnes causing a scene. *I just wanted to check that you were alright,* Caroline said. *And that you don't mind that I got involved. Better to have people helping, I always think.* Isla nodded, a brief flowering of pride at having managed something correctly, at having lucked into hiring someone responsible, and useful. Another adult in the room, which made two of them. *It's very good to see you, you know,* she said after a moment, and Caroline gave her a sympathetic look. *And you too,* she replied, and then, *I'm very glad I got to hear you speak at the funeral. It was interesting, what you said. About loving someone being no guarantee that they won't hurt you. I found it very moving indeed.*

The upshot to this was that Isla had asked her to come back as housekeeper, just to look in on the property a couple of times a week and ensure that nothing was falling to pieces. She couldn't entirely say why she did this, only that it felt important, to ensure someone kept a rein on things, to ensure that something was sorted, cleaned, organised, whatever Agnes later chose to do with the deed. She hadn't actually *told* Agnes about this, had felt rather bullishly like *let her find out.* It was, as she felt at the time, better to ensure that the house didn't fall to wrack and ruin until her sister made a move. If Agnes chose to move in, change the locks, sell the place, then so be it – they would cross that bridge when they came to it. Exactly why she felt this, why it felt important to pay for the upkeep of a place to which she had little in the way of positive connection, which she had dreaded the thought of inheriting, was anybody's guess. It simply felt better, calmer, to feel that she had this one thing taken care of.

Now, checking the clock in her office again, she wonders whether she ought to give Caroline a ring, just to check in, to make sure nothing is amiss. She reaches for the phone, considers for a second and then shakes her head, remembers that she has needed the bathroom for the past half an hour and gets up from her desk.

Irene

She's been working from home for the past few days, processing timesheets and updating accounts, which functionally means she has spent the best part of a week on the website where people role-play at normality. Nothing particularly wrong with that, of course, although occasionally she will look up and find that whole hours have passed in the keen perusal of plotless, pointless fantasies: *so the thing is that i have all this food lying around my house, i*

*don't know how i got ahold of it but i have all this olive oil
and eggs and like, imported cheese and ham and stuff from
all these different countries and i don't know what i want to
do with it exactly so i think maybe i'll just whip up like this
enormous omelette which would mean i can use everything
up all at once although actually i don't even need to worry
about food waste so it doesn't really matter what i make and
i'm not even going to recycle shit either i'm just going to
throw all the packaging away in the bin.*

She reads these threads at length, peruses one and then
goes in search of another, both because it's a distraction
from work and because it stops her thinking – thinking
being something she does too much of and is fundamentally keen to stop. It is preferable, on the whole, to stare for
hours at a website rather than to recall her sister's face the
night before the funeral, her sister's face right before the
slap. The money, of course, was something she'd never
intended to tell her sisters about; the reasons behind her
taking it and how easy it had ultimately been. She, Irene,
who had always protested and railed and argued against so
much of what her father was to them, of what he symbol-
ised. *I don't think that I should*, she had said to Jude when
her father first offered, and then, *you don't understand*, and
then, *we could move to a place that doesn't have subsidence*,
and then, *but I really don't think that I should. I don't want
his money, but I want you to have it, or something. Or I
want to have it with you.* Jude had looked at her. *Thing is*,
they had said, *if you want, it can just be 'fuck you' money.*

We can do what we want with it. We can take it and give it away. It's not his when it's ours, you know? But also you don't have to take it. You don't have to do anything at all. In the end, they had taken it and it had felt almost normal. Irene had paid off her student loan, bought a nicer sofa, started saving for a bigger flat, donated money. They had gone about their lives and not thought about it and it had been ordinary, clean, until she decided to tell Isla about it.

She is thinking about this – or rather, reading message boards in an attempt to not picture Isla's face, when the alarm in her building first sounds; glancing up from an extended screed in which one poster explains to another about being bored on a camping holiday to an unfamiliar racket ringing up from the corridor and bleeding in through the hall of her flat. It is not, as she notes after several seconds, the fire bell, being as it is both lower-toned and stranger, harsher; a sound blaring up from far below. For a moment she sits where she is and wonders whether it might just stop. Pulls her knees together and folds her hands, in confused hope that whatever is happening, whatever is making the noise, might fail to spot her where she is, might pass her over and leave her alone. It is a tremendous sound, a sound she seems to feel in her teeth, in the living cells at the roots of her hair. It reminds her of videos she has seen of hurricane sirens in small American towns, of warnings sounded to indicate oncoming tsunamis, too much noise to mean anything good. She wishes, abstractedly enough but with a violence that surprises her, that Jude wasn't still at work, wishes someone would come up behind her and place their hands over her ears to stop her having to hear it, this sound which isn't going away. It takes her too long to get up, to shut her laptop and move out into the hall, where the sound seems even louder. Too long to open the door to the flat and poke her head into the hall, where she finds a straggle of people already collected, neighbours whose names she half-knows, whose faces she recognises only in profile from standing in lifts together, waiting for the doors to close. Strange, to find them all out here at once – the woman from across the corridor who raises boxer dogs, the couple with the Peloton, the man whose well-trained contralto they sometimes hear spiralling up and down the octave at curious times of night. She stays where she is, half in and half out of the corridor, glancing between faces as the noise rages on. No one speaks, though one man works a finger into the depths of his ear as if to check whether he can be hearing things correctly. A pause, swollen with sound, with the screaming alarm that seems to get louder the longer you listen to it. Irene closes her eyes, opens them, tries to imagine what to do, how she is going to live if the noise simply continues and continues, whether they are going to have to sell the flat, move buildings, move to another city.

And then, of course, there is silence. Silence, just as sudden as the noise that preceded it, and Irene is so disturbed by the snap from one to the other that she staggers back into the flat and slams the door. For a moment she stands where she is, breathing hard, picturing the frozen figures in the corridor, ears ringing with the noise that has disappeared as sharply as if it had never been at all. Looks around at her dim little hallway, the shoes on the rack, the Japanese print and the coat hooks and the money tree in its tatty brass stand. Thinks to herself, out of nowhere: *don't do that*. Presses her hand to her heart and finds it going faster. She doesn't always like silence. It can bring up odd things, odd memories without a clear root or provenance. In the silence after the alarm, she recalls the sensation of waking in the night and hearing voices, the sensation of her feet on the carpet and not knowing who it was her mother was entertaining downstairs.

Later on, she messages Jude to tell them what happened. *I think*, she says, *it was some kind of alarm? Not the fire alarm, I know what that sounds like. Maybe it was some kind of a test for something. No one from maintenance came up, no one says we were meant to vacate the building. I don't know. I think it'll be ok now.*

She doesn't expand on what she means by *some kind of a test for something*, only continues to think about hurricane sirens and searches around for a video or two. It's possible, she supposes, that the alarm was installed whenever their building was first constructed but hasn't been tripped until now. It would be of a piece with the way things seem, just at present. She recently read online about a woman who reported hail so extreme that a chunk of ice the size of a fist had shattered her kitchen window, a man whose collection

of antique hygrometers had gone haywire, their dials spinning uncontrollably and failing to still. Looking out of the
living room window, she considers the weather; the rain
which, though she couldn't say with any real certainty,
might well be worse than it has been in previous weeks. She
does this, in the full velvet hush of the evening, in the quiet
after a terrible sound, and thinks again about something she
wrote in an essay long ago: about the silent years directly
after the crucifixion and resurrection, when people waited
for the promised return which never came about. *Did you
ever*, she once said to Isla, apropos of goodness knows
what, *read any of the weird shit that actually goes on in
Revelations? In the Book of Revelations, I mean. People
think it's just hellfire and brimstone, four horsemen and out,
but actually the end times go on and on and on.*

City

Strange times. Bad air and unpredictable pressure. The
moon, emerging in flashes between heavy banks of cloud,
grows vast and appears to turn on its side. Tipped downward like something snared by the tides and dragged into
closer orbit, it winks in and out of existence; great eye of an
animal caught in a net.

The cities appear fuller because they are. It might, in
theory, seem wiser to decamp to higher ground, to places
where the crush is less overwhelming, but in truth the cities

are often the only places capable of sustaining any infra-structure. It is hard to shore up places that have been left without insurance, without plans for a future that looks like this. People make tracks for rural communities, only to find them ill-prepared, ill-financed, and drowning.

The rain appears worse because it is so. Hard days of little respite, of downpours turning at last to hail and then back again. Lightning too, more often than usual. Families abandon rooms given up to damp, awake to leak-sprung windows and kitchens underwater. People throw them-selves into deepening water, people disappear. And more than this. Strange things blown in on inner-city waters; a man who calls a radio station reporting what he claims to be the body of a seal thrown up against his door. People reach into their gutters to unstick the scuttled shards of razor clams and strange crustaceans. Oystercatchers roost on washing lines strung out of upper windows, heads bent together as if comparing notes. A washing in, or a blurring together. One can picture the sea and the floundering remains of the city as less distinct, a bleeding in of lines once drawn in washable ink.

And on and on like that, like always. People migrate, move in, talk in circles about the Global South, about famine and panic and displaced populations, then just as suddenly cease to discuss them. Guilt at this, and a sense of dislocation. People watch reports on rapid mudslides, on communities thrown out on rafts barely made seaworthy, and don't know what to do or how to relate this to themselves. People twist, bed down, pack their ears and dream of lobsters black with roe outside their windows. Wide waters, sloe-black and dense with detritus: glass beads and tin cans and the bodies of cormorants, sugar packets and plastic spoons and shopping trolleys and the heads and tails of creatures blown off course and drowned for want of salt.

3.

Agnes

It is possible that the woman by the bar is staring at her, just as possible she's looking for a friend. The light is frantic; black and white and hard to penetrate. The music like something fed through a grille. She holds on to her drink and wishes that Stephanie would hurry back from the bathroom. Earlier, in the flat, they had discussed this. Agnes sitting up on the kitchen counter, Stephanie between her legs. The Compendium's sudden flurry of advertising: *COME ONE COME ALL 2 THE DROWNING BALL – going out of business SALE, end of a long sad SEASON, everything about us must GO.* Stephanie, squinting at her phone, wondering aloud whether this meant the club was closing, whether this was for safety reasons or whether the owners of the office building were turfing them out. *Landlords could have threatened legal action*, Beck said, sidling into the kitchen to fetch a fork and reading over

Stephanie's shoulder. Stephanie frowned. *Do we even know for sure they were squatting? I thought someone said they paid some kind of rent.* Beck shrugged and suggested they make a night of it. *Last night on the* Titanic, *we'll bring life jackets, make it a theme.* Casper, wandering in at this point with an empty plate for the sink, looked interested. *What are we theming?* Agnes snorted. Casper, who read miserabilist literature which always began with sentences like *have you ever hulled a pomegranate* and always seemed to come with titles like *The Life Cycles of Lesser Migratory Birds*, pulled a face at her. Agnes laughed. The new housemate was absent, sound of some peculiar arrhythmic music bleeding out from beneath her bedroom door. *We don't need to invite **everyone**,* Casper said, aimed a conspiratorial wink at Agnes. Strange, still, to be part of the whole extended ecosystem of a household. Strange to consider her name on the chore wheel, her presence uncontested and seemingly enjoyed. *We should go out,* she said, and Stephanie squeezed the tops of her legs and nodded.

Now, at the club, a sensation of some internal splitting. The black coverings are coming down off the windows, one of the spotlights hangs loose above the stage. Agnes looks around, tries to remember how long Stephanie has been in the bathroom and how long she should consequently expect to wait alone. Beck is nowhere to be seen and Agnes registers a curious sense of grief for her previous solitude, how easy it was to move through spaces as a single entity compared to the strange, hulling loneliness of waiting for someone with whom you arrived as a pair. It is easier, in some ways, to be single. Easy to move with the freedom of something untangled, bound for whatever brief destiny it likes. She has thought this, on occasion, wished herself away, alone and able to fuck whoever, and then frightened herself at the prospect. Turned over in bed and thought to herself several times *I want Stephanie I want Stephanie I want Stephanie*, until the words take the shape of an incantation.

She frowns, looks back towards the bar, where the woman still might or might not be looking at her. Hard to tell, in this light, from this distance. A face made uninteresting by a certain type of beauty – very symmetrical, pale eyes, the look of something cast in ice. Eyes that seem trained on her, a face which seems barely to move.

Sudden sway – someone has dropped their drink and people are shoving to get out of its path. She can't tell if the woman is staring at her, because so often it seems like people are staring at her. A silly paranoia, of course, but one that often seems grounded in fact. Turning in a queue to find eyes upon her, a face she hopes to recognise and then can't place. A man stepping back as if to peer into her window, a woman on the deck of a boat. People, sometimes, in the coffee shop, holding her gaze for a fraction too long, an explanation never forthcoming. The silliness key to a certain degree of its menace. Any of these incidents feel, alone, as if they could simply have happened. Odd little things, strange encounters that only mass and grow curious colours on closer inspection. A woman reaching for her hair, another woman throwing herself off the embankment. Difficult to communicate a sense of reasonable alarm when explaining one and another. *Don't you think*, Stephanie has said, *that the woman on the boat might not have been staring at you so much as simply **staring**? I mean, given what we know she was about to go and do? And the man you think was watching you the other day was probably just **looking**. That's a thing that men do, I'm told.*

The music has changed – something smoother – and for a second Agnes lets herself go with the heave of the crowd. The rain, tonight, is curious, saline on the tongue, crusting the bricks of the houses. You can watch it through the windows, where the black papering has come away, watch it as you rock with the music, riding a current away from its source. Sometimes, she remembers a face at a window – the central room at her father's house and a face looking in from without. Sometimes, when she feels that people are staring at her, she pictures this: the fact of the window between them, the blurring of the rain against the glass. She looks back towards the bar again and imagines this, throws up a window between herself and the woman who may or may not be thinking anything about her at all, thinks in a roundabout way that she wishes she knew what her sisters were doing, and as she thinks this she registers hands at her waist and Stephanie is back behind her, beside her, and the music has changed again.

* * *

Later: the night, the stairs of their building and Stephanie's hand at her wrist, dragging her upwards. They are drunk, or at least Agnes is, stumbling as she goes, a tight heat around the base of her throat, spreading downwards and settling in her chest.

'I'm showing you something,' Stephanie says, ignoring Agnes when she points out that they have already passed their floor. A frantic little giggle which Agnes catches and amplifies, their cackles bouncing off the walls of the stairwell as Stephanie pulls them further up.

They emerge on the top floor, faced with a door that appears at first sight to be locked, although Stephanie jimmies the handle with a confidence that implies she has been here before. Winking, she leads Agnes out onto a roof terrace of sorts – the gravelled top deck of their building which Agnes has never before considered, in the way one seldom registers the whole of a building in which one occupies only a fraction of space. The door to the roof is partially covered and Agnes squints around, aided by the hazy grey light of a couple of flood lamps, their illumination rendered tentative by the steady interruption of the rain. The terrace is almost flat, although it runs to a gentle tilt at each corner to ensure the rain is not allowed to pool but rather runs off into the gutters. Hard to tell how high up they must be, despite logically knowing how far they just climbed. Strange to think how seldom she has seen the top of their building from the ground, how often the high points of the city are obscured, lost to low cloud and the murk of constant downpour. A skyline incomplete without its crowning layer, a head snicked off at the neck.

'Come here!' Stephanie is no longer with her but has clattered out onto the wet deck of the terrace, immediately soaking in her club clothes and looking back at Agnes with a grin.

She beckons, turning away to gesture at something that becomes clear as Agnes approaches, edging her way past a graveyard of rain-bleached detritus: a disused barbecue, a couple of plastic folding chairs. The rain runs warm down the back of her neck, soaking fast into her t-shirt. Following Stephanie's gaze, she notes that a long blue tarpaulin has been unsnapped and discarded from where it was apparently once pinned in a rectangle along the far-right edge of the roof. As Agnes moves closer, she realises what the tarpaulin has left uncovered: namely a fair-sized swimming pool, about three-quarters full, sunk into the rooftop and painted a bright mouthwash blue. Agnes laughs, claps her hands without meaning to. She feels drunk, aware of being drunk, aware of the compulsion to tell a personal story, to declare herself, to twirl. Stephanie makes a funny little jazz-hands gesture towards the pool before putting her hands on her hips. She is pleased with herself, looking towards Agnes for praise, for reassurance, oddly butch in the moment, pushing her thumbs into the belt loops of her skirt.

'It was me,' she says, kicking out at the discarded tarpaulin. 'I mean, I came up this morning and took the cover off. To let the rain in. I thought you'd like it.'

Agnes feels moved, bee-stung by the shape of her, tall girl in the half-light, ghost-forms of the city beyond. The night is mauve, takes up too much space between them, and she rounds the pool at a half-run, grabs Stephanie's face and kisses her – stupid kiss, insincere with alcohol and yet simultaneously too earnest to exist at any other time. Stephanie stumbles backwards, laughs into the kiss, ducks her head and loops herself more tightly into Agnes's grasp.

'They don't let people come up here any more but it used to be a pool for residents,' she says, sweet breath from pouring ginger beer into her whiskey, long eyelashes, skin glossy from the rain. 'I think it got too unsafe or too expensive to heat or something. But I thought you'd like it – you're always complaining about having people around you when you swim.'

Agnes leans to bite Stephanie's neck, glances back towards the pool. She received an email just yesterday from the leisure centre, informing regular customers that, owing to rising energy costs, the pool would now only be open once a week, on Tuesday mornings. The rain hits the surface of the pool, working hard to fill in this only recently uncovered gap. She watches the surface, the water continuing to rise. Glances up, shielding her eyes as she does so.

The night hunches down around itself, hands cupped. The dark like something granted, like a kindness. *D'you ever wonder*, she asked Stephanie once – midnight, hands in her hair – *what you would have been? If things had been different, I mean. If you'd felt like you had more time or more opportunity or whatever. D'you think you would have tried harder, or wanted more, or done things differently?*

I think, Stephanie replied, *I would have been the same. Maybe my hair would have been better*, she added after a moment, *without all the rain, you know.*

They don't keep track of the time. Kiss until their clothes are sticking to them, until their shoes fill up, spring leaks around the rubber of their soles. After a while Agnes glances at the pool to find the water level significantly higher than before. She looks at Stephanie, tugs at her collar without first considering what she means by it, watches Stephanie take what she will from the gesture.

'Only if you're coming too,' she grins, tugging at Agnes's hand as she did when she pulled her up the stairs, and Agnes barely has time to register the turn the night has taken before her body has connected with cold water – brief swing through the air and then impact, her hand wrenched free from Stephanie's as she plunges down and then rises again, emerging chilled through and spluttering and clawing blindly. Her hand connects with something, finds Stephanie treading water and cackling, throws her arms around her neck.

'That was *terrible*,' she gasps, and Stephanie laughs again, yanks at the back of her hair and then kisses her as the water around them continues to rise.

'It wasn't so bad,' she counters, face close, the smell of her damp and acrid; ginger beer and menthol cigarettes, skin and night and dirty water, chewing gum and breath and heat and girl. Agnes monkeys up her limbs around her, held where she is and then pulled along as Stephanie pushes backwards, kicks until she drags them up against the far side of the pool. A sudden reversal – Stephanie is now bracketed, ducking down as Agnes rises higher, pressing her into the concrete deep-end wall and holding them both in place with her hands on the lip of the pool. Agnes feels the flip for what it is, the flash of Stephanie's intention. She can feel her heart in her knees, in the backs of her calves, her body like something hung from a hook, except that what she is hanging from is Stephanie.

'Come here,' she says, takes one arm from around Stephanie's neck and grips her face, tilts her head back a little. Their bodies mashed together, Agnes curled around her waist and moving her hand from Stephanie's chin to tug her hair, demanding that she stay there. Pulling away to dip her hand below the water, reaching for the soaked black hem of Stephanie's skirt.

'If you move at all,' she says – her voice, as she sometimes imagines it, more like itself, less invented in the dark – 'I'll stop.'

Stephanie's closed eyes, her head tipped back and frozen, the slick strong arch of her neck. Agnes moves aside her underwear with two fingers and finds what she's looking for. The quick gasp – she tightens her other hand on the edge of the pool – the tease, the certain press of something welcome, the momentary bite and then release. Stephanie shudders, sighs, and Agnes moves with her, pressing her down against the wall just as she is held aloft, the two of them moving in tandem, floating and drowning, fixed somewhere between.

I could be good with just this, she thinks in answer to a question she herself has asked. *If I could have this, I don't think it would matter if things had been different or we'd had a different world or more to hope for. I could be happy here.*

Isla

She is organising patient files on the floor of her living room. Jenny called early in the morning to tell her not to come in, that a flood barrier just west of the office over-flowed sometime in the night and the whole immediate area was currently inaccessible. *I've called your roster for today and told them you'll videocall them* – Jenny's bright voice, impervious to disaster – *two cancelled and the rest said they'll see you at their scheduled time.*

The files are mostly from patients who have long since terminated their therapy or otherwise moved away. She sorts them, scanning notes as they jump out at her: *Ms Weir is prone to delusions of grandeur; sometimes Mr Kline and I talk in circles on the same subject for the whole session; it occurs to me that one is stuck as an older sibling or a younger sibling forever and this can hamper the flourishing of a more adult relationship.* It feels necessary to tidy, the compulsion like a sudden cramp. She scans the shelves for files she's missed, pulls down one and then another: *Mrs Goshawk asks repeatedly for me to call her 'Bunny', which is a nickname someone gave her at school; sometimes I feel unusually certain Mr Epstein isn't in need of therapy at all and is simply vamping, or inventing past traumas, which of course is reason enough for therapy in itself.*

Yesterday evening, she had answered an unknown number to find herself on the phone with Morven. She had sat down hard on the sofa and asked what had happened to her old phone. *Broke so I had to finagle a new one –* Morven's tone, effortless, as though she was simply picking up a thread of conversation laid down only temporarily. *Where are you?* Isla had asked, not wanting to wait for pleasantries. Morven had explained in unhelpful abstracts: somewhere north, small community, high fells, strange lights. *So many people are trying to live differently,* she had said, *people planning for something, not just burying their heads in the sand. There is this whole community of people taking steps to make things seaworthy, these floating places, all these new ideas about how to live. I've seen this place where people have dug themselves into the hillside and live communally – reusing wastewater, growing things under oxygenated canopies, drawing power from composted scraps, etcetera etcetera. I've seen people living on the water – actually on the water – this whole community of people doing what they call 'buoyant living'. It makes me feel hopeful, for the most part, though sometimes I wonder if it might be less appealing if more people knew about it, if everyone was trying to do the same thing at once, you know? It's still hard though, all this pushing forward. Sometimes I think hope is a far less satisfying feeling than despair.*

Isla had picked at the cuticle of her thumb with her ring finger and nodded dumbly along with this, tried to remember the sequence of a poem she'd wanted to quote to a patient earlier in the week, about Old Masters and suffering: *how it takes place while someone else is eating or opening a window or just walking dully along.* The point, of course, being the whole bright dailiness of agony, the way Icarus in the Bruegel painting could crash to earth as little but a background detail while the bland spool of life went on in the foreground; the ploughman at his plough and the fabric of the day untouched, uninterrupted.

Do you care that you did this to me, she had wanted to say to Morven, had taken in the neat, dull shape of her room as she did so: the Bakelite clock and the armchair, the paperbacks on naval history, the magazines in a pile. She had asked instead why Morven was calling and received a frustrated sigh in response. *Well, ok, if we're doing that now, I wanted to ask why you haven't responded to my lawyer.* Isla had looked up towards the light fixture and wondered how long it had been since she'd dusted. *How does this work,* she had wanted to say, *you living this far-away fulfilling life and yet badgering me all the time about divorce? How does that fit into your plan to live better or something? Why not just get on with your life-changing journey and leave me alone?*

I've been busy, she had said instead, *I'm getting around to it.* A sound on the end of the line like a tongue clicked hard against teeth. *I'm really not asking for very much,* Morven had said, and then, all in a rush, *you know you think that you have this great moral trump card because I'm the one who left, but you don't. You don't win because I'm the one asking to end this. I tried, you know. I really did try. I tried for so long to be ok with things and not panic while everything got worse and worse around us. You going on as normal trying to organise your patients and trying to organise your family and trying to organise our lives and never looking outside for one second. Organise, organise, organise. You have no idea how hard I tried. You're so bedded into your life, what was I supposed to do? You could never imagine living another way.* Isla had looked again at the clock and wondered whether to simply hang up.

She is drinking, just now, which isn't wise but seems to be happening anyway. Just a dribble of the vodka she pinched from her father's (her sister's) house directly after the funeral. She has been trying to save this, supplementing with cheaper alcohol, shipped in from wherever she can get it. Fanning the remaining files before her on the floor, she takes a sip and considers the point of this exercise. *Organise, organise, organise.* It is true, she thinks – with the pointless candour of a realisation reached much too late – it is true that she always led Morven to believe she couldn't be moved from one spot. She has always liked routine, safety, certainty, has liked being able to provide it for others, however much the flipside of that can easily become pressure, a dogged need to keep the day running at all costs. She had thought – assumed, it appears – that this was what Morven had loved about her, that steadiness, the ability to plough on regardless of disaster. The fact, then, that Morven had ended up wanting to leave for this exact reason was destabilising. *You never **would**,* Morven said when Isla suggested quite desperately that they travel together, wherever Morven wanted to go. *You can't be without this box you've built yourself into.* And it is true, in a way. She has made herself into a person who organises, who runs a certain course, who doesn't say what she thinks, and now she can't unmake it. Reeling herself in, always, reeling herself in. She squints, looks down into her glass for a second. Makes a mental addendum: the night before her father's funeral, the blood and booze and the upset, the general sense of collapse. *Any minute now, any second, I could crash this whole day into the wall.*

She sighs, drains her glass and registers a painful stab of longing for Irene. Her sister, always resisting her steadiness, yet simultaneously demanding of it. Her sister, always reliably in need of an older sibling, reliably grudging about that need. Agnes too, of course, although that's different.

Harder, somehow, to know what she is to her, or ever has been.

You're drunk, she thinks, and pours herself more vodka.

*　*　*

They knew their mother was dead because someone came to the house to tell them. Wall-eyed stranger, craning over their father's head in the doorway as if to catch a glimpse of the house beyond. Isla, aged eleven and paused on the second step leading down into the hallway, watching her father's back, the way his hand grasped the doorframe and released.

It was late in the day, late enough that the automatic lights were coming on around the porch and the stranger's face was washed curiously featureless by the glare from the LEDs. Of note: the rain, and the smell of the dinner, and the fact that whatever television show Irene was watching was turned up loud enough to ensure she would never remember this part.

Their father told Isla that he was required to make a positive identification, pulling on his coat as he did so, blocking the stranger's view into the house. She would remain where she was (would, in some sense, always remain), on the second step and struggling to understand. Her father's dark woollen coat, too heavy for the season, the list of instructions he gave her: *don't wake your stepmother, take the soup off the stove before it boils.* She had looked at him and felt, for a moment, that she understood the whole grand span of his lifelong frustration, his inability to ever conceive of the motives or actions of others. *I won't be long*, he said – a bizarre thing to say, but then what would Isla, aged eleven, know about such things?

Their mother was found drowned in open water some thirty minutes from the house. Officials at the scene noted that it was more or less incontestable that the act had been planned, owing to the rocks found loading down both her pockets and, likewise, both of her shoes. She had been divorced from their father a matter of months, though the dissolution had been protracted. Her last few weeks in the house had been tense, frenetic. She had talked a lot and in circles about rituals and disasters and strange home remedies, had counted the breaks in the rain in hours and minutes, had suggested that the whole family ought to be doing more to stop what she seemed to hold as an evil sensation in the air. Skitter of images: their mother dancing in the kitchen; their mother weeping; their mother crouching by a wall. An odd memory – voices late at night and the thought that their mother was entertaining strangers. Later on, Isla would come to recognise a lot of what went on as symptomatic of her father's affair and the failure of her parents' marriage, though her mother had perhaps been unravelling long before that. She had been quite wonderful, and then quite difficult, and then quite frightening. Hard to define if her parents had ever exactly been happy, though at one point Isla had felt certain there was nothing in her whole life to worry about until all of a sudden there was. Her father had remarried mere days after his divorce was finalised, had kept his daughters from the wedding as he would later keep them from their mother's funeral, and the lack of control she felt over this brief span of weeks would sit with her long after the sting of the losses themselves had dulled.

What happened to their mother – and how – was always a little bit cloudy. It was a breakdown of sorts, though one that Isla would never feel best placed to analyse. Certainly a result of the divorce to some degree but also the result of a mind under heavy stress, under pressure that pushed her thoughts into unnatural positions, bent her body in ways it didn't use to go. She had fallen down into paranoia, had spent hours scouring the internet for information she wouldn't let her daughters see. Isla had done her best to keep the situation on an even keel. When their mother would take their hands and tell them, seriously, that they had to look out for evil influence, overturn their palms as if to check for hidden objects, Isla would let her do it and would later reassure Irene that it was simply a game. All the same, sometimes the expression on her mother's face, when she came to kiss Isla goodnight, would frighten her. The way she would talk about the rain, about danger, about catastrophe and the coming end. The way her voice had sounded, the time Isla heard her speaking to their father in the kitchen: *I feel I'm very close to cracking this, I'm really on the edge of something good.*

4.

Irene

She is working in the living room with one eye on the television; a group of people bearing placards about benefit
cuts and collapsing social care have walked into the foyer of
a dark-fronted building and glued themselves to the carpet.
The image on the screen is momentarily a chaos – arms
aloft, a lunatic swing of the camera – and then abruptly
switches to a man in a tremendous yellow raincoat, who
complains to an unseen reporter that if they really wanted
to get their point across they could think about being less
of a pain. *What does this achieve, other than pissing everybody off and getting shit all over the carpet?* The feed is not
live and his curses are censored on both occasions, although
the camera stays on him as he appears to realise his error.
*Sorry, p-ing everybody off. Sorry, sh-i..m uh – getting sh-tuff
all over the carpet.* A flutter of vox pops: a man explaining
that he's sympathetic to their cause, but that if they're that

serious about it they should try blowing something up; a woman who blinks at the camera, apparently unsure of what she is being prompted to say. *I mean, I hadn't really thought about it.*

The report shifts to offer an overview of the rising trend in trespass and occupation. Flashing between buildings – a financial office, an upscale hotel, each daubed with paint and strung with toilet roll. One particular building makes Irene grab for the remote: just one in a series of images, but still unmistakable: a restaurant built into the teetering eighteenth storey of a tower, its luxe interiors trashed, its central water feature gummed with imitation blood. Irene recognises the tower, of course, because she remembers the drawing, the plan which occupied her father's drafting table and, later, his study wall. The restaurant's founding concept had been the invocation of an anchorage, a haven plucked from air; warm wood and curving leather, the smoked windows that displayed not the outdoors but only a suggestion of the light, of external colour. *Not particularly clever,* as her father had said, *but the point is the sense of being away from things.*

Irene shakes her head, reaches again for the remote and changes the channel. She feels tired, creased along her edges. The previous night, the alarm had gone off once again in the depths of the building. She had lurched out of bed, thrown from a dream. Looking to her left, she had noted Jude, flat out and insensible, and wondered how anyone could sleep through such a noise. Had wondered if this was a noise only she could hear before remembering the figures in the hallway, the neighbours blinking at her. The next day, this morning, they woke to disaster: a bridge down some three miles from their building, uncontained flooding and warnings on the radio to stay indoors and work from home. She made a joke about heading back to bed and was snapped at – Jude, pacing in their office clothes, in the middle of a phone call to somebody from work. *I don't know*, they said into the phone and then, to Irene, *can you give it a rest for a minute?* Irene, bristling, waiting for the phone call to end and then pouncing. *There was no need to say it like that.* Jude looked at her, bit the inside of their cheek and looked back at their phone, a muscle going at their temple. *I don't think*— they started, passed a hand across their face and then changed tack. *I'm very happy you don't have to go to work but I **do**, you know. I mean, I **can't**, there's no way I can go, and I still have to.*

Irene registered a gentle ripping down the middle; the half of her that recognised the urgency of surrender and the other half, the half she knew too well. Too stupid, always – the desire to avoid a fight drowned out by other, more immediate urges. The need to be right, the devotion to her own indignance. *You can never just climb down from something*, Isla had once told her, *you like to treasure up a grudge like something you've birthed and fed and sent to an expensive school.* She looked at Jude and felt all her bad thoughts massing up about her, her face settling into something pettish and slappable, the demeanour of a person whose right to ill-feeling is beyond reproach. The problem with love, of course, is that it frequently asks too much of unlovable people. It can be hard, on even the best of days, to compel oneself to be selfless and patient and undemanding or even halfway reasonable when one is not given to any of those behaviours. But these are nonetheless the qualities that love demands.

She should not by any means have picked a fight but did so anyway, snapped that yes, they all knew that what Jude did was far more important than anything else in the world, to which Jude spluttered that that was not what they'd meant. And on from there – pointless, monotonous, cudgelling back and forth. Irene declaring that it was all very well to be virtuous but that one had to be bearable too. Jude replying that it was easy to get angry when one had nothing else to be upset about. On and on like that; tedious, unnecessary. Irene snarled, accused Jude of being a martyr, called them terrible names. Jude argued that Irene would know something about martyrdom given the way she insisted on behaving about her father and sisters. Irene snapped back that Jude *wouldn't* know anything about martyrdom because Irene was the one who had actually studied martyrs and if Jude was going to pretend to be anything resembling an intellectual then Irene would simply have to laugh. At one point, and in reference to something too tangled to parse, Jude put a hand to their head and said *how do you think people who can't afford these fucking psychodramas get from one day to the next?* The fight wore on until it ran out of oxygen, at which point Jude said that they were going to have to try to get to work one way or another and passed out of the flat as if uncertain how else the scene was supposed to end.

That was hours ago. Now, Irene gets up and moves to clear away her coffee mug, pauses and instead turns to shuffle through papers on her desk. She feels uncomfortable, overcrowded, the fight like a pressure at her hip bones. She frowns, pictures her insides, the tight wet cramp of her guts. Finds the fight embedded there, like a story she once read about a man swallowing a pine cone and growing a miniature tree on the lining of his small intestine. Why had she simply not shut her mouth when she knew she should have? Why was it so easy to pick at Jude – Jude, who is so tired they sleep flat out as though murdered, who barely woke to a noise that could shock Irene out of the depths of a dream?

She blows upwards into her hair, rubs her elbows, looks around for something to occupy her mind. She is trying not to think about the flooding or how it is that Jude found a way into work. She has typed out a text which she feels too embarrassed to send: *sorry for being a basketcase please can you confirm you have not drowned on way to office simple y/n will suffice i love you i'm tidying sorry bye x*

She ends up in the bonus room, looking around for something like a task. She has been meaning to organise in here – a gift to Jude, the image of opening up the door one day and crying out *ta-da!* She has been meaning to invest in a set of filing cabinets, to chuck what ought to be chucked and alphabetise the remainder. She crouches down at the closest box and paws through it, bringing up a handful of papers that surely don't need to be kept: a programme from a series of lectures on Gnosticism, a menu from a Chinese restaurant, a packet of old receipts. She sets these aside and decides to make piles.

At around three o'clock she comes across a paper which confuses her. She turns it over, frowning at the text, which appears to be a printout from some kind of blog or website, its top and bottom cut off: *the process of the Granting ensures that the intended object is offered over or, as it might be, exchanged. It is thought that by this act, a balance may essentially be purchased. One must remember that we are living in a period of such marked disequilibrium that it cannot be left too late to sow the seeds.* Irene stares at this paper, trying to decide whether it is perhaps an essay she wrote, or an essay she clipped and meant to copy, though it doesn't quite have the flavour of her past academia. Its tone is odd, curiously didactic – *we must*, it states at one point, *free ourselves from such binding tenets as 'shame' when it comes to an act of salvation* – and she finds it hard to imagine printing it out with the thought of referencing it later. It might, she imagines, have got in amongst her things when she smuggled papers out of her father's house – it has the look of something oldish. She roots through the stack again, wonders if she might have missed a further sheet, but comes up with nothing, only a fragment of lined card which she holds to the light to read the note scribbled across it: *it will all come good in the end, Marie.* She squints at this, then drops it, watching it flutter down into her lap. Her stepmother's name, though hard to tell if it was written by her or to her, the name just as plausibly an assurance as a signature. She tries to imagine how she ever packed this away without noticing, before remembering the tear at which she stripped her room, rooted through places she shouldn't, the thrill of finally getting away too close at last to foster anything but incautious behaviour.

She takes up the piece of card and the website printout and places them both quite deliberately in the pile of detritus intended for the bin. *No thank you,* she thinks to herself, and then turns to her next pile of papers, *none of my business at all.*

* * *

A house, at night, loses all its comfortable dimensions. In the dark, one might quite as easily be walking on the ceiling as the carpet. Windows recede, the knowledge of familiar corners grows less certain. One might come upon a room and find it twice as large, busy with right angles.

Irene, aged eight, awake on the stairs and uncertain of how she got there. Not a habitual sleepwalker and unsettled by this development, she looked downwards, considered the way every staircase sprouts an extra step in darkness. Moved quietly, soft-footed in pyjamas and socks. The voice she could hear was her mother's, though the dream-logic of her half-waking state wrapped around the back of her consciousness like a finger and thumb and pulled the thought out of shape, so the voice seemed at once her mother's and that of someone else. There were two people at least, she thought, her mother and another woman. A reverberation seemed to imply the voices were coming from the kitchen, chapel-echo of a room entirely comprised of smooth surfaces. In the hallway, she paused, listened. *The act*, said one voice, *will fulfil itself, the exchange will earn its own momentum. Progress can be painful, but the pain is our responsibility.* Irene wiped her nose on the back of her hand, considered going in to ask her mother for a glass of milk but decided against it. Another voice: *But my children.* Irene shuffled one foot in front of the other, wondered how one is really supposed to tell sleeping from waking. *It will be hard*, said one voice, *but trials are the direct result of failure. Straying has led to where we are now, there is only one way back to the path.*

Little else after this, a blurring of words into the night-time mumble of the house around her. *The time will come soon*, said one voice, *we will know what to do.* Irene stayed where she was for a while, aware of the sensations one feels more keenly in the dark: her feet on the carpet, her full bladder, the taste of her breath in her mouth. Later on, she would go back to bed, take the memory away and presently forget it. A story, recollected enough, becomes a fiction. She would know that she heard her mother in the kitchen.

Know, too, when she first met her stepmother, that she had heard her voice before. She would know this, but in time would cease to be quite so sure she knew it, the telling and retelling rendering it a dream, an act of childhood sleep-walking. She had simply made up a conversation between two women who should not, by rights, have known each other. She had stood, asleep and dreaming, at the bottom of the stairs.

Isla

The grid is down, dousing the lights in her house and the voice on the television. A room dim at noon is a curious thing – the sense of a stage set and awaiting its players, a scene without recourse to action or plot. Isla watches the rain wash by from the living room window and wonders how Irene is doing and whether the situation is worse where she is. It's been largely impossible to go out for three days, train lines blocked, power lines felled, trees down along the turn of the hillside. Things feel hectic, unstable. A news item trailed the possibility of a test government emergency warning being sent to the mobile phone of every-one in the country, then, when it happened, the message was universally scrambled: *do not go outsisefd7BN3bas.*

Periodically, Isla goes down to the cellar to check on a leak which appears to have sprung up sometime during the course of the week. She has taken a measuring tape each time to gauge the depths of the damage, although the third time she drops it and isn't able to retrieve it from the water, now knee-high and unpleasantly murky. She is worried about the house's foundations and unsure with whom to raise this issue. A nasty thought – swiftly dealt with – that her father would have known what to do. She can picture the act of asking; picking up the phone and dialling her father's number, waiting the requisite fourteen or fifteen rings that would bring him to think that a caller was serious. She can picture the way she would phrase the question, the pause, the shift on the line.

The greater part of adulthood, Isla has always felt, lies in the acceptance of oneself as a fundamentally lone ranger, a person adept enough at changing a bulb and making a sandwich to get along more or less without help. One can work at this kind of independence, come to it in stages or all at once, but however much one perfects the art of paying taxes and otherwise keeping afloat, the fullness of adulthood can never be realised until a parent is beyond one's reach. One might, at any time, sever ties and release a mother or father, might maintain such a rift for the rest of their natural lives, but death is irrevocable. Death, after all, puts an end to the argument, but it also prolongs the silence for good.

The windows chatter. The wind is getting worse. Isla looks around the living room, her neatly ordered shelves and the table with its fanned magazines, its coasters and woven-rush placemats. She feels, briefly, horrified by the stillness, by the Kansas pre-tornado cast of the room. In a room like this, she thinks, one could quite easily find oneself set in black and white and fastened to the carpet, frozen solid as the roof blows off. She doesn't have enough to distract her, was only able to see one patient via videolink today before the power died; a session which was frankly too combative to render much in the way of satisfaction. The patient, a woman she has been seeing on and off for months, has a daughter whose involvement in what she believes is a type of quasi-religious group tends to take up much of the designated hour. Isla has never been able to wholly get to the bottom of the group's stated intentions, only that the patient is concerned at the way that her daughter speaks to her and concerned, too, about certain things she has started saying within earshot (or rather, when the patient has picked up the extension to listen to her daughter's private phone calls). *She talks*, the patient said today, *as if something is at hand. She's always using those words – 'at hand' – like something's coming. She talks about some kind of big shift, some kind of act, and yes, before you say anything, I know we've had conversations about boundaries and space and I know I'm not meant to listen in on her phone calls or read her diary, but I'm worried about these people she's fallen in with.* Isla nodded, pretended to scribble something in her notepad, though in reality she simply drew a series of circles and then crossed them out. *Do you think*, she said, *that it's so much a question of disliking her new friends as disliking the fact of her moving away from you?* The patient's face glitched across the screen.

263

*They're not **new friends**, she said, *they've got her talking like a fucking kook. 'We'll Give and the balance will be reset, in time,' she said, 'the rain will stop, in time.' It's a fucking kook convention and you're telling me to put down the phone.*

Now, Isla moves away from the window, crosses to the table and picks up her mobile. She is considering sending a message to Irene but finds instead a text from Caroline, updating her on the situation with her father's house. This has become an embarrassment, the more she really thinks about it. She is worried about the house in a way she can't entirely parse, wakes from dreams where it washes away in the night, where it fills with a viscous substance which pushes out against the walls and shatters the glass towards the roof. When she dreams this, her father is often in the house as the flooding happens. When she dreams this, she is trying to rescue him and finding he refuses to get up from his wheelchair and go where he's bidden. She isn't clear on the root of this dream or the root of her worry, only that it feels better when Caroline's message notes that everything is as it should be. *All well*, Caroline's latest message reads. *Nothing's changed, no ghosts, no breakages. I can't see any evidence that anyone has attempted to move in or change anything, it all looks quite untouched. No one's pulled down a wall or upset the furniture, no one's overloaded the framework and sunk the house into the water.*

Isla sets down her phone again and looks at the ceiling. At the moment, whenever she allows her mind to clear for two seconds together, she finds herself thinking about

Agnes. This happened, at first, quite by chance. She was drinking (never a good sign) and looking at *Stephen Carmichael: A Retrospective*, flipping through the back pages, when she came to a photograph of two small girls and a baby positioned artfully in front of a series of scale models; the overall effect being that of a trio of giants preparing to take a city apart. The caption, very much in the overall style of the book at large, was a ridiculous confection: *the Carmichael sisters survey their kingdom.* Isla stared at this picture; the small her and the smaller Agnes, her hand on the baby's wrist as though intending to pull her back from something, Agnes reaching towards the sharp point of a model skyscraper with her other hand. Isla stared, and closed the book, and felt winded.

She thinks about this now, thinks about the fight before the funeral, her youngest sister snarling at her that things were just as bad for both of them. She thinks, too, about other things – Agnes, much younger, going missing for hours only to be discovered curled up in the minute space behind a dresser. Agnes, much younger, going days without speaking, wetting her bed at night and coming into Isla's room at midnight to tug at the collar of her t-shirt until she woke and went to sort it out. *I don't want to do this now,* she says to herself – not aloud, though it would have been easy enough to do so with no one here to hear. Thinks, again, about Agnes and her tiny hand reached out towards a sharp and unprotected point. Later on, she will fall asleep and, when she does, she will dream her usual dream of her father's house flooding, though when this happens it will be Agnes and not her father who she is unable to wrangle up out of the chair.

Agnes

She is at the cafe because Jason insisted; nightmare ride on the ferry cut short by debris in the water, back up and reverse to the nearest jetty, disembark, pause for orientation, inevitable long wet walk. There are, of course, no customers, despite Jason's decree that they show up to man their stations. She makes a cursory swipe at the counter with a J-cloth then turns back to the Gaggia, wondering whether to clean it now or save that for the umpteenth hour of her shift. Jason, of course, has not actually made it, having messaged some ten minutes after Agnes arrived to say that transport was simply too difficult and that he hoped she'd brought her keys. Liam is not here either, though he should have arrived half an hour ago. She glances at her phone, considers putting on some music and then dismisses it – too gloomy in an empty cafe, too much the atmosphere of some late-night place, a bus depot or petrol station, a place made eerie by its emptiness, by the fact that one ought to be safely elsewhere. It isn't late, it is actually still quite early, though the light is dim enough to render this inconsequential. The rain is loud on the roof and louder against the windows, glass misted over to such an extent that the precinct can barely be seen from the front of the shop, let alone from the counter. It is for this reason that Agnes initially misses the gesture, the shape that forms on the outside of the glass, the edges of two hands bracketed together, as if like a viewfinder, and pressed against the window. She stops when she notices, sets down her phone. The form beyond the glass is uncertain – ghost-shape, indistinct in condensation, a patch of denser mist like breath beneath the shadow of the hands. Agnes stands where she is, breath held, hands tight against the counter, stomach crawling down her leg. She is eight, and there is someone outside her father's house; she is twenty-four, and still there is no one coming to help her. One second, two, and then she starts to move again, takes up the J-cloth and swipes confidently at the Gaggia. The prickle in her arms, across her scalp, along her sternum. She hums a couple of bars of a song before remembering the empty cafe and stopping.

When she looks up again, the shape is gone, the circle of breath smeared sideways, as though swiped with the edge of a sleeve. She lets go a tentative breath and thinks of texting Stephanie. *Fucking weirdos*, she wants to say, to reshape the incident in lurid colours. A man looking in at a woman, of a piece with catcalling and hands thrust up skirts on the train. Unpleasant, unwelcome, but staunchly of the world. A recognisable ill, only made to seem otherwise by a veil of greasy glass.

She is typing out a message to Stephanie when the bell rings over the door, heralding the arrival of a man in green scrubs and cardigan, rattling an umbrella turned almost inside out by the wind. The commotion is welcome, a sudden burst of air rattling through her mental rafters, bringing her back to her perch.

'Filthy day,' the man says, as though Agnes might not have noticed, and orders a latte to go. She sets the order up for him, doesn't bother to request his name for the cup in the total absence of any other customers, hands the coffee off when he throws a few coins in the tip jar. 'Thank you,' he says, and pauses with the coffee in his hand. He looks at Agnes. 'Do you enjoy your work?'

She suppresses a sigh. This is not altogether unusual, men insisting on striking up conversations where a nod and a grunt would suffice.

'Not too bad,' she says, and busies herself with wiping down the counter.

'I imagine not too fulfilling either,' he says. 'Not much opportunity to make a great change.'

Agnes sets the dish towel down impatiently. 'What?'

'All in good time, I suppose,' he says, and smiles benignly. 'In time. Filthy day,' he says again, waving his hand in an odd manner that puts her briefly in mind of one of Stephanie's all-encompassing gestures, though he is presumably just referring to the rain. 'Might end soon.'

'Sure, I guess so,' she says, turning dully back to work as he leaves the shop.

It takes her several hours to realise. A fact, like something filtered, percolating, moving to the forefront of her mind. One moment oblivious, then certain. Restacking mugs as a means of passing time she registers a memory, pausing with her hand halfway between shelf and counter. The same man, of course; green scrubs and a cup of coffee. The outskirts of her father's death, the hospital corridor, and the way the man had spoken, as though he knew her, the coffee she had knocked from his hands. She stands where she is, unsure of what to do with this knowledge, uncertain how to lower her hand from the shelf. Cold shrink in the depths of her chest, reaching round towards her backbone. Any horror story could be said to work in two pieces: the fear of being wholly alone and of realising that one has company.

Irene

Several days in and she is making headway with her organising project. She and Jude have been at odds since their squabble, uncomfortable and barely speaking, and the papers feel like something to focus on. She wants to apologise and can't find the language for it, wants Jude to apologise but can't remember what she's actually angry about. On a couple of occasions, she has noticed Jude hovering in the doorway of the bonus room, looking around at the mess she is slowly fixing, and they have seemed a little pained, like they want to speak and are being physically blocked from it. A stupid thing, Irene thinks, to have allowed a silence to grow like this. Silence, which was once the whole point of her studies, now uncorked and spreading wet and sticky over everything it touches – her relationship with Jude, her sisters. *You should call Isla,* she will think sometimes when poring over papers in the bonus room, only for a competing strain of thought to interrupt and tell her *no, you idiot, you should talk to Jude.*

Jude is at work again now and Irene is on the last couple of boxes. She unearths a fair-sized pile of thesis notes, flipping through them with the somewhat leaden sensation one might feel when assessing old photos of friends one no longer sees or speaks to. *A certain distrust,* she once wrote, *pervaded early forms of Christianity when it came to the practice of silent prayer. Those who didn't speak their prayers aloud were subject to significant social prejudice. What, after all, could they be wanting to speak to God about that they needed to keep from everybody else?* Beneath this fragment, she had scribbled the words *silence and lying? silence and schemes?* followed by the semi-unintelligible musing that *if silent prayer is untrustworthy then what does that say about the God you're praying to?* Rough stuff, really, handwriting canted sideways as if she had been nursing a crick in the neck. She draws out a postcard bearing the image of a church set with bright-paned windows in a blazing Chagall blue. The memory is a neat-edged knife pressed tight into her ribcage – quick slit, a gentle downward slicing.

The plan had been a pilgrimage of sorts, although arranged around a strictly academic purpose. The church boasted a peculiar pedigree, as it was the site of both a series of well-preserved Norman wall paintings and a relatively famous murder (seventeenth-century poet and probable spy stabbed to death in the chancel and found in the morning with a handkerchief over his face, no obvious explanation). The murder remained unsolved; various historians and latterly podcasters had speculated that the victim had been a double agent, had been a Calvinist, had been in love with the local mayor's wife, but no official consensus was reached. Irene wanted to see the church less out of interest in the murder than in the strange black hole of afterwards, the vacuum of noise and knowledge where a solution might otherwise be. *Silence,* she wrote at one point, as part of a larger thought which she never got to the end of, *is not only a function of religion but of the Church as a whole. Silence pervades faith but more than that it pervades the institution, a constant deafening silence, a holding back of crimes, of secrets, of the many sordid things the Church would rather not be known.* She planned her trip with a dispassionate enough idea of doing her due diligence, though a subdued excitement at the thought of the windows, of the paintings, of the whole strange history of the place persisted. She pictured herself, standing in the swimming stained-glass light of the chancel, struck dumb with some sudden divinity: the solution to the murder, a clear path through her thesis, a clarity that could hardly help but come upon her in such a certain blue.

She remembers the boat she took out to the west of the city, beyond what had once been fenland, only to find to her surprise that the area she had imagined to be walkable was not so and that she had to take another public boat and then a water taxi. The day was filthy, clammy as well as wet, and she sustained herself with pictures of the church drawn up on her phone as the taxi took her across increasingly sodden marshland and into the valley beyond.

The discovery had been inevitable, a sharp ache settling down to grim acceptance. The church was gone, of course. Both it and its surrounding parish first evacuated then abandoned to a reservoir which had overflowed its dam and flooded the valley, swiftly uncontained and just as swiftly settled. An open mouth, great Charybdic swallow. The valley was too low, the town positioned too perfectly in its basin. The whole area was now underwater with little enough to indicate the recent presence of a working community besides the church's finial, which still protruded some half a metre, visible from the left-hand side of the water taxi, which Irene could only induce to approach within a few hundred yards for fear of scuttling. She stared at the finial tip from the window and thought of the shape things take in water, the way that forms appear less certain when pushed beneath the surface, outlines growing lesser, growing loose. She thought this and pictured the sunken shapes of spire and belfry, pictured blue glass and Norman stonework, altarpiece and offertory and carved sedilia; thought, too, and for no clear reason, about the scene in the movie *The Omen* where a pole is flung from the roof of a church in an act of malign-seeming randomness to pierce the chest of a man standing far below.

She went home and cried in earnest. Tried to explain the way she felt and only managed to express to Jude that she felt despair, unmoored from her studies and yet panicked at the thought of abandoning them. Panicked, too, that a whole mapped and plotted and navigable place could have drowned without her notice, that no one had thought to tell her, that she hadn't thought to check. Jude pulled her into their lap on the sofa and talked to her gently, eased her down out of tears, pulled her hair from the collar of her shirt and kissed her and told her it was entirely right to be upset. It was difficult, they said, to have put so much thought and effort into a project only to find yourself met with resistance, with bad results. It was hard to keep faith in a project that felt so intentionally confounding, hard to feel it was worth all the time you would never get back. *Sunken church fallacy*, they joked, and then made a face about the joke, and Irene laughed in a way that felt sore in her throat but nonetheless better than crying. *I'm aware*, she said, *that this is less a tragedy for me than it is for the people who lost their literal homes*, and Jude looked at her. *I wasn't asking you to convince me of that, you know*, they said. Irene shook her head. *I know, but sometimes I worry.* She gave up on her PhD four months after this, and it felt like a kind of relief.

Now, Irene sits back on her heels feeling suddenly sick of herself. Moving to switch on the television, she flicks through news stations, pausing on a livefeed of several people being airlifted from a flooded office block. Further updates follow: a building collapsed in the financial district, power outages away to the west, a man trapped on a jetty not twenty minutes away from their block and apparently still awaiting rescue. The next channel is midway through a programme in which people attempt to date each other by kissing for long periods of time and then deciding whether or not they liked it. The couple just coming up for air look slightly bewildered as the camera looms in on their faces. The girl wipes her mouth, appears to dig her tongue around the back of one of her molars. *It was ok*, she says after a moment, *but it didn't feel like you were really there*. Irene mutes the sound, raps her knees with her hands and then goes back to her papers, reaching for her phone before she does so and tapping out a message to Jude.

5.

City

There are rumours of a great wave, though this of course is nonsensical. People pass along the image anyhow, spread the news like something learned; a truth that becomes more itself the further it moves from its origins. A great wave to the south – so it goes – heading inland, some twenty feet or more across. The size shifting as the story shifts, the wave expanding, gaining momentum. A wall of water, people say, perhaps a mile from end to end. It blotted out the sky, they say, filled up the whole horizon. When it hit, you could have forgotten you were ever dry in your life.

This didn't happen. Or rather, whatever did happen was less dramatic, more diffuse. A series of coastal places have receded, fallen, dropped down into the water or otherwise been wiped away like sums sloughed from a blackboard. Rumour floats up, gathers in to plug the gaps. It is, perhaps, less of a stretch for the mind to contemplate events via the lens of the kind of films one might have watched in the dark at the age of seventeen; asteroids, louring skies. Easier to tell a story with a beginning, middle and end. Disaster movies, after all, come complete with pending resolution: the dash up the hill to avoid the falling rubble, the turning tide, the core of the slowing earth ignited at the cost of six courageous lives. Heroic flights, Hail Mary passes, et cetera, et cetera. The rescue is the point, or at least the idea that reversal is still imminent. There is little the imagination can do with an ending that is already assured.

Agnes

The noise hits her like a sudden searing. She is in the kitchen at home and drops her mug, puts her hand to her head and turns towards the window in time to see – nothing – no change to the fabric of the world outside, no alteration in the weather. She squints, presses her face into the glass and looks out, looks downwards. The traces of the sound remain in her teeth, singing up through her palate and out into the bones of her face.

'What the fuck?' She turns to find Stephanie standing in the kitchen doorway, staring out towards the window.

'I don't know,' Agnes says, and finds she badly wants to offer some excuse, as if she might be blamed for the disturbance. 'I heard it too.'

'It was an explosion, right?' Stephanie crosses to the window and joins her in looking out at the rain. 'That's what it sounded like.'

'I don't know,' Agnes says again. 'I thought it sounded more like something landing. Or falling down.'

Stephanie frowns, scrubs at the glass with the sleeve of her shirt and peers outward. The rain is heavy, falling today with a hectoring quality that makes it feel more than usually malign. When Agnes went down earlier in the day, she found the lobby flooded to about knee height and swiftly turned around to run back up again. This discovery now coupled with the noise is unsettling, if not to say wholly without precedent. Casper has taken to playing news items aloud on his phone in quiet moments: the power plant evacuated to the north of the city, the tower that came down in the flood. The new housemate does not seem to like this, has often got up from wherever she is sitting in the middle of these broadcasts and made for her room, closing the door. They have received several emails from their local councillor which make no imme-diate sense: *stay indoors unless that is not feasible, in which case do not stay indoors.* Agnes has heard sirens, more than once, sirens too loud for what she pictures when she thinks of sirens: ambulances, helicopters, isolated tragedies. This latest noise, whatever it was (and how even to describe it? *the boom, the blast?*) falls in with a larger percussion, the sense of a city shuddering itself apart.

'Seems ok,' Stephanie says now, leaning back from the window and glancing down to where Agnes's mug has hit the laminate and shattered. 'Are you alright?'

Agnes nods, tries to smile and wonders how many times Stephanie has asked her this question. Days ago, she asked what was wrong when Agnes came home feeling rattled, crashed about, picked a fight about the dinner and the sheets not being changed. In stages, Agnes worked around to an explanation, climbing down from her temper and shifting into something like apology. She explained the man who had come to the cafe, the way that she had seen him once before. Stephanie listened attentively, passed a hand across her face in a gesture that could have read like impatience but on Stephanie only seemed like another gesture, a gentle pass and then release. *We do see people more than once*, she said, *I mean, if you think about it. You saw me at the club and then you saw me near the cafe. It's just what happens. Cities can be smaller than you think.* Agnes bridled against this and then just as swiftly gave in, accepted the futility of her own alarm. It felt good to lean into Stephanie's outlook, the idea that nothing terrible was about to happen, was perhaps already happening now. *Are you alright?* Stephanie asked her sometime later, and Agnes nodded and more or less meant it, which felt like something new. Since then, there have been a few little things – a woman who seemed to be moving very swiftly towards her across a crowded walkway, another woman who, turning a corner and coming upon Agnes in an understocked supermarket, declared *Oh! Oh!* and caused Agnes to immediately swerve her trolley away. Agnes has tried to reframe these things in her head, applying Stephanie's voice to her anxieties. *Small city*, she has thought, *bad times, hysterical fucking people*.

She imagines the noise again now, lifts her hand to one ear without thinking, as if half-convinced there'll be blood. She wonders, despite herself, whether her sisters heard the same noise in their own respective sections of the city, whether it was loud enough to reach all three of them at once. She shakes herself out of this thought and catches Stephanie working her fingers under a flake of paint at the windowsill, realises she loves her, can't find a gesture to couple with this fact. She has felt it, perhaps, but never found the space to know it. The sensation now is like discovery, like something caught in her peripheral vision and pulled at last towards the light. She tries to think of what to say and draws a blank, smiles stupidly. Stephanie bends to gather up the pieces of the mug and Agnes puts a hand on the top of her head, holds her there for a second.

'What was that?' Stephanie asks, smiling and then frowning as she straightens. Agnes looks at her, finds the words lodged tight against the roof of her mouth. Love, it seems, is bizarre in its moment of realisation, too blatant to speak aloud. Now she thinks it, the fact feels obvious, the fact of their life together; the vacuum and chore wheel, shampoo and conditioner, the time spent in bed and the time spent undressing, the meals and bad dreams and rent cheques and gas bills and toothpaste and sex toys and laptops and sweaters and bras and woollen hats and umbrellas and everything else together. Love, then, as something she should have clued into, a fact against which she's been willingly blind. We love people before we notice we love them, but the act of naming the love makes it different, drags it out into different light.

She looks at Stephanie and says nothing. Thinks, absurdly, that the words might be kept for a rainy day.

'What are you smiling about?' Stephanie asks, and Agnes shakes her head, tilts up to kiss her and then glances back towards the window. The noise is still in her head, and a fresh splinter in the glass towards the base of the sill bears a trace of its impact. She presses a finger against it, following the line of the fracture. It shuttles up from the edge of the frame, tiny split like the pop of a seam; nothing more dramatic. She looks at it and imagines a cartoon window, blown out in comic fashion by a note sung far too high.

Isla

She is reading the news on her phone, scrolling past reports of explosions to the west of the city; something to do with a dam and an overloaded generator, a factory up in flames. She pays only scant attention, scrolling further in search of a story she can't seem to find. The house next to hers appears to have sunk several yards down the hill overnight and the family is currently outside assessing the damage. She hasn't been out to offer assistance, though she knows this would be the neighbourly thing to do. She is too alarmed by the speed of the sinking. Too alarmed, as well, by the water still accumulating in her cellar, the increasing conviction that whatever is fixing her house in its place could be rapidly losing its grip. Finding nothing concrete on any respectable news outlet (*family of four in domestic landslide, neighbours assured it won't happen to them*), she throws her phone aside and peers out of the window. The family consists of a man, a woman and two children, although beyond that she knows very little, can barely remember how long they've lived there. Morven, she reflects, was always the one who handled introductions, presenting herself to new neighbours with a carton of milk and the bright-eyed conviction that no one, on first moving in, will have thought to stock up on essentials. *They were nice*, she would typically say on return from manoeuvres. *You should come with me next time, we said we'd do drinks.* Isla would nod and smile and this would be the last she'd hear of it, until a neighbour moved out and Morven commenced the whole operation again. Outside, the man appears to be setting a futile shoulder against one side of the house, as if to shove it back into place. The pressure of his shoulder appears to achieve little, though he persists, leaning back and then hammering the wall several times with his body, until a window tumbles out of its frame and shatters in the mud.

She turns away, walks a tight circle of her living room and pauses, poised on the balls of her feet. She feels rattled, shot through with iron filings. Her skin, if touched, feels like it might quite easily cause injury. She pictures this, scraping up against another person's surface, grating steadily away until she's caused sufficient damage, until the person scatters soft across the floor. The other night, she finished the majority of a bottle of wine and called Morven over and over again until she picked up. She can't remember now what she said when she finally got through, although she woke this morning to a message telling her to take care of herself, please, but also not to call again if she was going to talk like that.

She shakes her head. *This*, she reflects, *is what happens when you don't see your patients*. It's been three days with only intermittent power, still impossible to get into the office, patients crying off sessions that can only be conducted via patchy video. Perhaps, she has reflected, it is simply easier for her patients to mistake her for a decent therapist when there are items in the room to distract them. The desk and calendar, the Barcelona chair – all these elements combined to sell an overarching competence. Without them, she is little but a face on a screen, disseminating bad advice and then charging for it. Therapists are supposed to have therapy, although Isla hasn't done this in a number of years. She is worried that her supervisor might revoke her licence, might call in all the therapists from surrounding practices – *look what we've got here*.

She is thinking this when it occurs to her that she ought to call Irene. A feeling out of nowhere, longing like a kick in the stomach: to be anything to anyone. She stands where she is and tries to imagine what she would say if she called, whether she might beg her sister to treat her like a competent older sibling, to at least make a show of considering her thus. *Do you have any problems you need fixing? Could you maybe invent one and send it my way?*

She picks up her phone, clicks on a number in her contacts and then pauses. *I'm scared*, she imagines herself saying, *that my house is going to fall down the hill with me inside it. I'm scared of the water in the basement. I'm scared that, if I was my wife, I would have left me too.*

She looks at her phone. Outside, she can hear a painful shuddering, the creak of foundations shifting on unstable ground. She imagines the man flinging his shoulder up against the wall of his house, imagines him forcing it back, preposterously, up the hill, up along the distance it has slipped.

'Hello?'

She has dialled without meaning to and now stands with her mouth half-open, white spot where her thoughts ought to be.

'Well, what is it?' Irene says. 'If you're calling to ask if I needed very extensive reconstructive surgery after you hit me, be assured you'll be getting my bill.'

Isla exhales.

'How are you?' she says, and hears a noise which might be Irene clicking her tongue.

'I'm ok,' she replies, and then, 'Well, you know. I'm worried.'

'Are you?' Isla responds, and then wonders whether she sounded too eager. 'Can I – do anything about that?'

Irene makes an odd sound, possibly a laugh. 'Oh, Isla, you're such a fucking fruitcake.'

Isla pauses, struggles to feel offended. 'Um. Sorry?'

'No, I just mean ...' – and here Irene again seems to be stifling a laugh – 'I mean we don't speak for months and then here you are, talking like this.'

'Talking like what?'

'Like yourself. I don't know. Maybe it's comforting.'

Isla snorts, puts her hand to her mouth as if to prevent something falling out, worries it might be her heart and swallows.

Irene

She sits cross-legged on the sofa for a long time after hanging up, fiddles with the corner of one nail until she rips it and has to get up to fetch a cloth. She has torn the nail towards the quick and it is bleeding gently. Her sister had sounded *off*, inasmuch as Isla always sounds off but seldom quite so obviously. She had talked about the basement of her house, and the news, and about trying to work with only intermittent power, and Irene had listened and nodded and tried to remember how it had felt to be slapped. It is, it turns out, harder than she might have expected to hold a grudge when presented with the actual chattering fact of her sister, combined with her own immense guilt, and she feels proud of this – absurdly so, as if it were the direct result of something she's been working on (which, in a sense, it is). Irene, optimised. Irene, the kinder sister, leaving rancour in the dust.

I'm feeling like I need to take a break, Isla had said, and then, as if something had whispered to her to say it, *I think you should too, if you're feeling the way I am.*

I'm ok, Irene said, and then, *well, worried, like I said. And I'm tired, I think. I know how you feel.*

They had talked like this for a while and Irene had felt odd, as if she were the older sister. She had pictured Isla at some former juvenile age, the way she had used to react to embarrassment with outsized actions: slamming her own arm in a door or cutting her tights up with kitchen scissors.

I think, Isla had said at one point, *that I've probably been unfair to you*, but then hadn't expanded on this, going on to talk instead and with unwonted openness about something Morven had said to her. *I'm getting divorced, you know*, she had said, but carried on before Irene could remind her that she already knew this. *I remember*, Isla said, *how she used to talk about the things she was afraid of. Like the earth curving, like taking a wrong turn one day and coming to the end of the world.*

And she used to say, 'What if that happens, what if you come right to the edge of something and then you just fall and fall?' And I'd say, 'Well, the issue here is that the earth is round', when I guess what she was actually asking was whether I'd pull her back from the edge or something. I think that was what she wanted. I don't know. I think I tend to miss things.

Irene had listened and wondered what had happened to set Isla thinking along these lines. *I think*, Irene had said at one point, *that you're probably overworked*, to which Isla had laughed.

I've been thinking, Isla had said, *that I behaved very badly with Agnes. I've been thinking that in general*, she had added, *but with Agnes in particular. I didn't tell you but I've been paying Dad's housekeeper to keep an eye on the house. It's not even mine and I'm paying her to look after it because I thought Agnes wouldn't. Or because I wanted to know whether she'd moved in or something, I don't know.*

I think you're turning into the wrong DuBois sister, Irene had replied, and then, *sorry, that's not very helpful, is it?*

You aren't very helpful.

Well, you're insane.

Isla had huffed a laugh and made a soft slurring noise and Irene had wondered whether she was drinking.

I've been thinking, Isla had said, had seemed to lose the thread of her sentence and had to start again, *I mean to say, I've been thinking about Agnes a lot. And Dad a lot. Both of them, I mean. Sometimes I think of them together and then I get confused. But I've been thinking about her, and I feel embarrassed about how I behaved before. I think I got so angry, I've been so angry with her, and now I feel so ashamed. Do you know what I mean?*

Not particularly, Irene had said, *but then you never make much sense.*

But don't you think, Isla had said, *that you've done the same thing, over time? Don't you think you've been angry too?*

I don't think I'm angry at Agnes, Irene had said and then wondered at the baldness of this statement, the futility of the lie. *I'm angry about certain things – about Mum, about Marie – but I think they're more or less separate from her.*

Do you ever worry about ending up like our mother? Isla had asked. This, unprompted, thrown down in the manner of something unwelcome.

Irene had sat where she was for a minute, searched her mind for an answer that resembled the truth. Their mother, grown outlandish in her bedclothes, banned from the house computer by their father because, he said, she was spending too much time on silly websites, getting cracked ideas into her head. Their mother, pushing Irene's face into the water when she combed her hair for nits; the eternity of seconds during which Irene believed she'd never let her up.

Sometimes, she had said, without adding how often, without adding that sometimes she pictured her mother spreading across her like lichen, like something resembling skin.

I guess it's not Agnes's fault, Isla had said, *that all of that happened. We probably make it her fault more than we should do. I think maybe we should talk to her.*

Later on: the hum of the quiet that is never exactly quiet. Irene glances up at the sound of the door. Jude comes in, shrugging off their jacket and looking at her. Since the fight, since Irene texted her tentative apology, they have both been tense, tender in the manner of something burned and poorly bandaged. Irene's finger throbs where she ripped at the nail and she looks at Jude and wishes she knew how to stop making messes of things. The problem, it occurs to her now, is anger – the huge, heavy, futile weight of anger and how good she and her sisters have always been at it. Anger and silence, as always, the way they allow it to rage out of all control. She thinks about Isla, almost certainly drunk on the phone: *I've been so angry, and now I feel so ashamed.* She tries to layer the thought of her own voice over her sister's. *I'm getting divorced, you know* – she tries in Isla's voice, in her voice, and her mouth runs suddenly dry.

'So listen,' Jude starts, and Irene shakes her head, gets up off the sofa and hurries towards them.

'I think it's ok now,' she says. Draws them in, puts her hands in their hair. 'I want it to be ok.'

Loving someone is easier in theory. She has known this a long time but still comes upon it occasionally as if unawares. She hadn't thought, when she saved the eggshells from their first night together, that what came after would be what it was. She hadn't pictured so much tiredness, so much

bickering and scrapping, or the many little nicks and insin-
cerities that amount to a normal sort of life. Even so, the
truth of what she hoped for remains, lodged safe in the sink
of Jude's shoulders, in the way they kiss her, the easy
manner in which they carry her to bed. It is, after all,
enough to have this and be happy, if only in the fleeting
moments that all other thoughts recede. It is, after all,
enough to be thrown down and forgiven, enough to pull
Jude down on top of her and kiss their neck and tell them
she loves them, that she'd hate it if they ever were to leave.
It's hard enough to live, she sometimes feels, without also
having to think about it. Hard enough, amidst panic and
boredom and drastically shortened horizons, to simply
treat a person nicely, put your hands into their hair until
they shiver, until they push their face into your chest.

She has wondered, before now, whether thinking about
God is part of this. Wondered whether endlessly circling
the same topics, harping hopeless and uncertain on God
and on silence and deep, drowning lack have simply func-
tioned as ways to keep her unhappy, keep her tight in the
grip of an answer she can't help but seek. Perhaps, after all,
God is simply a poached egg and a yolk cooked just as it
should be. Perhaps God is being fisted by the person you
love most in the world, being taken apart one finger at a
time until the whole of you is fucked out and pulled like a
cord strung tight, white-eyed and waiting for crescendo.
Perhaps God is all of that and kissing afterwards, kissing
most of all, sore-mouthed and messy, half-asleep and trying

to remember if you locked the door and if you need to set your phone alarm for seven. Perhaps God is all of that and an apology.

*   *   *

The lights go and don't come back on again. She lies in the dark for a moment and listens for the siren, hears it sound in the depths of the building for a span of a second and then cut. She looks at Jude, still sleepy with their arm thrown across her. Without light, the night is ungentle, darkness fixed hard and heavy in the corners of the room.

She kisses Jude's temple and pushes herself upright, walks naked to the window and looks out. Blank city, snuffed and featureless. She squints out to find nothing, not a window or doorway, not a light strung loose across an awning as far as she can see. She blinks, imagines herself flung into space, thinks of the science books she used to pore over at school that tried to document the colour of the galaxy, glossy photos taken by telescopes showing the great blank stretch between stars. She jumps when she feels Jude at her elbow, turns to find them wrapping an arm round her waist.

'What is it?'

'Grid's down again,' she says, 'or I *guess* it's just the grid. I don't know. Could be the whole city. Looks like no lights for miles.'

'What's that then?'

Readjusting her gaze to follow Jude's finger, she registers an uncertain glow; something like the emergency light that one sometimes sees in municipal halls and stairwells during a mains power cut. It seems to blink out and then back again, dispersing and forming like something blown out and relit. She squints, tries to gauge how far away it might be, though perspective collapses in darkness, dimension tipped over into something less assured. The light seems to float, hover vague above the blankness of the city. Blue light, blue like Cherenkov radiation, like church windows in water, like the colour that comes before black.

'Look at that,' she says, although Jude is the one who pointed it out. 'D'you think it's meant to be some kind of warning?'

'Could be,' Jude replies, nudging their face into her hair and then shrugging. 'Could be like the alarms going off all over the place – some kind of emergency light – could be a gas explosion, could be someone's got a generator and they're having a party, I don't know.'

'Could be.' Irene tries to bring herself to feel more immediately curious. The problem, of course, is that there's always something, and it can be easier on occasion to ignore it and take your partner back to bed.

Isla

She is watching when it goes. Next door's house. It has clung on all day and then slipped, slid down and shuddered to pieces; it collapses as if from the inside first, the way tower blocks do when demolished. She has been watching from the window, squinting for any sign of movement. The family appears to have decamped, likely taken in by some friend or relative. She should probably have evacuated herself, but no one has come to her door and told her to, or declared her house officially unsafe, so she hangs on where she is, clamshelled into the corner of the hill with the basement steadily flooding and no idea whether staying is correct. She was supposed to be fairly protected, up in this higher point of the city, safe in her affluence, in her house that still sits on solid ground. It is hard to climb out of that assumption and to know what she ought to do next. A church hall perched somewhere to the north of her little enclave has been operating a temporary shelter for people whose homes have been rendered unliveable by the recent surge of bad weather. Camp beds laid out like dominoes, a trestle table and tea urn and earnest curate talking about *community effort* and *everyone doing one's bit*. Isla went down there the other day, took a bundle of tins and a box of teabags only to find everyone there bemoaning the loss of three-storey houses and gym equipment and reupholstered vintage club chairs. She offered her tins to the curate to take and immediately felt stupid, turned around and went home again and wondered what sort of charity she had been picturing and how she had thought it would make her feel.

The neighbour's house, when it goes, is almost nothing. Sudden slip and collapse, like a turned ankle, like something lost in mud. It slides some twenty feet, foundations shuddering, creak and groan of beams and grinding girders, upper windows falling out. No one is around to watch it go. No one but her – unevacuated, uncertain in the foundations of her own identical home – watching it go with her torch to the window.

Agnes

She isn't sure of the time, clambers up to the roof with the hazy intention of swimming. The city below; shifting soft like an agitated creature, spikes of grey to the easternmost edge of the sky. Before sleeping, she and Stephanie lit candles to set on the bedroom floor and pretended a restaurant, Stephanie setting out plates and paper napkins and asking whether she'd like her cheese sandwich single or sliced. *I assume this is what people mean when they talk about 'dating' someone*, Agnes said, and felt like laughing, and laughed, and Stephanie pulled a face that aimed for deadly serious. *Well yes, of course this is a date, I can't believe you aren't feeling appropriately romanced.* They ate that way, soft-lit in the swaddle of a power cut, and after a while Agnes shifted around to sit at the end of the bed beside Stephanie, dipped her head to give her a look. *Is this a move*, Stephanie said, setting the last of her sandwich aside, beginning to laugh and then catching her breath as Agnes slid an arm onto the bed to rest her cheek on her fist and look at her more intently. *I'm giving you a date*, Agnes said, and smiled, and continued to look at her, *I'm giving you the moves I'd pull on a date*. Stephanie smiled, bit her lip, and Agnes felt suddenly hot and shivery. She has never really dated, missed out in large part due to lack of opportunity, lack of places to go and people she really yearned to take there. She can imagine it now, can imagine the fact of wanting it, at least. After dinner, they started to fuck and found Stephanie on her period; Agnes tasting blood and surfacing to find Stephanie grimacing through a cramp. Dismayed snick of the head. *But your **moves***, she groaned, and Agnes wrapped her up in the duvet and hurried out of the room in a t-shirt to fetch paracetamol. Brief shock: the new housemate at her back when she turned from the kitchen cabinet, moving away half a step and then blinking when Agnes expressed her surprise. Kitchen gloom, the whole flat thrown into uncertain angles in darkness, the housemate too close and too unfamiliar. *My fault*, she said, which made little sense but still seemed to conclude the matter. Left the kitchen without seeming to take anything with her.

The roof is more bedraggled than it was the last time she came up here. The swimming pool, still uncovered, has overflowed into the gutters and drains and what excess there is spills across the terrace. The disused garden chairs take on a shipwrecked look, the barbecue close to floating. Agnes thinks about the damp which stickers the walls of their kitchen and bathroom, the semi-drowned foyer, black mould left unchecked in the hall. How long, she wonders, will this building remain vaguely habitable? Even if she drains the pool, the rain will continue to overwhelm the guttering, will seep, in time, through stone and porous membranes, will find its way into the fabric of the walls. Where, then, will they go, and how will they manage? She has listened to the radio, heard pundits speculating about a *crisis point* (a term she has been hearing since childhood), heard people arguing that this or that statistic is exaggerated, that nothing is changing, that everything is already lost. They recently had an email from their landlord floating the possibility of a rent increase owing to an *unstable financial climate*, whatever that is supposed to mean. She closes her eyes for a moment and thinks of her father's house, the deed that was transferred across to her and sits untouched. *You're a selfish cunt*, she has said to herself more times than she can keep track of. *You should sell it and give the money to someone who needs it. You should keep it and drive a boat through its big glass wall.* There are, she has often felt, no answers to inheritance, to the slick black suckered thing that at once shoves you up and drags you inward. Inheritance, both in the sense of what is owned and what is embodied, the sense of herself as indistinct from the influence of those who came before. She does not want, nor has she ever wanted, to own her father's house, but nor does she relish the thought of handing it over to some architectural trust for preservation, even less the idea of selling it on to someone to live held tight and safe above the flood. She wants, or thinks she wants, some other way – some veiled third thing – but resents the task of discovering it. She thinks of a girl she used to fuck, a girl with long hair and a wrist tattoo, whose bumper sticker pronouncements were only rivalled in enthusiasm by the speed with which she would down a litre of water after having sex. *It's so hard*, this girl had said once, *to want to save the world when you feel that you shouldn't have to.* A stupid sentiment, but nonetheless one which Agnes thinks about now, and then feels embarrassed for thinking. *Stop being a dick*, she thinks, and then, *no one cares about what makes you guilty.* Looks around at the rain, at the mess of the roof and the dark of the city beyond, and thinks, in a way that she can't entirely follow, *I don't want to be responsible for any of this.*

She shakes her head, peels her t-shirt off and moves across the roof in her bra to get to the pool. The rain is cold, hard against her skin like a shower of pennies. She slips into the overflowing pool and feels the gentle swell of displacement, her body pushing water to either side. Cold shrink of her skin flowering into goosebumps. She ducks her head, kicks her legs and pushes off from the edge, swims a width and then reorientates, opens into breaststroke. She isn't sure how long she swims, relishes the easy hum of her thoughts as she pushes herself back and forth. The rain hits the surface of the water. She thinks, vaguely, about Jason asking her to follow him into the coffee shop storeroom and showing her a line of what appeared to be sea anemones growing rough along the grouting of a wall. She thinks in snatches, about movies she has seen and people who have said things that entertain her. A voice from an old TV advert declaring that *I am the spirit of dark and lonely water*, the lyrics to a song by Frankie Valli, and *behold I stand at the door and knock*. She thinks all this and then thinks nothing, pulls herself up out of the pool again after who knows how much time to see that the grey of the morning is streaking down across the sky and the rain is a little less heavy than it was. Hugging herself, in her bra and wet trousers, she looks out across the city, grey-tinged and tired like something sunk in bedsheets. She watches the uneasy thread of light through raincloud, the way a morning, in wet weather, is only very slightly different from the night. Notices the next thing all at once and cannot, for a moment, quite compute it. Rubs her eyes the way people do in movies and looks again to note that what she has seen is indeed a flock of pelicans wheeling through the sky from somewhere over to the west. Vast birds, pinkish in dawnlight, the cramped camber of their necks and strange Jurassic bills and bodies, the way they tilt and ride as if in tandem, all at once. She watches them pass between the buildings, tries to understand whether they might have flown off course, blown east from San Francisco or the Gulf of California or some other drowned-out place. She watches and says nothing and shortly after goes back down to towel her hair and dress in warmer clothes and crawl back into bed with Stephanie. Later on and for no very obvious reason she will switch on her phone and find she has a message apiece from *I (1)* and *I (2)*, one reading *I'm sorry, I think I was a bitch to you* and the other reading *hey, so Isla told me that she thinks she was a bitch.*

City

Nearly there now.

You can hear it if you listen; the slow dissolution, the panic becoming something else.

Picture this: a man holds a candle to a window; a woman picks seaweed from the corners of her kitchen tiles. A shoal of eels knotted hopelessly in a storm drain, a sea slug, a shiver of crabs on a wall. Somewhere in the city, a group of people raise their hands to mark an offertory, a man enters the bedroom of his sleeping children with a pillow in one hand. Some people are throwing a party, though without power it is difficult to play music and hard, therefore, to set an appropriate tone. Someone wedges their phone into a mug in the hopes that this will act as a kind of amplifier and plays show tunes until the phone dies. A woman slips from her bedroom window to be swallowed by the water outside. The rain, as always. A building slides into blackness. A group of girls watch a movie on a battery-powered camping television, throw a duvet over their heads to further the illusion of being outdoors. The man on-screen seeks a missing girl whose existence people repeatedly deny. As the movie progresses, he exhumes the girl's purported coffin, to find only the body of a hare inside.

People do what they have always done, in the knowledge that choice is limited. Strange alarms go off in various parts of the city, once installed as a means of warning against something which no longer requires pointing out. In one block, a group of tenants get together to dismantle the lobby alarm with a stepladder and broom handle, kick it between them like a football until the noise gives out. Elsewhere, two women wash each other's feet with something like obligation. Elsewhere, a man holds a book to the light.

The night is wide, unstill, implacable. The city like a wishbone, ready to break in two.

6.

Agnes

It is strange to be here. Strange, for one thing, to be somewhere that still reliably has power, as the generator keeps the lights in her father's house warm and solid as though nothing is even slightly amiss. Strange too, of course, to be here at all when she told herself she wouldn't, when the thought of the house made her sick with a kind of bewildering dread that had no clear source or antecedent. Dread only at the thought of the furniture, at the thought of the air, at the thought of the whole slick shape of the place and her inside it and the sound of the rain without.

They sit across from each other a little awkwardly, as though each is somehow interviewing the other for a job. The reasoning was simple enough: Isla had suggested neutral ground but it is increasingly difficult to find somewhere open or able to keep the lights on, so they had decided to come here instead. Stupid, really, and hardly convenient, although there is a roundness to the overall moment that Agnes can tell appeals to her oldest sister, a sensation of something cyclic and neat. *We could even*, Isla had said on the phone, *cook something. If you wanted, I mean. I could bring something, there might be something useful in the larder. Only if you like.* Isla had come with frozen pizzas, three of them stacked on the kitchen island, telegraphing a sense of festivity that none of them feel. Their phones sit side by side on the coffee table, all three plugged in to the nearest extension. *Should have brought everything I have that needs charging*, Irene had said, *should have brought my toothbrush and my power bank and everything else.*

Agnes assesses them both. Irene looks alright but Isla looks bad, somehow depleted, as if in the aftermath of their father's death she has met with the edge of an eraser, the whole of her somehow less total than before.

'The thing is,' Isla says, pressing her palms into the coffee table, 'that I don't want to be fighting. It's not that I'm not still angry or that I suddenly feel ok but it occurred to me the other day that I really wanted to know how you both were, which is something, isn't it?'

'That's a beautiful sentiment,' Irene says, and then bites her lip like she hadn't intended to speak. Irene has not come in her usual stupid coat and looks cold in her t-shirt, somehow skinned, as though, perhaps, she was right to be wearing her coat all along.

'I just think,' Isla says, ignoring Irene, 'that what happened was the exact opposite of what I intended. I know you laugh at me when I say we should present a united front and maybe we shouldn't – maybe we never have – but I never wanted us to be at the mercy of something our father decided. I feel embarrassed, now,' she adds, 'at the way I reacted. To the news about the house, the money, everything. I feel embarrassed that his decisions are still governing the way I behave.' She pauses. 'We don't have to like each other or want to see each other. We don't have to be family in the way I've insisted – I think I understand that now. I just don't want the reason we aren't a family to be anything to do with him.'

Agnes looks at her sister with brief affection, swiftly doused but nonetheless unusual in its clarity. Before leaving the flat this afternoon, she had put her face in Stephanie's neck and kissed her, nosed her hair aside to breathe her in. Stephanie, still down with cramps, had hummed and shifted over as if to encourage Agnes to get back into bed. Agnes has never been very good at delineating emotions. The fact of Stephanie, of loving her, is still discomfiting, like discovering a skill she never imagined she'd have. Kissing her shoulder again, she had thought to herself, *I'll tell her later, I'll tell her tonight*, and then gone out of the room and away through the kitchen and living room, Casper singing behind his closed bedroom door, the music the new housemate's been playing flipping off as she passed. Having identified one emotion, she wonders whether it might be easier to pinpoint others. Looking at Isla now, and from Isla to Irene, she tries to sort through the murk of her feelings towards them; the jostle of love and resentment, nostalgia, familiarity, the feeling of barely knowing them at all.

'I don't know if that's exactly an apology,' she says to Isla now, 'but I accept your apology.'

Isla nods, glances towards Irene as though in expectation.

'You hit me in the face,' Irene says smartly, shucks her hands up her arms and watches as Isla opens her mouth.

'Well, I can understand the impulse,' Agnes says before Isla can say anything, and for a moment it seems like all three of them might laugh. If this were a film, she reflects, this conversation would end with them hugging and dancing around to a song that they all remember. The camera would pan out like someone watching from beyond the windows to see the three of them twirling around the sofa in the warm electric light. She tries to conjure a song that all three of them might like. Draws up the opening bars of 'If Not for You' by George Harrison and then loses the thread.

'Do you remember,' Irene now says out of nowhere, 'when he left us alone for four days and it was just – fine? I would have been fifteen so I guess Isla was sixteen? And—' She gestures towards Agnes, makes brief eye contact and then blinks. Agnes thinks, not for the first time, that it's more than likely that Irene has no idea how old she is. 'I remember that,' Irene continues, looking around the living room, the golden pendant lights, the juxtaposition of soft and hard.

Agnes nods, shakes her head, tries to remember. Five years old and aware of a change in the atmosphere, a sensation of an overthrown regime. There had been no misrule, only a kind of alteration; a memory of Isla clambering onto the kitchen counter to reach things down from high cupboards, of Irene skidding up and down the corridor in socks. Hard to pin the chronology of four days in place, if four days was what it really was. Only a series of snatches: the unfamiliar sensation of being held when she fussed and demanded attention; a childish effluvia of handwashed underwear hanging limp from the shower rail.

'I remember you made us this huge pasta dish,' she says to Isla now. 'I remember you took everything out of the cupboard and threw it in.'

'I don't remember that,' Isla says, resting her elbows on her knees and frowning at the coffee table. There is something etched in the wood towards the top left-hand corner, a miniature vandalised face with a mouth scratched wide. *When did I do that*, she thinks. 'I remember that I kept thinking I heard the door, opening and closing. I kept thinking it meant he was back but when I went down there was nothing, there was nobody there.'

Agnes can remember more; the way the house seemed to take on a different shape during that period, less austere, less incomprehensible. Moving around the place, she had imagined gentle breaths, a whispering skylight, pictured kisses in the swinging of a door.

'I remember,' Irene says, 'that when he came back – he'd been on-site at some project, never even really thought about not leaving us – you went up to your room and locked yourself in for twenty-four hours. I could never figure out whether you were angry because he'd gone away or angry because he'd come back.'

For a moment Agnes assumes Irene is speaking to Isla but then looks up from her hands to find her looking at her. She doesn't remember this, tries and finds only a blank of lost footage. Her marshy child's imagination, sucking down occasional memories wholesale and throwing up less certain things in their wake. *I remember*, she wants to say, *the idea of a woman at the window. I remember*, she wants to say, *an idea of being watched*. Even throughout the blurred childish memories of those lonely four days she can feel it; the sensation of eyes, of something watching. This might, she supposes, be her mind's way of reckoning with being looked after, of her sisters taking over in her father's absence. There would be a certain logic to this – her sisters keeping watch, sudden hands at her back when she almost overbalanced coming down the stairs too fast.

'We watched movies every night,' Isla says. 'That's something I do remember, although I don't know what they were or whether we thought about them being appropriate for you.'

Agnes snorts, tries to picture her slick little brain at age five, age six, and comes up only with clouds that feint towards emotion. The suggestion of being sad, of being lonely, of waiting for another shoe to drop.

'I don't know why I thought about that anyway,' Irene says now, 'that week when he left us. Maybe it's being here again, just the three of us. Feels the same. Feels like waiting for him to come back.'

Isla puts on the pizzas because it never seems natural to her to let a moment lie. She hops about the kitchen, pours wine she has produced from somewhere.

Agnes sits on the kitchen island and watches her, glances to the left and sees her father – just for a second, a shade that collapses under her gaze. He is in the doorway and then he isn't, and then Irene is there instead, complaining that she's cold and that it's never once been a normal temperature in this house. Agnes shrugs off her jacket and offers it to her. It is actually Stephanie's jacket, the first thing she saw to grab when leaving the flat, and she hands it over with a pleasant recognition of its smell. Irene puts it on, nods, gestures to the wine.

'So are we all having some or what?'

The rain is a hard continuous rhythm; the rattle of the wind like a voice, like several voices. On first approaching the house, Agnes had tried to gauge how much higher it had risen since last time, how many of its minute adjustments it must have made to remain as it is, serene atop the surface of the water and tethered in place. It feels as though the water must be higher than last time – the surrounding landscape is diminished, sinking low – but the great trick of the house has always been normality, the sensation of something at ease and undisturbed by environment. They eat their pizzas standing up in the kitchen, each apparently uncertain of how to continue the conversation. At one point Isla looks up as though startled out of a reverie and turns to Agnes.

'I've been paying a woman to clean,' she says. 'I'm sorry. I think I should have run it by you. I don't know why it bothered me so much at the time, I just wanted to make sure this place was being cared for. I really don't know what I was thinking.'

Agnes looks at her, tries to process this information, to explain how little she cares about something like this.

'I didn't even notice it was clean,' she says, and then looks around the kitchen. Sees her father again – a shape that reveals itself to be nothing in the window, long strip of absence in the dark reflecting glass. Life, she understands, is a collapsing down, a succession of memories held not in sequence but together, occurring and recurring all at once. She's in her father's kitchen at the age of twenty-four, but so is she at aged five, aged nine, aged eleven. She is standing where she is with her sisters and her father is here, and yet he isn't.

'It's just that the house is yours,' Isla is saying now, 'and I feel like I overstepped.'

'I really don't care,' Agnes replies, and meets her sister's eyes, tries to explain what she means when she says this. *I have this idea,* she wants to say, *about what I want to do with the house. I've been thinking about it a lot and now I want to tell you.*

The windows are black, the night shifting inward from the shadows of the evening. They take the wine back into the living room and sit as though in the cosy confidential period that follows a dinner party. The room seems unusually friendly for a second – the lamps and coffee table, the large, rectangular Persian rug. Agnes thinks of texting Stephanie that she'll be heading back soon, reaches for her phone but pauses when Irene opens her mouth.

'Do you think,' she says, 'that the problem was Dad, or did we just use it as an excuse for everything?'

Agnes looks at her, turns to Isla, who shifts on the sofa, sets her glass down on the coffee table and rakes a hand through her hair. Agnes curls her legs beneath her, drums her fingers on her knee and considers for a moment, opens her mouth to reply and then pauses. She has tilted her head to the left, which is why she sees it before her sisters; which is why she is a fraction ahead of Irene, who will shortly spill her wine on the sofa, or Isla, who will shriek and jump up as though shot. Hard to tell, in this light, how many people there are, how many faces looking in from outside. Hard to count the hands pressed to glass, the bodies on the platform that rings the house and sits gently on the surface of the water. Ghost-forms becoming solid as she looks at them, dark figures, people staring in from without. The key in the lock is unexpected, the sound of the door thrown back, the footsteps, the figures in the hall. Agnes looks from Isla to

Irene, finds herself unable to speak, unequal to the moment. *This is the wrong genre*, she thinks, and a figure in the doorway is smiling at her and there will never now be time for resolution, to finish the conversation they were trying to have.

Isla, Irene, Agnes

The fact, of course, is that they knew and then forgot. All three of them, clairvoyant in their way and yet oblivious. Irene, who heard the voices in the kitchen. Isla, who dreamed (or thought she dreamed) the face with bloody lips. Agnes, who saw the figure at the window and ran upstairs to hide. Pieces of a blueprint rendered incomplete by time and memory, by the way a recollection formed too early loses shape, transforms itself. They knew, inasmuch as any five- or six- or twelve-year-old can ever really know, the core untruth that crouched amidst the litter of their childhoods. Knew that the totality of their father's power was always less than he might have wished it.

They were children in a house ill-made for children and allowed the wrongness of this feeling to explain too many other strange, wrong things. Isla's assumption, for instance, that she heard her father's mistress entering the house one day, when in fact their father was not in and what she heard was her mother making for the back door to let a stranger in. Irene's failure, for instance, to recall googling *catholic stuff* on her father's computer and seeing her mother's browser history in the process: *afraid about things ending; what to do; scared end of the world; bad energy; bad thoughts; ways to stop it; groups to join; what to do.*

What they never wholly managed to grasp amidst all this was a sense of being watched, a sense of something courted, let inside. Agnes, perhaps, caught a whiff of it on occasion. A simple fact: that one mother veered off course because of ill-treatment, because of anxiety, because of the state of things, and agreed to hand her family over to another. That a second woman took over only as a conduit, to have a child for some veiled purpose, one which she duly abandoned to a house grown increasingly cold. In the absence of this understanding, the sisters were only ever able to amass a list of more trivial things: a handprint on the outside of a window, faces scribbled on walls and tables, the words *in time in time in time.* Life collapses down and it is easy to imagine certain events as having happened at almost any point. Easy to remember the voices at night, the creaks on the stair, as universal aspects of a childhood rather than moments rooted in time. A night when two women came together in the dark.

What happened, then? Two mothers and a father. Three sisters and a house. A house which, once invaded, could not be closed again, was left open to the elements, to whomever wished to come inside.

*   *   *

There are too many people in the room, people shaking off wet coats, pushing hair back from foreheads. A face amongst them that might be that of the man in scrubs who once came into the coffee shop, who once spoke to Agnes in the hospital.

Isla, having screamed and stumbled backwards, now stands dumb, staring at the people filing into the house from outside. Caroline (for of course it is Caroline, a fact that hits Isla like something known and long avoided) lifts a hand to her and smiles.

'I have to thank you,' she says, 'for being so accommodating.' Raises the keys that she holds in one hand and shakes them, sets them down on the mantelpiece.

There is nothing to make sense of it, the preposterousness of the moment. Irene thinks, hysterically, that the wine she just spilled on the sofa is going to stain. The people stand ranged around the room and she pictures her mother, finds her face bleeding instead into the faces around her – her mother's eyes, the shape of her mother's mouth, each feature incorrect the more she looks and finds them lacking.

'Agnes' – and this is Caroline again, Caroline whom only Isla really recognises, though they all saw her however fleetingly at the funeral, a funeral so full of unfamiliar faces, the same faces now filing into this room. Caroline speaks as calmly as she did at the funeral, as she has every time Isla has called her for an update on the house. 'We're so grateful to you, Agnes, for bringing us all here.'

Agnes shakes her head, tries to speak, wants to ask whether these people might have simply come to the wrong house. But then, another scatter of faces that it dawns on her she recognises: the new housemate, Liam from the coffee shop, a woman who once stared at her at the club. The world seems to tilt, swings back, and she sees it more clearly. The faces she has known and seen, the constancy of watching.

'I want to apologise,' Caroline says now – it occurs to Irene, as she speaks, that her voice is priestly, liturgical, someone leading others through the Catechism – 'I want to apologise to you for the lack of restraint some of us have shown in recent months.' She is speaking to Agnes, though as she does so, she gestures around at the surrounding interlopers. Another woman Agnes recognises: the one in the purple dress who pulled her hair at the funeral, insisting she looked like her mother. 'I know there have been others,' Caroline continues, following Agnes's gaze and nodding at the woman in a manner that appears to reproach her, 'people who have approached you or otherwise lost their grip. I can only apologise for this. If I had to blame it on anything' – and here, a woman sings through the air in Agnes's memory, mounts the embankment and then streaks downwards to splinter across the jetty – 'I could only put it down to excitement. Anticipation, maybe. Everyone has been so very keen to meet you. That's no excuse, of course.' Her voice is uncannily reasonable. 'We've always been here, so we should really have better control. But, things being as they are, I think some of our number can be forgiven for abandoning their manners.'

There are nods. The woman who pulled Agnes's hair at the funeral dips her head apologetically, a man sets his palms together as though to pantomime contrition.

'What the fuck is going on here?' – and this is Isla, finding her voice with her hand still high at her throat. The people gathered take very little notice, their attention trained on Agnes, to whom Caroline is now advancing with one hand raised to shoulder height.

'We're so grateful,' she says again, and then, 'to your mother for the Gift and to you for the Granting. The world is out of step, you know, and the Granting will put it back in order.'

Somewhere in Irene's memory, a glitter of words gleaned from the website printout: *the process of the Granting ensures that the intended object is offered over or exchanged. We must free ourselves from such binding tenets as 'shame' when it comes to an act of salvation.*

'You can tell, can't you?' Caroline continues. 'All these last long months you've been able to feel it – the downturn. The weather and the city, the terrible way things are. We've all been waiting, hoping for you to give us the signal, to travel here of your own accord, when things are at their worst. It was useful, to have learned so much about you from your father. He talked about you often. He felt certain, when he made up his will, that you would come. Not that he knew why that was important, of course.'

'I think we need to stop this,' Irene says, raising her hands as though talking someone down off a ledge and then feeling useless, idiotic, wishing with a fierceness that guts her that Jude were here.

'We are grateful to *your* mother too, of course,' Caroline adds, her gaze shifting swiftly from Irene to Isla before fixing tight upon Agnes again, 'for the grace of her sacrifice. To set up an act of this nature takes not only years but a certain flexibility. You need a person born for the purpose, you see, born to someone wedded to the task. We are grateful – of course we are – to your mother for stepping aside. Though it was a terrible thing that after all her sacrifice she felt unable to stick around to see our work completed. She will miss out on a wonderful reckoning, but perhaps she was simply overeager. We will all give ourselves, in the end.'

'What the fuck are you talking about?' Isla says, trying to ignore the fact that the surrounded group have taken up a quiet but perceptible humming, a low tone like the churn of some bass instrument pushing an orchestra along.

'Your mother,' Caroline says, with a wave of the hand that implies impatience, 'she found us, shared our way of thinking, came to see what needed to be done. She understood that, to restore balance, we would need to make sacrifices, to give something over to the cause. Wonderful, of course' – she gestures around – 'to have all this at our fingertips. Wonderful to be able to use this house – such a suitable blend of vision and hubris. I'm sure if your father had ever had any idea he would have been delighted.

Nothing he loved so much as the idea of moving things up out of the water, of finding a way forward, of changing our luck. The perfect conduit, really.'

She has been moving towards Agnes so calmly that her steps resemble nothing so much as the blocked-out pattern of a dance. She reaches Agnes now, takes her hair in one fist with a gentle grip and then smiles at her. '*Your* mother was one of us from a young age, you know. She gave us to you,' she says now, 'and you to us. It will be very easy, my darling, you mustn't worry about that.'

'Don't touch her,' Isla says, moving forward, and then, 'What are you *doing* here?' as if asking enough times might render up an answer she can use.

'We've been here a long time already,' Caroline says, tightens her fist in Agnes's hair and smiles again, almost benignly, as Agnes meets her gaze. In the second before she attempts to rip herself free, Agnes understands her father for the red herring he has always been and her life for the accident it isn't. Sigils on the walls and floors and tables, her photograph laid out in its frame, the whole house set up like a sound stage for a long-intended final act. It occurs to her to ask if her mother is here, to explain that she wouldn't recognise her if she were. *Perhaps Isla and Irene would know*, she thinks, insanely, *perhaps I should ask them.*

'Please let go of me,' she says instead, and Caroline shakes her head gently.

'I'm afraid, my darling, that we really can't let you go.'

What happens next – the scene like one thrown into forward motion. Agnes lunging away and Caroline grabbing again for her hair, dragging her backwards. Quick unsheathing, glint of something sharp in Caroline's hand. The shift and the struggle, Irene throwing herself forward and clawing at Caroline's back. Too many people, the swell of the surrounding group and hands reaching, grabbing at Irene, grabbing at Agnes, Isla catching up her wine glass and throwing it, the tilt and heave of the room, the hammer of the rain and Isla screaming as someone catches her, drags her away from Agnes, Irene lunging again. The humming still, even as hands reach them, grab them, even as someone tears them apart. It occurs to someone – possibly Isla, possibly Agnes, possibly all three of them – that this house was never made for this many occupants. The humming growing louder now, like a rising, swelling, a noise threatening to spill.

What happens next – Agnes screaming and trying to bite, two men reaching towards her, faces she knows, people who have always been watching. Caroline holding her own temple where someone appears to have grabbed at her hair, Agnes kicking out and missing, kicking out again and feeling her foot connect with bone.

What happens next – there are too many people. The article Irene's mother once quoted for her ran as follows: *The building is lightweight and built for family – one might marvel at the tensile strength of the mounted structure, the legs that extend to a seemingly infinite degree. There are issues to raise here, of course. Theoretically, the higher the structure is lifted, the more unstable it becomes, particularly when perched on what amounts to little more than a set of extendable stilts. The number of occupants, the weight of the house, the height of the structure might all, in certain circumstances, be an issue. However, it would be churlish to dismiss such a project in pursuit of a theory that is unlikely to require imminent testing.*

What happens next – someone holding Agnes by the elbow. Irene again, dragging her up and away, trying to pull her towards – what – the sofa, the door. *Agnes, Agnes*, she says, and then—

What happens next – humming still, humming turning into gasping. The sharp object in Caroline's hand – a knife – and Irene dragging Agnes away. Their father's wheelchair stacked safe in the corner, the oxygen canister beside it and someone grasping it up, lashing out, missing, lashing out again. The unfamiliar Persian rug, which some of the intruders have rolled up and set aside without her notice, revealing a vast rectangular pattern of sigils scratched into the concrete floor. Agnes looks down at this, as if from a very great height – the faces and markings gouged deep, the words written and overwritten: *in time in time in time in time in time.*

What happens next.

Agnes falls when the canister hits her, falls where the Persian rug had been, where the rectangle of sigils now catches her like a net. White lights and a pain in her head and the room off its axis. Dark, for a moment, and a thought that the world is terrifying in its greyness, its lack of absolutes. Nothing else. She lies where she has fallen and tries to think. Cannot do so. Something that feels like the floor. All the people around her at an odd angles, too tall and to the left of her and somehow very far away. They are gasping now, mouths wide, some strange circular breathing as if starved of oxygen, as if they have run miles and miles. Her head pounds and she wonders if she also ought to be breathing like this, if that might make it easier to see.

Somewhere amongst the crowd far above her, she imagines she sees her father and knows that she doesn't, wonders if she sees her mother and knows there is no way to tell. She thinks about Stephanie and wishes she had a voice to tell Irene that the jacket she is wearing contains Stephanie's address written in pen inside the collar. Somewhere, somewhere, Irene shrieks, though the sound is swiftly muffled. Agnes blinks, finds she can see little and imagines she is swimming, barely reacts when hands hold her down.

What happens next.

The house seems to lurch – or perhaps it doesn't, perhaps that is just Agnes's head.

Caroline's voice – or a voice very like hers – *come here, come here now*. Indistinct struggling noises and Isla's voice again, Isla shrieking. The house lurches once more, a strange grinding noise from below. Irene's voice, somewhere far away – *fuck, fuck, what did you do to her*. Caroline's voice occurs again, just next to her ear this time, the glint of the knife so close: *when I hold your mouth at each side it's because I want you to breathe in. It may hurt, it may bleed, but you have to be open to it. Breathe in the way we do, my darling. Breathe in and it'll soon be done. We think of it as taking the old life in and letting the new life out. We need you to do this for us. Do it quickly and it'll be over and everything will change.*

There is another lurching sensation, cold concrete floor rattling, and Caroline slips to the side. Rights herself quickly, grabs hold of Agnes's face. *What was that* – someone says, as someone else says *nothing, stop it*. The floor shifts, groans, and everything is suddenly off balance. Agnes struggles against the pressure of hands on her face, hands moving to the corners of her mouth. The floor creaks, the whole building seems to hum, and she thinks in a voice that is so far away that it might as well be someone else's: *this house has grown far too high now, there shouldn't be so many people here.*

Thoughts occur the way they do when she swims: her head and how it aches and the fingers dragging the corners of her mouth open; the smell of drilled teeth, of bad friction; the thought of the evening; the flat and the walls and the sound of bed linens thrown over; Stephanie's hands and her dusty-soled feet and the way that she kisses; the shape of a bird in the clouds.

Irene and Isla: each caught up and tangled, watching as Caroline, crouched on the floor beside Agnes, begins to speak. She talks as the house creaks and staggers. Tells Agnes to breathe in and out, drags at her mouth as if to assist the process. Irene looks towards the windows and notes the unreality of the water rising against the windows on one side as the house sinks down, imagines its mechanical legs giving way under their own height and the weight of the structure they're built to support. She looks around herself, tries to locate any sense that what is happening is wrong on one of the surrounding faces. *The house is sinking*, she thinks, *what are you doing, the house is sinking*. She thinks of elevators, submarines, then shuts off from these thoughts entirely, tries to school her mind into something useful and draws only a blank. There is, she knows, a panic button by the fireplace, but what on earth would be the point of that when the house is already falling down. The building screeches – metal on metal – holds for a second, sinks further, and it feels preposterous that the water would possibly be this deep, could possibly rise enough to cover the windows.

'We are,' she hears Caroline say, yet again – a voice that dips down into tenderness, a hand that reaches for a knife – 'so grateful.'

The light has changed, the dark of the water on the sinking side of the house solid, unlike the dark of the night. Somewhere to her left, Irene can see Isla caught by the arms by a man who looks towards the windows with a wide, placid expression, like something wiped clean. All around them the company are gasping, drawing in and letting out air, their mouths wide circles, the noise of it growing in speed and in volume. The house groans around them.

'No air,' someone says, and another repeats it, three or four voices taking it up in canon, repeating and then dying down, taking up the gasps again. Whispers as the lights dip and recover, a creak at one window, another. Air drawn in and released, gasping, gasping. And then.

Isla. Caught up and struggling, a wild array of white nothings slashed hard across her brain. *What do I do*, she thinks, and then, *why did I bring us here*, and then, *why did I think all those stupid squabbles were important.* The house is listing wildly now, one end dipping dark into the water, and she feels rather than hears objects toppling from tables, a lamp tipping over, furniture screeching down across the floor.

'Please forgive us' – this from Caroline, not intended, it seems, for Agnes or Isla or Irene but elsewhere, spoken outward, and just as the crack in the window appears. *The pressure*, Isla thinks to herself, turns to Irene and tries to say it but stops as the crack spreads fast and the people standing around the room start to groan, start to raise their hands, and Caroline is still holding Agnes on the floor, now pressing the knife against her neck, their foreheads dipped together. *I think all of this is my fault*, Isla thinks to herself, tries to remember when it was she last thought this. *I think I was supposed to sort this out.* Her sister at her side and her sister on the floor and all of them, again, in this house that wants to kill them. All of them together and yet never enough on each other's side to save them from disaster. The floor groans again, shudders, and Isla knows it is the legs of the house giving out, the shriek of metal against metal, a terrible screaming and rending, and as the window bursts inward there is nothing Isla can do but stumble sideways, throw herself away from the person holding her and crash her body into Irene, dragging her with her as they go.

The flood is immediate, the room filling, the lights drifting out all at once. The house in freefall – a leg gone, plunging down into the water, and Isla ducks under with it, pulls Irene after her, tries to swim as the water rises.

Wide dark, drowning dark, the room filling rapidly towards the ceiling. People stagger into each other, thrown off balance – a knife dropped, kicked away in confusion, and Caroline screaming as it goes. Isla gasps, tries to picture her house, the house beside hers falling into the water, tries to think herself back there and safe. She swims blindly towards where Agnes was when the flood started, can't see well enough to find her way. Irene, she thinks, is somewhere beside her, the two of them reaching out to where their sister had been, to where Caroline had been holding her. Bodies in the flooding dark around them – these people who have chosen, for whatever reason, to stay here, to drown. She reaches with her hand, swipes out, feels sure she connects with something – a hand or a foot – feels sure something reaches for her and then retracts, pulling back into darkness. Her lungs burn and she writhes, registers sheer rage at the thought of her youngest sister, who she has never had time enough to love, being taken away from her. Grabs for Agnes again and feels her hand connect and yanks, drags on a sleeve and pulls. Tries to fight off the nearly irresistible urge to breathe in.

The water. The dark. She kicks and struggles wildly against resistance. Another hand at her wrist – Irene's, pulling her sideways – and she twists underwater, pulls the dead weight of Agnes with her, pushes her, lifts her, makes Irene take her. Agnes goes – the slack shape of her, Irene taking hold of her arm, kicking frantically, heaving them up towards the broken window. A brief lightness – Agnes slipping from Isla's grip as she kicks up, kicks harder, tries to remember which way to go. The hand on Isla's ankle is a surprise. Someone else, someone wrenching her downwards. Someone else reaching out for her. She kicks her leg, but the hand holds tight, pulls down. (*I have you*, her mother said once, grabbed her hair in a game of tag, pulling it tight before kissing her shoulder.) *No*, Isla thinks, and then, *I'm not going to fucking drown*. And then, *I was supposed to sort this out*. And then, *I was meant to*. And then.

Surfacing into the night, they gasp, try to breathe. Irene, treading water, coughs and spits and starts to scream. The night is vast, the house still staggering downwards, drowning, dragging things into its rip tide as it goes. Irene grabs Agnes and scrabbles her legs in the churn and tries to stay afloat.

'We're not going to fucking drown,' she says, yanks at Agnes's arm and pulls her sideways, 'we're going to swim.'

Agnes, bleary, opens her eyes to stare at her. Her mouth is bleeding at the corners, her expression barely there.

'What's—' she says, and then nothing.

Irene treads water, tries to hold on to Agnes and thrash her free arm around.

'*Isla*—'

Isla is nowhere to be seen. Irene kicks her legs and calls for her, struggles and feels Agnes slipping and tries to catch her up again.

A noise shudders up from below, the house now covered over with water, moan of metal grinding to a stop. Irene gasps, spits water and tries to think, screams for Isla again.

'What do I do,' she says aloud to no one, repeats herself, holds on to Agnes and tries to remember how to swim. 'What do I do?'

There is no one to tell her. There is debris floating up from below – a section of something like timber cladding. She swims towards it with Agnes, clings on tight. A minute, then two, and the water is dark, and no one is struggling up to the surface. She holds Agnes against her shoulder. Thinks *what do I do* again.

'I'm ...' – and this is Agnes, slurred against her neck – 'what's ...' She peters out again and Irene looks at her, follows her gaze.

The feeling is unfamiliar at first, a sensation both new and too old to easily recognise. Drenched as Irene is, it takes a moment for her to see what Agnes is responding to; that it is no longer raining, that the water is so cold around them. That what is falling from the sky is something other, something gentle and strange. Looking up, she can feel the chill of it light on her cheeks. Snow, falling soundless and easy, like something that has always been the case. They float there – the two of them, unable to speak, unable to move from the spot where their father's house was, where their sister was, only minutes ago. They watch the snow fall and Irene thinks *Isla* and then doesn't know how to finish the thought; *Isla no, Isla wait, Isla help me*. She holds her sister – her other sister – up against her chest and tries to picture what comes next.

What comes next will be trickier, of course. Snowfall and a drop in temperature, a world tilting, the suddenness of something new. Best to keep on, wherever this is possible. Best, in time, to swim back from a drowning place and continue, struggle back into dailiness, and to live with the icing-over of windows, the frozen pipes and bad wiring and increasing impossibility. Better, in whatever small way, to go on until it becomes too cold to do so. Better to hold one's hands to whatever warmth there is, to kiss and talk and grieve and fuck and hold tight against the whitening of the sky.

For now, however, they drift between the water and the snow, the sky above them broad and starless, absent of rain and yet busy with snowfall that doesn't stop but only seems to grow more insistent. For now, they stay where they are and listen to the unwonted quiet, the hush in place of rain-fall unfamiliar, the silence like a final snuffing out.

Acknowledgements

To Kishani Widyaratna and Caroline Bleeke, with infinite gratitude.

To Sam Copeland and Honor Spreckley, who field every query with kindness and patience.

To Naomi Mantin, Sydney Jeon, Niriksha Bharadia, Alex Gingell and everyone else who took on a piece of the endless work that getting a book to print always is.

To every writer who has supported this book or inspired me by being a thousand miles better than I am.

To everyone I love and adore.

To Nick Armfield and Emily Down, whose big year this really is.

To Sarvat Hasin and Isobel Woodger, always and forever.

To Martha Perotto-Wills and Avery Curran, whose book this is.

To Tiggy, I guess.

To Rosalie Bower, to whom I belong.